SHORT SQUEEZE

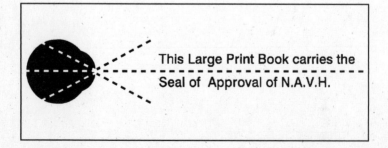

This Large Print Book carries the
Seal of Approval of N.A.V.H.

SHORT SQUEEZE

CHRIS KNOPF

WHEELER PUBLISHING
A part of Gale, Cengage Learning

GALE
CENGAGE Learning

Detroit • New York • San Francisco • New Haven, Conn • Waterville, Maine • London

GALE
CENGAGE Learning™

Wheeler Publishing Large Print Hardcover.
The text of this Large Print edition is unabridged.
Other aspects of the book may vary from the original edition.
Set in 16 pt. Plantin.

LIBRARY OF CONGRESS CATALOGING-IN-PUBLICATION DATA

Knopf, Chris.
  Short squeeze / by Chris Knopf.
    p. cm.
  ISBN-13: 978-1-4104-2590-4 (alk. paper)
  ISBN-10: 1-4104-2590-8 (alk. paper)
  1. Southampton (N.Y.)—Fiction. 2. Large type books. I. Title.
  PS3611.N66S56 2010b
  813'.6—dc22   2010001932

Published in 2010 by arrangement with St. Martin's Press, LLC.

Printed in the United States of America
1 2 3 4 5 6 7 14 13 12 11 10

None of my favorite female friends were spared in the making of this book. You know who you are.

ACKNOWLEDGMENTS

As always, thanks to Mary Jack Wald for connecting me with another fine editor, Peter Joseph at Thomas Dunne. And to Anne Collins at Random House Canada, editor par excellence. Special thanks to Bill Field for the style and content of a gamer's casino experience. Thanks to Bob Willemin for lessons on short selling and other financial shenanigans. Thanks to Cindy Courtney, the only female lawyer I know who could give Jackie a run for her money, for legal subtleties. Thanks to ace readers Randy Costello and Sean Cronin for early-stage editorial guidance. And Heidi Lamar for digital-reality checks. As always, indispensable assistance by Anne-Marie Regish. Last, but hardly least, thanks to Mary Farrell for putting up with all this.

The cure for boredom is curiosity.
There is no cure for curiosity.
— Dorothy Parker

1

I don't know how to dress. It's easier to just say, "Oh, you're right — this skirt and blouse have no business being together on the same body. That's what I get for dressing in the dark."

I feel that way about my life in general. I know it doesn't look very good, but I seem to be missing the specific talent to do anything about it.

Getting through law school was probably the only thing I ever did on purpose that might have been a good idea. Even a lousy lawyer can usually make enough money to stay a little north of the poverty line, and I'm not a lousy lawyer. I'm unconventional. A little spotty at times on the finer points, but I usually do okay for my clients. Nobody's asked for their money back. Not yet, anyway.

Maybe I'm just a product of my environment. I've lived in the Hamptons my whole

11

life, minus the time spent in college and law school. That period away taught me that standard notions of reality aren't always applicable to the East End of Long Island. The outside world thinks living here requires a Bentley, a face-lift, and a shingle-style home the size of Buckingham Palace. The truth is a lot more complicated than that. You see a lot of swells in capped teeth and riding boots, but also dusty valiants in tool belts, and long-legged, high-heeled salesclerks, like you'd see anywhere. But dig a little deeper and you're as likely to find a saint — or a Mensa genius — as you are a deviant or certified nut job lurking right below the surface.

I know this because these are my beloved clients.

I used to have a home office, but I'd made the house such an unlivable pile of crap that I moved into a room over a row of shops along Montauk Highway, the traffic-clogged two-laner that strings together the Hamptons. The town I'm in is called Water Mill. I like the place because there's a coffee shop and a Japanese restaurant within a few seconds' walk, and I can look out the window at a giant windmill whenever I don't want to look at the brief I'm writing, which is most of the time. I can also see the gates to this glorious old estate right at the head of Mecox Bay that's been a nuns' retreat for as long as I can remember. The word is they're going to sell it off to a private group of jillionaires, which explains how such an incredibly valuable piece of property could still be undeveloped. They just hadn't gotten around to it yet.

Being Irish Catholic, I can't help wondering if the nuns threw in a few indulgences as part of the deal. I think that kind of thing as quietly as I can, so my dead old man doesn't hear me and try to reach out from the beyond and whack me on the head.

Disappointing my old man was a reflex of mine. It almost killed him when I gave up a solid Irish name like O'Dwyer for Swaitkowski when I married that adorable dope Potato Pete. That's what we called him in high school because his family owned the biggest potato farm on the East End. Which, like the nuns' place across the street, got the attention of real-estate developers, and soon after got converted into a tidy fortune, a chunk of which my husband used to buy the Porsche Carrera he flew like a jet fighter into a big old oak tree.

I sort of almost loved Potato Pete, so I kept Swaitkowski after he died as a kind of memorial. I also think it makes sense for me to have a name nobody knows how to spell or pronounce and gives me license to kick the shins of any chowderhead who thinks Polack jokes are funny.

Like everyone else, Sergey Pontecello had trouble with the name when he introduced himself to me one day in early fall at my office in Water Mill.

He'd made it through the door, which was an accomplishment of sorts, given all the junk that somehow got piled up everywhere. I could see him wondering where he was supposed to sit.

"Just call me Jackie," I said to him, shoveling a stack of paper off one of the chairs I'd promised myself I'd keep clear for visiting clients.

"People have trouble with Pontecello, too," he said, trying to get comfortable in the old leather chair. "It's the *c.* You'd think they'd know better. Anyone ever play a sello?" he asked.

"You drink coffee?" I asked him. "Tea? Orange juice? Martini? Just kidding."

He smiled weakly.

"The martini sounds very good, but I should wait until at least four o'clock."

Sergey wasn't a very big guy. Thin, with a long nose and a missing chin that would encourage a cartoonist to turn him into a rat. His hair was too black to be natural, especially given his age, which I guessed to be late sixties. His eyes also didn't fit the hair. They were either yellowy brown or yellowy gray; I can't remember. But they didn't make him look all that healthy, or happy.

"I'm sorry, Mr. Pontecello. Here we are just meeting and I'm making stupid jokes."

"It's fine. I was warned," he said, smiling.

Not wanting to pursue that, I slapped the top of my knee and asked, "What can I do for you?"

"I need legal advice."

"I will do my best," I said gravely.

"I need to perform an eviction. Things have finally reached that point. It's intolerable."

"Rental property?"

"No, my own home. The home I shared with my wife for more than thirty years. My late wife. As of quite recently. She had an unfortunate fondness for tobacco. She'd convinced herself that a cigarette holder obviated the effects."

"I'm sorry."

He seemed to drift off somewhere for a second, then snapped back.

"It's her sister. She doesn't seem to understand the situation."

"She's in your house?"

He nodded, the gray cloud that floated around him darkening a shade or two.

"I'm told real estate is your speciality."

He pronounced the word *speciality* like they do in England. It reinforced his distinct accent.

I didn't let him in on the fact that real estate was every lawyer's speciality in the Hamptons.

"Oh, yes. You might say real estate is my forte," I said, dropping the second syllable in case he was actually a Brit who knew the proper pronunciation.

"So, how do I toss that miserable woman out on the street?"

I sat back in my chair.

"When you're discussing an eviction, try not to say things like 'tossing' and 'out on the street.' You never know who's listening."

"I suppose you're right. But 'miserable' will have to stand."

That's when I got a cup of coffee for myself and one for Sergey, whether he liked it or not. I needed the caffeine and a chance to decide whether I should listen to more of his story or pass him off to one of my less favorite competitors. I decided on the story, but only because I was bored, sick to death of reviewing title searches, slightly sorry for the old rat, and prone to making reckless

16

decisions, none of which were good enough reasons, but that's me.

"So, give me the rundown," I said, clicking a ballpoint pen over a fresh yellow legal pad. "Nice and slow. I write like a third grader."

He was wearing one of those old-fashioned rayon shirts with the sleeves a different color from the body. Reminded me of Howard Hughes. His slacks might have been made of the same fabric. There wasn't a wrinkle to be seen. He put a hand on each knee when he talked.

"The house in Sagaponack has been in my wife's family since the early 1930s. Her father was a professor of medical history at Fordham. I don't believe they even have that curriculum anymore. In those days, a man of fairly average means could actually have a summer home out here, if he was willing to drive the four hours out from the City."

Yeah, yeah, I said to myself. Heard it a billion times. Geezers wallowing in future shock. Sorry if that sounds unkind, but you'd get tired of hearing it, too, if you lived out here.

"So she inherited the house? Her and her sister?" I said, wanting to jump to the obvious.

His face reddened.

"Of course it went to the children. Elizabeth, my wife, and her sister, Eunice. Both Hamiltons. That's never been in dispute."

"Okay," I said, writing down the words "okay" and "both names begin with an 'E.' "

"Elizabeth and I were the only ones who cared about the house. Eunice ended up in Arizona married to some Bohemian so-called artist."

"Bohemian with a beret or a guy from Czechoslovakia?"

"Both, from what I understand," he said, looking disgusted. "Anyway, since we were maintaining the property, and the sister seemed to have little or no interest, she agreed to sign quitclaims giving Elizabeth the house. Elizabeth and me, her husband, I might add."

He touched the tips of his fingers to his tongue and then ran them over his oiled hair, his hands betraying a slight tremor.

"Seems pretty straightforward," I advised. "I assume there's a will. Are you the only beneficiary of your wife's estate?"

"Of course. I'm sure it's in order. Elizabeth took care of all those matters quite capably."

"You haven't looked at the will?"

"Of course not. Everything that was hers

18

is mine. Nothing has changed. Why should I bother with a will?"

There were so many reasons, I didn't know where to start.

"So who gets the house after you?"

"We didn't have children, so charity, of course. Don't ask me which. As I said, Elizabeth took care of those things. I couldn't be bothered."

"Do you know why Eunice believes she can take possession of the house?"

"Who knows? She tells me the quitclaim is invalidated by Elizabeth's death. Which is absurd, of course."

I thought it was, too, based on what he was telling me. But one of the things I've learned getting to the ripened age of thirty-eight is to be suspicious of everything my clients tell me, at least at first. The sad fact is they rarely tell you the truth and never nothing but the truth, whether they swear to God or not.

"You have the quitclaim, I assume?" I asked him.

He looked displeased by the question.

"Of course. In a safe-deposit box. Do you have any idea what that document is worth?"

Another thing I'm sick of hearing is how much somebody's house in the Hamptons

19

is worth. Especially when they give you the spread, the basis to current value. Five thousand to five million is not uncommon.

"No. What is it worth?"

"At least five million dollars."

I could have told him property owners were registered with the tax office, so I didn't need the quitclaim itself to assert a claim. But why spoil the fun of a safe-deposit box?

"Okay, Mr. Pontecello, I'll need to make copies of all your documentation. We can do it at the bank, so don't worry about losing anything."

This clearly pleased him.

"Splendid. So when do we arrange for the eviction?"

He said "the eviction" the way other people might say "festivities."

"Well, technically, I don't think this falls into the eviction category. That's more like when you want to remove someone from a separate rental property. Is the house your official residence?"

"It is. We gave up the place in the City years ago."

"And she's not paying rent?"

He chuckled an evil little chuckle.

"Oh, no. But she's threatening to charge *me*."

"Cheeky."

He nodded and took a deep breath, struggling to maintain forbearance. "I invited her to stay at the house for the funeral. She hadn't been there for, Lord, decades, always choosing to stay at the club in Southampton. Having her at the house seemed like the appropriate thing to do under the circumstances. That was a month ago and she's never left. Last week she reports to me that she likes the air on Long Island and has decided to take possession of the property, thank you very much. She offered to pay the movers to pack and ship our things to wherever I wished. Our things. The whole house is *our things.* How ridiculous can you get?"

I had an answer for that, too, which was a lot more than you could possibly imagine, buster, but I didn't say it. Instead I asked, "You said 'our' things. Does that include Elizabeth's?"

His face shifted slightly from outrage to grief.

"Yes. I'm only now going through her unopened correspondence. It's not a pleasant process."

"Do you know if Eunice has a lawyer?" I asked.

He shook his head.

"No. I don't know. No one she's told me about. Not that we're talking. She's talking, I'm not listening."

I spent the rest of Sergey's free hour getting his vital statistics and breaking the news that he'd have to pay for all the other hours, beginning with the first eight paid in advance, by personal check if he wanted, but not to expect me to do anything until it cleared. This was one of the few practical things I learned from my father, who had a civil engineering practice Up Island. Never work off your own money. If customers aren't willing to commit up front, they're getting ready to stick it to you.

Sergey took it all pretty well. He had to, after making such a big deal about owning a five-million-dollar house. Claiming to own. When I asked him why he didn't already have a lawyer, he told me he used to, but the guy had died.

Ah, I thought, great new marketing strategy. Outlive the competition.

I stuffed one of my business cards in the chest pocket of his Howard Hughes shirt and gently shoved the beleaguered old guy out the door. After being reasonably sure no fresh clients were about to appear, I took a break to finish the latte from the morning that I'd stuck in the refrigerator for some reason and an inch-long roach I knew was lurking in the ashtray under a week's worth of stubbed-out Marlboro Lights. I like the idea of smoking dope and drinking coffee at the same time. Let the caffeine and tetrahydrocannabinol fight it out. Winner gets to pick whether you go uptown or down.

I was going to use the break time to stare at the windmill, but instead found myself pecking at the computer keyboard, wandering on to the Town of Southampton municipal site, then using the password they gave me as an officer of the court to sneak into areas where I didn't belong, like where the tax department kept their property records.

The database was easily accessible by typing in either owner name or address. So I put in both.

There it was. Sergey and Elizabeth Pontecello, 34 Hunter's Plain Road, Sagaponack, New York. The tax map told me more. The address was in an area where five-million-dollar houses were a regular thing. In fact, five million was probably the cost of the ante.

So Sergey was telling the truth, at least to that extent. After copying down the name and address, I clicked out of the screen and headed over to the first stop on a routine title search. It looked like Sergey's taxes

23

were all paid up. He was about to get reappraised, the result of which would probably come as an unpleasant surprise. It always did. Reappraisals are a good governor on the urge to brag about how much your house is worth, especially in earshot of the appraiser.

I was about to get back to my paying work when for the hell of it I checked for mechanics' liens. Not an unusual thing for an older, longtime homeowner to get into it with a contractor, now that the price of a kitchen rehab used to buy the whole house.

And there it was. Not a mechanic's lien, but something I hadn't expected. A mortgage. Actually, one mortgage in the form of a credit line for $45,000 and a personal note, totaling $4,685,000. Most of the value of the house.

Lien holders Harbor Trust Bank and Eunice Hamilton Wolsonowicz, respectively.

I burnt my fingers putting out the nearly extinguished roach. Good lesson. Never mix curiosity with cannabis. Nothing good ever comes of it.

2

I know there's a lot written about women living on their own. I don't know what any of it says because I can't stand to read it. I try, but after the first paragraph I'm getting all choked up and before I know it I'm weeping like a rainy day.

And I like living on my own. Most of the time. After my husband died, I spent about two months doing nothing but sobbing, listening to Pink Floyd, and smoking about two acres of grass and half the state of Virginia worth of cigarettes. Every grief counselor in the world advises you not to do any of those things, but it worked for me.

It was realizing that my biggest fear was living alone in the house, which after two months I began to like, that started me on the cure. That and a lot of legal work God gifted to me as a distraction.

I don't know why magazine articles that're

supposed to make you feel better about whatever lousy thing you're dealing with make me feel even lousier, but that's what happens. So I never read that kind of stuff, or self-help books, and never watch television except for cop shows. Plus, I never join organizations that might put me in the position of having to talk about what it's like to be a widow at twenty-five and an unmarried woman in her late thirties. Because, frankly, that's nobody's business but my own.

One of the best things about living alone is getting off the bra and scratching that poor, tortured skin under my boobs that no matter what kind of bra I buy always feels itchy and chafed at the end of the day. You can't do this with full satisfaction in front of somebody else, I don't care how long you've lived with him. There's no such thing as a bra that fits and looks good at the same time. Anyone who says there is owns a bra factory or is lying through her teeth.

Some people in the Hamptons, either crazy old-money types or tasteless slobs flush with undeserved good fortune, name their houses. They put out signs such as DUNE VIEW or BUY LOW, SELL HIGH. If I were going to do that, I'd call my house Cognitive Dissonance.

It's a horrible, horrifying mess. My brain has no idea how it got that way and how anybody could possibly live in such squalor. My heart loves it.

This is another advantage of living on my own. I only have to make excuses for the house to myself. Since I'm easily swayed by my own arguments, the conflicts are more fleeting and less destructive to the relationship than when there was a whole separate human being to contend with.

I was there in my squalid house trying to remember how to run the VCR, which I was determined to get some use out of before replacing it with a DVD player or whatever dazzling technology they came up with next, when my cell phone rang. I usually remember to turn it off at night, so I found the sound a little disturbing. I answered it anyway.

"Why can't I just call the police?" said Sergey, after I said hello.

"You can. But they'll probably tell you to take a sleeping pill and go back to bed."

"It's the same as having an intruder. They'd do something about that."

"They would, but this isn't the same. Not technically. Can we talk about this tomorrow? I'm sure we can work something out, but I don't think now's the time. Bold accusations in the middle of the night, however legitimate, can only work against us."

He was quiet on the other end of the line.

"I suppose you're right. It's only that she's taken over the master bath, put all my toiletries in a paper bag, and locked the door. She's in there now, I'm sure of it. I've been standing here holding my damn toothbrush for an eternity. It's beyond the pale."

A tiny traitor part of me urged the more sensible part to ask about the lien the dirty bathroom hog had on his house, but the sensible part shut her up. Nothing was going to happen between now and tomorrow, which would be soon enough to confront that issue. All that was needed now was more wine.

With the cell phone held to my ear by my shoulder, I was able to open another bottle and pour a big girl's glassful.

"I'm going to immerse myself in your case first thing in the morning, Mr. Pontecello. You are my highest priority. I'm sorry about the bathroom, but I'm sure there are other places around the house to brush your teeth. Just console yourself with the fact that these indignities are nearly at an end."

He was quiet again for a while, which, of course, I interpreted as hurt feelings, but then he said, "I suppose I could continue organizing Elizabeth's papers."

"You could. It's not an easy thing to do, but it might be therapeutic."

"You are a thoughtful person, Miss Swaitkowski. I am grateful. Thank you."

"You're welcome," I said, matching the gravity of the moment. Then I hit the end button.

I went back to the VCR, which rewarded me about an hour later with a tape that started jumping around right at the moment the serial killer was using a skeleton key to jimmy the heroine's apartment door lock. The cell rang again just as the door clicked open and the music turned Hitchcock. I looked at the screen and saw Sergey's number.

"Sorry, dude, done for the night," I said, and let the phone ring itself out. Then I turned it off like I should have done in the first place.

I downed the wine and refilled. I tossed the remote for the VCR back on the landfill in the middle of the room and lit a cigarette. I scratched my head as a totally ineffectual way of dealing with that other itch growing in my brain. The one no amount of scratching would ever relieve. That jittery, nasty, unscratchable itch of curiosity.

Like a girl attached to someone else's

remote control, I felt myself lugging wine-glass and cigarette out to the dank and moldy sunroom off the back of the house where I had my home office, now more a museum dedicated to my early professional inadequacies. The old computer was still there, however, still hooked up to the Internet and eager to please.

I snuggled my butt into the office chair and fired up the old HP. The feel of the mouse and keyboard was comforting, like the busted-in driver's seat of a paid-off car. I shoveled off a clear spot on the desk for my wineglass and waited for everything to boot.

First I searched for Eunice Hamilton Wolsonowicz. Which yielded nothing on her but a few hundred thousand bits on Antonin Wolsonowicz, the painter. I'd never heard of him, but a lot of other people had. He'd come from a well-off family in Czechoslovakia, owners of a furniture business that he was supposed to take over, but instead he ran off to Paris to be an artist. Whatever conflict this might have caused was settled by the Munich Agreement, which basically handed the country over to Hitler. Mom Wolsonowicz was a Polish Jew who'd turned Catholic for her husband but wasn't about to take any chances. They were lucky

30

enough to sell the factory and split for Paris, where Antonin found them a villa in the outskirts of the city. It was a great gig for Tony, a rising star of the salon, with his doting parents and their deep pockets still out there in the burbs, within easy reach.

Great gig until Hitler was back on their doorstep and once again they had to get out of town. This time they opened up a little more air, escaping through the Azores to Havana, and from there slipping into Miami as the guests of a drunken American war correspondent they'd known in Paris who by all rights should have been Ernest Hemingway but instead was a guy named Edgar Staltz.

The rest of the commentary featured Tony W., as he became known, showing up in all these American cities where he was a dazzling success as an artist, a rakish bon vivant, an A-list partygoer, and all this other stuff that went with being rich and famous and that always sounded made-up to me. Though I know sometimes it's not. Some people just end up living those kinds of lives. I know this because I've lived in the Hamptons all my life, and I've met a few of those people, some I actually like.

In 2000, a month into the new millennium, Tony dropped dead at his studio in

Scottsdale, Arizona. This made me sorry for him but glad for my research. I dug up the obituary and finally found evidence that he had a wife named Eunice, who was fifteen years younger, a daughter named Wendy, and an adopted son named Oscar. The subtext of the reports was that he'd sold a lot of art in his life, and bought a lot of real estate with the proceeds, leaving Eunice, Wendy, and Oscar pretty free to grieve in the comfort to which they'd become accustomed.

The kids had both moved to Long Island after college. Mom kept the house in Arizona as home base, while maintaining a membership at the Gracefield Tennis Club in Southampton — complete with residence privileges — inherited from her parents. The second thing the English settlers did when they got to the Hamptons, after thanking God for the great-looking real estate, was to found the Gracefield Club. Anyway, that's what the club wanted you to think. The place was so exclusive the members would exclude themselves if they could figure out how.

There was more I could have read, but I'd finally tired myself out, which was part of the strategy. I need to be completely exhausted to go to sleep at night. I need to feel myself nodding off at the desk or on the sofa in front of the TV. Otherwise I might be in bed with my eyes closed but my brain still dangerously in gear, revving up for a nighttime of psycho-insomnia.

This is another key to living alone. Never go to bed with your hopes and fears still awake. Make sure they're beaten unconscious before you get within ten feet of the bedroom.

Which is what I did successfully that night. Teeth brushed and lights out, the alarm set with a half-hour snooze already programmed in, flat on my back on top of the covers in my favorite pajamas, the ones plastered with pictures of tropical drinks, about to pass blissfully into the abyss.

Then my home phone rang. I keep it on the night table on the left side of the bed. So when it rings and I'm half asleep, I stick the receiver to my left ear.

What happens then is nothing, because I'm totally deaf in my left ear. The eardrum and all the cute little bones that make it work are gone.

The night table's always been on the left, and I can't seem to muster the energy to move it to the other side, partly because there's so much junk piled on top I'd need a wrecking crew to move it.

When I realized I wasn't hearing anything, I rolled all the way onto my stomach, stuck the phone to my right ear, and rolled back again.

"Uh," I said eloquently into the receiver.

"Hey, Jackie," said a cheerful male voice. "If you're doing something I don't want to hear about, I'll wait till you finish up."

"Jesus."

"He doesn't want to hear about it, either."

"Sleeping. I'm trying to sleep."

"If that's all, I need you down here right away."

It was Joe Sullivan. A Southampton Town plainclothesman and conditional friend. I usually cooperated with him on my criminal cases, when I wasn't trying not to, which was why the friendship had always remained conditional.

"Where's here?"

"Sagaponack. Got a stiffy with your name on it."

"What?" I asked, finally relenting to the inevitable by sitting up and rubbing thwarted sleep out of my eyes.

"Dead guy in the middle of the road. Has your business card in his pocket."

I held the phone with my shoulder as I stood and dropped my pajama bottoms.

"A little more detail would help," I said.

"We got a call from a lady in Sagaponack about a guy lying in the street. She thought we might want to know so we could put up protective barriers or something. I was in the neighborhood, so I took the call with Danny Izard. Your card was in the guy's shirt pocket."

By then I was all the way out of my pj's and riffling through the central clothes pile for jeans, a clean shirt, and cowboy boots.

"I mean the guy. What's he look like?"

"Older guy," said Sullivan. "Approximately five-eight, dark hair, maybe one-forty, wearing the remains of a two-tone shirt and some kind of silk pants. Pretty chewed up."

For some reason I'd already heard that description in my head before he said it. It might have been the timing or a legitimate premonition. I don't know, but it didn't make it feel any better.

"Aw, Christ. Sergey."

"Russian?"

"Just give me directions. I'll need about twenty minutes to get there."

I grabbed my purse — too elegant a word for the battered feed bag I hauled around — and jumped into my trusty Toyota pickup. Another legacy of my time with Peter Swaitkowski that I couldn't seem to part with. I didn't even like the thing. I'm more of a Volvo station wagon than a Japanese pickup kind of girl. But as long as it refused to die, I couldn't find a way to part with it.

Sagaponack is a made-up village southeast of Bridgehampton with the dubious distinction of having the highest average property values in America. They didn't have the highest top end in the Hamptons, but they'd managed to draw the borders in a way that kept people like me from dragging down the mean.

I like driving through there in the daylight. Lots of open space despite the sprawling mansions and towering privet hedges. Most people like me who are born and bred and forever stuck in the Hamptons spend lots of emotional energy fretting over how it's changed. They don't seem to realize that everything's changed everywhere, including places like North Dakota, where everyone's moved out. Don't get me wrong, I miss a lot of what used to be here, but I'm not going to ignore some of the good things that have come in. Like clueless clients willing to pay decent money to local real-estate lawyers.

I'm not so crazy about driving in Sagaponack at night. Too easy to make a wrong turn and end up stuck in a cul-desac. Though, that night, I just followed the flashing lights illuminating the trees. A few hundred yards out, a pair of cruisers and a few saw horses established a roadblock. I recognized one of the cops.

"Hey, Danny, waz up?"

He leaned halfway into my window. I leaned back.

"Whatcha doin' here, Jackie, ambulance chasin'?"

"Christ, that's insulting, Danny. I don't chase ambulances."

" 'Course not, Jackie. You race 'em."

"Sullivan called me. I'm supposed to be here."

Danny pulled away from my window.

"In that case, Miss Attorney, you oughta go on in."

"You think? Ambulance chasing. Jesus Christ."

"Don't start gettin' the way you get," Danny called to me as I accelerated away from him. "Just makin' fun."

Yeah, bullshit, I said to myself as I ran through the notchy gears of the old bucket of Japanese bolts.

A car, I said to myself. What would be so wrong with having an actual car? With comfy seats and an automatic transmission. A radio that works and a parking brake that actually stops the thing from rolling down a hill. What would be so wrong with that?

I ran into another blockade a hundred feet down the road and had to go through the same rigmarole.

"It's a pretty unpleasant scenario over there, miss," said a cop I didn't know. "You sure you want to be exposed?"

"Please inform Detective Sullivan that Attorney Swaitkowski is here," I said, then rolled up my window in his face.

The cop stood there looking through the window for a minute, then knocked on the glass.

"I guess you really want to go in," he said when I opened the window again. "Go ahead."

Joe Sullivan was standing in the middle of the street outside a corral of yellow police tape. His back was to me, but I knew it was him by the general shape: round head and bulked-up body without a neck in between. He had his hands on his hips and was staring down at the person lying perpendicular to the solid yellow line, facedown.

I walked up and stood next to him. He kept staring.

"Hey, Joe."

"Hey, Jackie. Anybody you know?" he asked.

I looked down at Sergey Pontecello. I knew it was him from the shredded remains of the Howard Hughes getup, blackened with filth, not from his face, which was turned away and floating in a pool of blood. I felt something tighten at the top of my throat. I took a deep breath.

"What happened?" I asked.

"I don't know, but looks like severe assault followed by ejection from a rapidly moving vehicle."

I knelt down so I could get a better look.

"Did you get his wallet?"

"All he had on him was your card. And this envelope, in his back pocket."

I looked at the envelope in Joe's hand.

"What's in it?" I asked.

"In what?"

I sighed loudly enough to wake the neighbors.

"The envelope. What's in it?"

"I don't know."

"So why don't you take a look?"

Sullivan glowered at me.

"That's forensics. We don't do forensics."

"Oh," I said, "you just call it in and wait for the smart people to show up."

He glared at me and opened the envelope to look inside. After a few moments, he closed his eyes and turned away.

"Christ," he said, handing it to me. "Help yourself, you're so gung ho."

I looked inside and tried to figure out what was in there.

"It's a nipple," said Sullivan, tired of waiting.

"Oh my God."

"Why don't you just go home now, Jackie. We'll take it from here."

I threw up in a big blue hydrangea bush, but I didn't go home. Going home would have been like running away, something I was never very good at doing.

3

One of the problems with being a lawyer in small-town America, which is really all the Hamptons are if you live here year-round, is nobody's sure how to behave around you. The uneducated think you think you're too smart for them, and the overeducated are afraid a simple conversation could get them sued.

This can lead to being left out of a lot of things. It's isolating. Not a good thing for a woman who was never particularly artful at connecting with people to begin with. Not just the lover kind, even the regular day-to-day kind.

The other thing that happens, partly because of all the above, is the only people you end up talking to, besides your clients — who you really want to avoid talking to as much as possible — are other lawyers or paralegals or prosecutors, or if you're lucky, a cop or two or a private investigator. You talk to judges once in a while, but there's nothing to love about that. In other words, you can get up in the morning a creature of the American legal system, stay that way until you go to bed, and never talk to anybody who isn't ass-deep in a lawsuit or putting somebody in jail or about to go there themselves.

This leaves you without a lot of friends. In fact, I have only one by the standard definition, and even he's sort of connected to the law, though not in the usual way. His name is Sam Acquillo, and I'd either defended him or simply consulted with him on a few criminal entanglements he'd gotten into, all slightly extralegal and definitely ex officio.

The man has learned more about more things than anyone else in the world, but he's also the most frustrating and difficult person I know. He used to be a big-time corporate whiz, an engineer like my father, but he'd managed to screw that up, along with the rest of his life. He lives in a cute little house, inherited from his parents, at the end of a peninsula that sticks out into the Little Peconic Bay. He has a dog and a beautiful girlfriend named Amanda who lives in the house next door. So no, he's not that kind of friend.

Since he got up early to hold down his

current position as a carpenter, you'd think it'd be too late to call, but this guy isn't big on sleep. So I thought, What the hell.

"What," said the voice, or rather the growl, on the other end of the line.

"Nice way to answer the phone."

"The only way to answer after midnight. Especially when you're asleep."

"You're never asleep."

"Not with the phone ringing all the time."

"I was hoping we could chat. I've got a situation," I told him.

"I don't chat on the phone."

"Is Amanda there?"

"Just Eddie. He doesn't chat on the phone, either."

"I was thinking of coming over."

"Oh, goody."

"Be there in twenty minutes. Time to uncork a bottle and put out the nice linen."

I hung up and concentrated on driving the cranky old pickup over to North Sea, the woodsy area north of Southampton Village that used to be the only place regular people could afford to live out here, until there was no place regular people could afford to live out here.

I was trying not to think about ignoring Sergey's call only hours before he ended up dead in the road. I could barely stave off this massive cloud of guilt that was forming over my head. All my law professors would say it's unprofessional to take these things personally, which was a pretty dumb thing to say. Like you're not supposed to be a human being with personal feelings.

Of course, there's also the Irish Catholic thing. We're supposed to feel guilty about letting the milk curdle.

Eddie was sitting there, waiting for me in the driveway. It was as if Sam had said, "Hey, Eddie, Jackie's coming over in a few minutes. Do me a favor and give her a nice greeting."

He wagged his long tail and rubbed all over my legs, then trotted off as if to say, "Job done, got other stuff to do."

"A sight for sore eyes," said Sam when I walked in the door. "Literally."

Somewhere in his mid-fifties, Sam's one of those guys who looks weather-beaten and sturdy at the same time. You can see he's had some hard miles, but his handshake tells you turning your fingers into little splinters wouldn't be that much of a challenge.

He still has most of his hair, kind of a curly battleship gray. He's actually not bad looking, though time in the boxing ring as a kid and some fun and games later in life had roughened things up a bit.

"Wine for you, vodka for me. Eddie can have what he wants."

I followed him to a winterized sunporch that faced the Little Peconic Bay. He had two easy chairs, a kitchen table, and a daybed out there — just add a refrigerator and a hot plate and he'd never have to leave.

I started by telling him about the nipple in Sergey's pocket and worked backward from there. I thought, rightly, that would get his attention and keep it there long enough to get through the whole story.

"What about Eunice?" he asked when I was done.

"I don't know. Haven't met her."

"Hard to know anything till you talk to her."

"But I know almost nothing about Sergey himself," I said.

Sam swirled the bottom half of an old chrome art deco tumbler that he'd filled with vodka and ice.

"Do you think hiring you got him killed?" he asked.

Sam has some really good qualities, I keep insisting to people who meet him for the first time, but tact wouldn't be high on the list.

"Aw, crap, Sam. That's a big help."

He might have winced a little.

"You have to think about it. I'm not saying I would. Probably wouldn't. But you asked. Kind of."

"I'll keep thinking about that," I said. "Meanwhile, I'll go talk to Eunice. What're you going to do?"

"Me?"

"Yeah. What're you going to do?" I asked.

"Go to bed."

"Then tomorrow you're going to get Joe Sullivan to tell you who belongs to the nipple."

He swirled the art deco tumbler again. "Not likely."

"He's your friend. You've done plenty of favors for him. He'll do it for you. And I'm your friend who's done you thousands of favors."

Sam once saved my life at great risk to his own, the ultimate favor, which he had the good manners not to point out.

"I'll talk to him," said Sam, grinning at me for no good reason.

That's when Eddie came over and put his head in my lap. Sam got you to do that, I said to myself, just to distract me. Then I said to myself, You can't just tell a dog to do that. He's a dog. Even if you could, how do you tell him without saying anything? A

46

secret signal? Telepathy?

"Good boy," said Sam on his way to the kitchen to pour himself another gallon of vodka.

4

I like to gaze at my face in the mirror. Not out of vanity but relief.

I'm ashamed to say the worst thing to ever happen to me wasn't losing Potato Pete. It was getting blown up along with a table full of hors d'oeuvres when a car bomb went off outside the restaurant where Sam and I were having lunch. It was a kiss on the cheek by a big salad bowl that did the real damage, taking out my left ear and leaving me looking like the Phantom of the Opera's little sister.

The relief comes in two installments. If it hadn't been for Sam, I'd be dead. And if it wasn't for a team of wiseacre plastic surgeons, I'd be a mangled mess.

The kicker is they improved on the product. I had all the work done at a hospital on the Upper East Side. Count the number of face-lifts they do per day versus reconstructive surgeries and follow the logic.

We're not talking Greta Garbo, but it could have been a lot worse.

The bigger challenge is the hair, which I can't even blame on the explosion. It's called strawberry blond, which means some people think it's red and some think it's blond. Either way, there's way too much of it. They say every woman hates her hair. I don't hate my hair; I just can't do anything with it but pretend it doesn't look like an orange Brillo pad the cat's been playing with.

Or as my nurturing dad used to put it, "Ya look like an Irish Rastafarian."

I suppose I could cut it all the way back, slash it into submission. But then I worry about the face, still sort of round despite the clever nip and tuck.

The morning I went over to see Eunice Wolsonowicz I brushed it out as best I could and shoved on a hair band, my go-to solution since grade school.

The house wasn't far from where they'd found Sergey's body, but it took a while to find it. One problem was the mailbox. There wasn't one. And no street number. Just a driveway interrupting a wall of tangled vines and brush that grew along the road. Halfway down the drive was a little green-and-white sign that said PONTECELLO. If you didn't

49

know where you were before turning in the driveway, you had no business being there.

The house was Hamptons cedar siding with white trim and ivy climbing all over the place. The shingles were the old style — really wide and nearly black with age. But the house was only an anchor for the landscaping, the main attraction. It took my breath away. Big old trees with trunks the size of sequoias, a putting-green lawn, and mountains of flowers in every color nature and genetic engineering could connive. Arch-top gates, picket fences, stone walls, and pergolas knitted everything together, and a tall privet hedge toward the rear of a side yard surrounded a swimming pool that looked like a pond in the middle of Sherwood Forest.

A pair of pickups with trailers was parked in front of the house. I parked alongside and went up to the door to ring the bell.

"Not here," came a voice from one of the trucks.

"Oh, hi," I said. "I'm looking for Eunice Wolsonowicz."

"Still not here," said the guy in the driver's seat, sipping from a travel mug and chomping on a wad of cinnamon bun.

I walked back down the path and leaned on the door of the truck.

"I didn't see you there," I said.

"That's 'cause you didn't look."

"You know where she is?" I asked.

"Nope."

"When she's coming back?"

He shook his head.

"What do you know?" I asked.

He let his head drift over in my direction.

"More'n you, apparently."

I reached in the window and patted him on the cheek. This is the kind of thing young women can often get away with. Usually the guy on the other end likes it, and this was no exception. He thought I was giving him a compliment, which I was, sort of. I was saying, Of all the people I've met lately, you are the dumbest.

"What can you tell me about Sergey Pontecello?" I asked him, feeling I had nothing to lose.

"He's dead."

I wanted to pat him on the cheek again, only with a little more force. I thought better of it.

"Before that. What was he like?"

"Who wants to know?" he asked, looking over my shoulder as if there were a team of reporters standing behind me.

"I'm an officer of the court," I said, my trusty line. It's an absolutely true statement that sounds incredibly impressive and holds zero authority out in the regular world. It just sounds like it does.

The guy in the truck started looking more serious.

"Mr. Pontecello was a good enough boss," he said, as if I were recording his statement. "A little particular about some things but polite enough. More than I can say for his wife," he added, then looked as if he regretted it. "Not that we're talking about her."

"What about her?" I said.

He looked longingly at his cinnamon bun, as if no longer authorized to eat it. "More particular than her husband, let's just put it at that," he said.

"A bitch."

"A bitch. But you didn't hear that from me."

"Any ideas on who'd want to hurt Mr. Pontecello?"

He shook his head vigorously, as if he were warding off evil spirits.

"No idea. Can't imagine it. Terrible thing."

I leaned back from the window and looked over the beautiful property.

"What do you do around here?"

"Grounds maintenance. Been workin' here for years. If it's outside, it's mine."

I nodded, impressed.

52

"Plenty to do around here."

"Got that right. Something nearly every day."

"Were you here yesterday?"

"Yep," he said.

"Yep?" I repeated. "Yep means what?"

He pointed to the house.

"Cleaning gutters, mostly. Lotta trees around here. Toss a lotta crap all over the house. And fixing up the rotten wood around the windows on the second floor."

"So you're still on the job," I said. "Who's paying the bills?"

"Mrs. W. took over where Mrs. P. left off."

I plucked the cinnamon bun out of his hand, tore a piece off an unchewed section, and handed it back to him.

"Help yourself," he said unhappily.

"Can you do me a favor?" I asked.

"Do I have a choice?"

"If you think of anything at all that might shed light on Sergey's death, call me. You can also call me when you see Eunice back at the house. I want to talk to her, too."

I handed him one of my business cards.

"Part of an ongoing investigation?" he asked, proud of a line learned from TV.

"Ten-four."

I started to walk away, then went back to the truck.

"I gave you my name. Who're you?" I asked.

He reached out the window and pointed to a sign on the door panel.

"Ray Zander, like it says. 'Ray Zander Estate Management. Since 1984.' "

"Good year."

"Me and George Orwell," he said, turning his attention back to the mutilated remains of his cinnamon bun.

I was on the way back to my office when my cell phone rang. I almost killed myself grabbing my purse off the passenger seat and digging around for the phone.

"Fuck," I yelled at the crappy little thing.

"Love to. Name the time and place," said the voice on the phone.

"Who is this?" I asked, still yelling as if it were all his fault.

"Nice to be recognized," said Harry Goodlander, stoking my guilt before I even had a chance to feel any.

I slammed on the brakes and pulled off the road, barely missing a big sign that said PICK YOUR OWN STRAWBERRIES, under which some charmer had written WHILE YOU PICK YOUR NOSE.

"Harry," I said.

"Jackie. Long time no hear."

I took a deep breath and tried to calm myself down, something I was never very good at.

"Where are you?" I asked, hopefully in a level enough voice.

"Grand Central Station. You?"

"Half in a field of strawberries. Where else?" I said.

For all my whining about lack of friends, I'd forgotten about lack of lovers. Though the same impediments were there. Plus, for me there was the strange problem of the dead husband. I can't truly say he was the love of my life, but he had some redeeming qualities, mostly expressed in private situations that were hard to replicate.

Until I met Harry Goodlander.

"Where are you heading?" I asked.

"Southampton."

It seemed fitting that Harry would call me right when I was grappling with this Sergey thing. Two flavors of emotional torment blended into one zingy cocktail.

"Are you just coming here or are you, like, here here for a while?" I asked.

"Here here forever, I hope."

"I didn't think I'd hear from you again," I said.

"You told me not to call."

I put my hand on my forehead, a gesture I

hoped he'd see over the phone lines.

"I said, 'Don't call,' " I said. "But then I said, 'Call when you get back.' "

"I must've forgotten the second part. But I did anyway, so there."

"I meant, 'Call when you get back next week.' Not 'When you get back two years from now.' "

"When were *you* ever on time?" he asked.

I didn't know what to say to that. So I just sat in the silence.

"I miss you," said Harry, finally.

"Yeah, yeah."

"I want to see you."

"Sure, sure."

"Friday night. I'll pick you up at seven-thirty."

"Okay, okay."

"Great. I'm really looking forward to it."

"Bye-bye," I said, and hung up.

Shit, shit, I said to myself.

The phone call from Harry must have stirred my imagination, because a few minutes later I had a nice hunch. Even if it didn't pan out, it was an excuse to call Burton Lewis, a friend of Sam's and legal backstop par excellence.

I do a lot of work for Burton's criminal practice, especially on the cases he picks up on the East End. For him personally it's all pro bono, but he pays his staff, most of whom work out of a storefront in Manhattan. I've worked on every cat and dog case he's ever thrown at me, no matter how busy I was at the time. Lawsuits, divorces, parole violations, B and E, child custody, probate, foreclosures. Representing arborists, tennis pros, car mechanics, haberdashers, investment bankers, cross-dressers, you name it, I've worked it. "Take every Burton referral" is one of my few inviolate principles, right behind "Always work off the client's money."

Burton's an incredibly elegant guy, graceful and decent in every way. I always want to give him a hug and mess up his hair, even though he hates it when people invade his personal space. He's also richer than stink and gay as the day is long, which is fine with me. Takes that man-woman thing right off the table from the get-go.

I called him on his cell phone.

"Lewis," he answered.

"Swaitkowski. How're you doing?"

"Splendid, Jackie. Who's been arrested?"

"Nobody I know."

"There's a turn for the better."

"I'm looking for a rich old lady named Eunice Wolsonowicz."

"Tony W.'s widow," he said without hesitating.

"See. I knew you'd know."

"Though I don't know where you could find her," he said.

"She's a member of the Gracefield Club."

"I believe you're right," he said. "The membership's been in the family since before the professor, her father."

"I wonder if she's there now."

"Perhaps. I could call."

"God, I can't ask you to do that. Sure, okay, why not. You're a prince, Burt."

"Perhaps you could tell me what this is all about."

I summarized the situation, describing Sergey's death and related details while trying not to babble on too much, which is something I often did with Burton. I blamed that on him. Too easy to talk to.

After that, he made the call.

Coming back on the line, Burton said, "Apparently she's having lunch right now." I took both hands off the wheel so I could give a proper cheer, but only for a second. The Toyota hadn't been aligned since the last century.

"Man, I'm a genius," I told Burton.

"Indisputably."

"Can you get me in there?"

"Already arranged," he said. "Go to the front desk in the main building and ask for Marcello. He'll take it from there."

"Burton, you *are* a prince."

"Not at all, darling."

Getting into the parking lot was the easy part. To avoid suspicion all you needed was a Benz or a Rolls-Royce, or a beat-up pickup truck like the help drove. Just don't try it in a new Chevy station wagon.

The main building looked like any of the older mansions built along the shoreline. White trim, monster blue hydrangeas, millions of gables and dormers, and cedar siding so gray with age it was almost black. A porch deep enough to hold a square dance ran across the front of the place. It was furnished in white wicker, of course, arranged on Oriental carpets with wicker coffee tables holding bouquets of fall flowers and copies of *Impossibly Wealthy and Obscenely Privileged Quarterly.*

Marcello surprised me. I was expecting a gorgeous Latin, slim and refined. What I got was an ordinary-looking Asian guy, slightly chubby and refined. He wore a spotless white suit and a tie with the most beautiful iridescent colors I'd ever seen.

"Miss, how do you say . . . ?"

"With difficulty," I said, then pronounced Pete's last name.

"Ah. Of course."

"Great tie, by the way. They don't happen to make that in a scarf?"

He gave a little bow. "A pity, no."

He looked left and right, then over his shoulder.

"Mr. Lewis told me of your plan," he said, lowering his voice. "I am honored to assist you, though you realize this is highly improper and must never be discussed. It would mean instant dismissal."

"I'm totally cool with that, Marcello. I'm an attorney. Discretion is my middle name."

"So I understand. Mr. Lewis told me I should retain your services to help with a little misunderstanding I'm experiencing with your immigration."

I slid him my card.

"Absolutely, Mr. . . . ?"

"Machado, at your service."

"The service is all mine," I said. "So."

He took a pen out of his breast pocket and clicked the button with a pretty little flourish. Then pulled a small pad out from behind the desk.

"I'll draw you a map. We're here. Mrs. Wolsonowicz is here on the east patio having her usual lunch. She used to stay here

60

for a month every summer, but now she just has lunch. The same lunch, every day." He checked his watch. "She'll be finished now, which means she'll be having a double Dewar's on the rocks while she does the *Times* crossword."

I followed Marcello's map down the hall and through a series of sitting rooms to an outdoor patio covered by a giant green awning. I wormed my way across the patio, pretending to admire the flower arrangements stuck on all the tables.

"Red roses. You gotta stop and smell 'em," I said, startling some poor old sot when I bent down to give his vase a sniff.

"I'm sure you do," he said.

Eunice Wolsonowicz's vase was filled with curly stalks of bamboo. Not much to sniff. I sat across from her.

"Mrs. Wolsonowicz? I'm Jacqueline Swaitkowski."

She looked up from her crossword.

"What sort of a name is that?"

"Same sort as yours, I guess," I said to her.

"I like yours better."

"Thank you. It was my late husband's."

"So was mine."

"I'm really an O'Dwyer."

"I'm a Hamilton," said Eunice.

"There you go. Common ground already."

"Two fools who can't hold on to a decent name."

"I'm Sergey Pontecello's attorney. Or was, anyway."

"Oh, dear," she said. "I hope you weren't friends."

"We were just starting out. I'm sorry for your loss."

"I'm sorry, too. Though 'loss' doesn't exactly describe it. By the way, Mrs. Swaitkowski, are you a member here? I haven't seen you."

I shook my head.

"Nope. Pulled a string."

"Must have been a very strong one."

"The strongest."

"Interesting. Pardon me for asking this, dear, but do you feel it's entirely appropriate to join me at my table without an invitation?"

"It's entirely inappropriate. You can tell me to get lost anytime you want. But I'm really hoping you can talk to me for a few minutes about Sergey Pontecello, who, by the way, has just been murdered."

"That's what the police are telling me, though I find it hard to believe."

"Really?"

"Who would bother killing Sergey? Not a

62

bad sort, underneath. My sister never brought home sick puppies or injured birds, but she did have a taste for tin-plated European nobility like Sergey. The surprising thing was she married this one, probably because he came with some independent wealth. Modest, but enough for them to live reasonably well without actually doing much of anything."

"So if they had money, why the mortgages?" I asked.

"Had money. Past tense."

"Where'd it go?"

"I thought you were his lawyer. Surely you discussed this with him," she said, neatly cutting off that line of inquiry. While I thought about how to get back on track, she said, "I think you're getting the wrong idea, Miss Swaitkowski. Despite myself, I liked the little prig. Somewhat full of himself but harmless."

"He thought you were trying to heave him out of his house," I said.

"Sergey was terribly upset with me, and I can't blame him. It wasn't his fault that he lost his house."

"I looked up the tax records. Sergey and your sister are still listed as owners of the property," I said.

She smiled a kindly smile.

63

"A formality, dear. I was trying to break it to him gently."

"You're holding paper on the place. That's also in the records. Was Sergey aware of that?"

"Awareness wasn't the man's strong suit."

"So with your sister dead, you're reclaiming the place," I said.

"One doesn't reclaim that which one already owns. It's our family home. It belongs to my family."

"You and the kids? Don't they live around here somewhere?"

Something moved across her face, but it went by too fast to interpret. She covered the moment by seeming to discover there was a half inch of scotch left in her glass.

"I have all the information with my attorneys. Including my sister's will. You should probably speak with them," she said.

"Sure. Who are they?" I asked.

"Atkins Connors and Kalandro in East Hampton. Ask for Sandy Kalandro. I'm sorry about Sergey, I truly am. But I shouldn't discuss this any further. You're an attorney. You understand."

She looked at her watch.

"This may seem silly to you," she said, "but I now only have fifteen minutes to finish my crossword. Doable, but difficult."

"Not silly at all. Routines are important," I said, as if I thought that were true.

She smiled at me with the type of forced smile that would stick there until I got out of her hair. I was far from done with her, but I had to be happy with what I had.

"Thanks for your time. Sorry to bother you," I said, jumping up from the table. "Just one thing."

"Yes?"

"Did you really lock him out of the bathroom? All he wanted to do was brush his teeth."

She leaned back in her chair and lost the smile.

"Mrs. Swaitkowski, please, sit down."

I did.

"Before I committed myself to humanitarianism, I taught anthropology at the University of Arizona," she said. "Before that I earned my Ph.D. in organizational psychology, focusing on corporate power structures."

No shit, I said to myself, but acted as if I knew that already.

"There is nothing known of the intricacies and convolutions of human behavior that I haven't studied in fine detail," she said. "From the jungles of New Guinea to the City of London I have literally seen it all. I cannot be intimidated, manipulated, or charmed. I am sorry for what happened to Sergey Pontecello, but it was only the final, though surely the most dire, misfortune to befall him. I will not feel guilt or remorse or suffer the insult of recrimination."

"That's fine with me," I said. "I'm a lot simpler than you. I hardly know anything about human behavior, least of all my own. I just want to know one single, solitary thing."

She leaned across the table and moved her ice water out of my reach.

"And that would be?"

"Shouldn't be hard for you to guess."

Superiority flowed at me from across the table. If I hadn't been holding on to my chair, I'd have washed away.

"You want to know who killed Sergey Pontecello. If, in fact, he was."

I gave her the thumbs-up.

"I do."

Then I got up and walked back through the patio as if I did it every day. Right after I knock back a couple bottles of beer and read all the funny papers.

As I drove away from the Gracefield, I felt my mood tilting toward the dreary. It wasn't Eunice so much. It was the accumulation of strife. I'm no braver than the next person, but I'm usually late to realize I'm in any kind of physical danger. Blood and broken bones I can take in stride, but dead bodies make me want to puke or pass out. Or both.

Seeing that ridiculous old guy mashed up on the road wasn't even all of it. It was the way I'd treated him when he was still alive. Not poorly, exactly. But dismissively. That's what I did. I dismissed him.

I knew why. It was a bad habit of mine, which made me feel that much worse. Whenever I get a client who's got a little money or wants to act like they do, I have this reflex reaction. Like, you got all this money, what do you need me for?

But then I think about Burton Lewis, who's the best person I know. And a lot of my wealthy clients turn out to be great people. Just like some working folk can be completely unscrupulous, evil assholes.

It's prejudice, pure and simple. And I know where I got it from. My old man. He always had a bug up his ass about people he suspected of putting on airs. Financial or otherwise. I don't know if it was an Irish thing or a class thing or what. The funny part is he had a good education, and did fine with his business. We were well-off compared to a lot of people, and he didn't mind spending a little money on the house and cars and things such as new TVs and stereo components.

My father had been born poor, so maybe that was it. The hardscrabble stuck to him. And some of it shook off on me.

5

As soon as I got back to the office, I lit a joint and stuck my face in the computer.

In about twenty minutes I found Fuzzy, Eunice and Antonin's adopted son, whom they'd named Oscar, which is why they shouldn't have been surprised that he picked up a nickname. I was an open-minded kid, but even I would have given shit to a boy named Oscar.

I not only found Fuzzy, but I also found his personal Web site, blog, and a half dozen other sites where he starred as a frequent responder under the name FuzzMan. A powerful creepiness factor became apparent after reading only a few entries of his vitriolic commentary. It was a rotten stew of dystopian survivalism, goth anarchist fantasies, and early-twentieth-century bigotry. This sort of ugly rant and rave isn't hard to find within the blogosphere, but even by that standard, Fuzzy was a standout. I kept going deeper into prior postings, and was charmed to find headings like "100 Ways to Serve Boiled Nun," "Hey Terrorists, Call Me When You Want to Nuke New York," and, my favorite, "What Do You Call 5,000 Lawyers at the Bottom of the Ocean? A Good Start."

I'm not hip to all the nuances of cyberspeak, but from what I read, there was nothing warm and fuzzy about Fuzzy.

I'd also nailed down his address, so the logical thing was to take a ride Up Island and pay him a visit. And maybe bring along a little company. Actually, not so little.

My cell phone had a record of the number. I pushed the send button.

"Ya'ello."

"Hey, Harry."

"You're canceling."

"Why'd you say that?"

"Because I disappeared for two years and you can't get over it."

"I'm curious about where you went and why, but that's not why I'm calling."

"Okay."

"Do you have a car?"

"I do," he said. "I have a Volvo station wagon."

Most excellent. A real car. A safe, roomy, comfortable car. With shock absorbers and power windows.

"What're you doing tomorrow?" I asked.

"Distributing mainframes."

Harry moved stuff around for a living. Big stuff, like full-scale manufacturing facilities prefabbed in Japan and assembled in Massachusetts. Or lots of stuff, such as forty thousand cots, ten thousand tents, a lakeful of water, and enough food to feed thousands of earthquake survivors for a year. This is how he explained logistics. Or rather, rhapsodized about it. Harry loved his work.

"How would you feel about shipping me to Atapougue and back?"

"We call that custom handling."

"No handling, buster. Just lively and engaging conversation."

"Still have the old truck?" he asked.

"I might."

"Should I be feeling used?"

"Yes. But appreciated. How does nine sound?"

I first saw Harry at the Memorial Day parade in Southampton. Or more precisely, the middle of his back, which was completely blocking my view. I reached up and tapped on his shoulder and he almost knocked me over when he turned around. At a little over six foot eight, with the wingspan of a condor, a bald head, and black wraparound sunglasses, he looked like an alien sent down to monitor the ritual customs of us pathetic little earthlings.

Until he blasted me with a smile that somehow conveyed the totality of his big-sky, earnest, mirthful — though slightly obsessive-compulsive — self.

Six months later we moved in together. Six months after that, I was putting his toothbrush, silk dental floss, extra-hypoallergenic sweater, special imported teas, and They Might Be Giants CDs in a box for him to pick up off my doorstep. I thought almost immediately that was a mistake. Mine, not his. But I didn't know I'd have to wait two years to properly calibrate how bad a mistake it might have been.

"Nine is fine. Though I'll have to stop along the way and jump on the wireless. IBM will want to know where their computers are."

"Of course, hell yeah. Plenty of time for that. You're still a mensch, Harry. You can't help it."

"You're still a commotion," he said.

"And you mean that fondly. Don't answer. See you at nine."

I might've been using him. But I also wanted to see him. I thought a ride in the car in the daylight might be a better way to catch up and reorient than a dark restaurant where I had to chitchat and chew at the same time.

Plus, as I thought about it, having him along to meet the nasty FuzzMan in the flesh wasn't such a bad idea. You can rent cars, but it's pretty tough to dig up six-foot-eight aliens whose shoulders are too wide to fit through a normal door but could still fit into his army fatigues. At least the last time I saw him.

I worked until after midnight to catch up and then get ahead of my regular client load. The people who were actually paying me to do things for them, boring things on the whole, but usually not to them.

So I slept late, and when nine in the morning came around, I wasn't exactly ready to go. I was mostly wet, with a towel on my head and a bathrobe sticking to my skin, when I answered the door. But there he was.

"Hey, Harry," I said, straining my neck to look him in his sparkly blue eyes.

He'd still be able to fit into his field jacket, that was obvious. And that bald pate still shone like a glazed vase. And when he lifted me off the floor and kissed me on the forehead, he still switched on that little electric switch. Damn him.

He set me on my feet and stepped back a bit. I felt around my robe to make sure everything was still contained like it was supposed to be.

"Hi, Jackie. Looks like you're ahead of schedule. For you."

Harry was born with a clock in his head. It was so accurate I sometimes thought his head *was* a clock. And it mattered to him, being on time. Sticking to schedules. Executing exactly what you planned to execute before you launched your day.

I understood none of these things.

"My alarm went off at the wrong time," I lied by reflex.

"You have the worst luck with alarms. Coffee?"

I cleared a spot for him on one of the couches and made a pot of so-called fresh ground bought at a supermarket a month before. Then I attacked my wet hair with the industrial-strength hair dryer my hairdresser had bought for me, probably breaking a solemn covenant that could banish him forever from Fire Island.

When I got back to the living room, mostly dressed and ready to go, Harry was sitting with his mile-long legs nestled in a pile of magazines on the coffee table, reading a lingerie catalog I didn't know I had.

"*Playboy*'s got nothing on this stuff," he said.

"You look great, Harry," I told him honestly. "I'm glad you called."

He lit up a half-powered version of the Big Grin.

"Me, too, Jackie. Let's roll."

I spent the first half hour in the car messing around with stuff on the dashboard, adjusting my seat with little buttons that offered infinite variation, programming the radio to something beyond AM news and indie rock, setting the climate control to precise temperature and humidity, and testing the ability of the windows to suck out cigarette smoke.

"I'm thinking of getting one of these," I said. "Just checking it out."

"That's okay," he said. "My eight-year-old niece does the same thing."

I sat back and concentrated on looking at the Long Island scenery. We were going through the Pine Barrens, a lot of which had burned in a big fire in the 1990s. A carpet of new growth had formed, but it looked so new and the stalks of sizzled pines so forlorn. I said as much to Harry.

"The sandy soil provides limited nourishment," he said. "Trees grow more slowly,

75

and can only reach a certain size. It's like a bonsai forest."

"And now it's all burnt up. How sad," I said.

"Why sad? The trees don't think they're deprived. They're still alive, growing fresh new branches up from the root system. The carbon freed from the fire enriches the soil, and the burned-off canopy lets in lots of light, diversifying the undergrowth. Critters love it in there. It might look like a wasteland, but in fact it's ten times more biologically vibrant than a mature forest."

For Harry, the glass is half full if there is a molecule of water vapor floating nearby. When we were together it got to be a private game show of mine: *Guess the Bright Side!* starring Harry Goodlander. I blamed it on his being an air force brat, growing up around can-do guys whose ultimate aspiration was to fly faster, farther, and more recklessly than the other guy or die trying — falling to a fiery death singing "America the Beautiful" and/or whooping loudly.

"So, what're we doing?" he asked as we crossed into the strip-development paradise of western Suffolk County. "Or is that client confidential?"

I filled him in on every detail I could remember about the case with no effort to protect confidences, client or otherwise. I even told him how I felt about Fuzzy Wolsonowicz, leaving out my own wimp factor. I might've been more secure having him along, but I wasn't about to reinforce stereotypes. Even with an enlightened guy like Harry.

I'm terrible at finding my way when I'm driving, but I'm a homing pigeon if I can read a map in the passenger's seat. There wasn't much else to look at in that part of Long Island anyway. Dirty white, gray, and beige buildings, mostly grimy and shopworn, gaudy neon, and potholed streets. Tiny ranch houses with vans and pickups filling the driveways, a few with all four tires.

When we got to the address I'd pulled off the Internet, I had a crisis of confidence. Mostly because we didn't see a house. There was just a two-foot-high rectangular slab covered in weathered tar paper, a Porta Potty, a rusted-out Datsun coupe with vanity plates that read SHRTSLR — shirt seller? — and a pickup that made mine look like a new Range Rover. And a mailbox with Fuzzy's street number and the word *OW*.

I jumped out of the car and Harry followed me, unfolding his lanky limbs like a praying mantis.

"OW," I read. "Oscar Wolsonowicz?"

Harry looked at the slab. He walked over and leaned down for a closer look. Without standing up, he waved me over.

"Look for a door," he said.

We circumnavigated the slab from opposite directions, meeting on the other side at a metal Bilco hatch, painted black, with a sign that said LOSE HOPE ALL YE WHO PASS THROUGH HERE.

Harry pounded on the hatch door.

"What the fuck!" yelled a trebly, electronic voice a few seconds later.

We looked around and Harry spotted a speaker next to the hatch. Seeing no way to reply, he pounded on the door again.

We waited almost a minute, then heard the sound of the latch being pulled back, followed by the hatch door opening, groaning on its raw hinges.

A square-headed pale white guy with slippery black hair, a thin beard, and thick, plastic-rimmed glasses poked out. Unhappily.

"What. The. Fuck," he said.

I squatted down to get on his level.

"Mr. Wolsonowicz? I'm Jacqueline Swaitkowski. An attorney and officer of the court."

I handed him my card. He took it like it was a free ticket to next Sunday's Declare

Your Sins for Jesus tent revival.

"Yeah? And?" he asked.

"Your uncle, Sergey Pontecello, has died. There are issues relating to his estate I need to discuss with you."

His nascent sneer grew into the real thing.

"Who the fuck cares," he said, reaching to pull the door back down. He got partway there before Harry caught the edge of the door and pulled it back up.

"Ah, come on, fella," said Harry. "She just wants to talk to you for a minute. Why not give it a chance?"

Fuzzy looked up at him, which from that perspective was a very long look.

"What do you want me to say? I don't know anything about him. Married to my mom's sister. Hardly ever talked to me. What did he die of?"

"They found him on the road," I said.

He smirked again.

"There's a news flash. Drove like a drunk old lady."

He looked at Harry again, who was wearing a white band-collar shirt, a gold earring, and a pair of round wire-rim glasses through which gleamed ice blue eyes. Before going bald at about twenty-five, Harry'd been a platinum blond. So now, at about forty-five, his eyelashes and eyebrows were snow-white, making him look almost hairless. This took some getting used to, though if you looked at him long enough, you'd notice he was actually sort of cute.

"You a lawyer, too?" Fuzzy asked him.

"Strictly transport."

"You said estate. There's money involved?" Fuzzy asked me.

"Like the man said, we just want to talk. Can't hurt. Might do you some good."

Fuzzy clenched his eyes together and shoved his shoulders up against his neck like kids do when their mothers tell them to eat all the green stuff off their plates. Then he popped open his eyes and threw up his hands.

"Okay, what the fuck," he said, walking back down the steps.

We followed.

Fuzzy's place was more or less what you'd expect. Dark, damp, dirty, and crammed with junk. Electronic junk — beige, black, and gray boxes covered in buttons and dials and flickering lights. Every kind of monitor, from the old green screens stacked three at a time to gigantic flat LCDs hanging on the walls. The furniture was basic couch. Big couch, little couch, convertible couch, leather, velour, Herculon, and unidentifiable synthetic couch.

The walls were a charming concrete. No paint, no wallpaper, no art, no decoration at all. There was mood lighting — depression being the mood encouraged by little task lights with opaque metal shades scattered around the ceiling.

I liked the refrigerator in the middle of the room. Always kept you close to cold cuts and beer. He had a fan blowing on the refrigerator's coils, and every shallow window had an air conditioner struggling to hold the temperature at about sixty.

"What happened to the house?" Harry asked, pointing at the ceiling.

"Burned down."

"Bummer," I said.

He shrugged. "Nothing says you have to build it back again."

"Except for a few dozen state, county, and municipal statutes," I said.

"She's a real-estate lawyer," said Harry.

"I thought this was about Sergey's estate?"

"Mind if we sit?" I asked.

He shrugged again.

"I don't care. Grab a couch," he said as he plunked himself down on an office chair in front of a computer screen, a big one, on which some sort of online game was running. I picked a leather couch. Less likely to hide things that bite.

Fuzzy noticed me looking at the big screen. He spun around and rested his hands on the keyboard.

"I'm in the process of scouring the Free Earth Quadrant of alien hostiles," he said.

"Really."

As a presumed resident of the Free Earth Quadrant, I was grateful for his success. Harry bent down to take a look at the monitor.

"You made it all the way to level twelve. Impressive. I've never gotten past ten."

Fuzzy scoffed.

"Twenty-two is my personal best, making me one of three Grand Warlords in North America. There's only one son of a bitch in the entire world who's made it all the way to level twenty-five, and he's like a Tibetan monk or some shit."

"So, anyway," I said, "we're here to talk about something important."

"Like this isn't. Just a stupid video game. Kid stuff. You try it sometime. NASA scientists'll tell you getting to level twenty is statistically impossible."

Harry nodded. "He's right. Grand Warlords aren't minted every day."

"Oscar," I said.

"Fuzzy," said Fuzzy.

"Fuzzy. I need to tell you something about

your Uncle Sergey."

"He wasn't my blood uncle. I just called him Sergey. Or sometimes Dipshit."

"He didn't just die. He was murdered."

Fuzzy shook his head as if trying to shake a thought out of his brain. Despite the twitchy reaction, there was little surprise behind his eyes. "You're shittin' me."

"I'm afraid not. The police think somebody beat him up, then threw him out of their car. Tough way to go."

"Yeah, I guess," he said sarcastically. "Even for a miserable little prick like Sergey."

"No disrespecting the dead. It'll come back at you."

"Legal advice?"

"Spiritual," I said.

"So now you're a priest?" he asked. His voice had moved up a notch in register.

"Any idea who did it?" I asked.

He jumped out of his chair. "So now you're a cop? What the hell is this?"

"Why don't you sit down, Mr. Wolsonowicz," said Harry, his voice a lot calmer. "We are."

Fuzzy didn't seem to have a firm grip on his movements. As if coordinating thoughts, feelings, and facial expressions wasn't the automatic thing it should have been. I had trouble fixing his age, especially with his potbelly pushing out from under an untucked Pepto Bismol — colored shirt, and his black peg-legged jeans and white Velcroed sneakers. But I figured early thirties.

He sat down.

"So what do you do for a living?" I said, looking around the basement. "Looks like something with computers."

"You think? Yeah, something with computers. Everything with computers. Nothing matters but computers."

I felt myself about to leap down his throat, but Harry slipped in front of me.

"Boy, you got that right," he said. "I live on the darn things. Used to just help my business, now it *is* my business."

"Oh, yeah," said Fuzzy, warming to the hint of empathy.

"Harry's logistics on computers," I said. "I'm legal on computers. And you're what again, Fuzzy?"

"Everything you can do. Hardware, software, rants, blogs, columns. And trading, of course."

"Trading?"

"Day trading. The WWF of capitalism. Raw and rude. Trench warfare in the battle of chumps, champs, and suckers. The haves and have-nots. The insiders and outsiders. Kill or be killed. Pure play roulette made out to look like some sort of legitimate commercial enterprise, a rational exchange of wealth based on sound and sacred economic principles. Bullshit. It's a blood sport."

Here was the FuzzMan I'd come to know. He finally sounded like he wrote, though a toned-down version.

Harry grinned and pointed at Fuzzy.

"Now, that's a rant. You are a writer, for sure," he said.

I probably should have let Harry's diplomacy soften him up a little more, but I'm not a terribly patient person.

"So who do you think did it?" I asked.

Fuzzy looked confused.

"Did what?"

"Killed old Sergey."

He did another of those head shakes. I expected to see something fly out of his hair.

"I haven't seen him in years. I was supposed to go to some service when they planted Aunt Betty, but I was all tangled up in shorts — selling short, not in my own shorts — and couldn't let my eyes off the screen. In the time it takes you to hit a key, a stock can shoot up ten percent."

"I thought that was good."

"Not when you're caught in a short

squeeze," he said. "When you short a stock, you bet on it going down. Going up is very, very bad."

I wanted to comment on his priorities, but I was trying to take Harry's sympathetic, nonjudgmental lead.

"So no guesses. On Sergey," I said.

"Not even a wild-ass guess," said Fuzzy. "What do you think the cops are going to ask? Same thing?"

"What cops?"

"They called yesterday," he said. "Asked me about Sergey but didn't say anything about any murder."

I didn't tell Fuzzy to get ready for the hostile, suspicious, and highly judgmental approach of Joe Sullivan. Let him learn that for himself.

"So you heard about all this from the cops? Your mother didn't tell you?" I said.

Fuzzy stared at me, his face a mask.

"My mother?"

"Eunice didn't tell you about Sergey?"

His whole face turned into a snarl.

"For her to tell me something, I'd have to talk to her. I don't talk to her, so no, she didn't tell me. All I know is what the cops told me, which was the old freak was dead."

"How come you don't talk to your mother?" I asked.

He looked at Harry as if to say, "Could you do something with this broad?"

"How come?" I asked again.

"Tell me again why I'm talking to *you?*" he said.

" 'Cause I politely asked?"

"That's polite?"

"Advice on manners, from you. That's a good one," I said.

"I invited you into my home."

"Is that what this is?" I asked, looking around.

I could hear a low rumble of disapproval coming from Harry, but I was done with diplomacy. It can only take you so far.

"What the hell was so bad about Sergey?" I asked. "Or for that matter, your Aunt Betty? You couldn't tear yourself away from your damn computer long enough to go to her funeral? Why so heartless?"

"You can't call me names in my own house," said Fuzzy.

"This isn't a house, it's a crypt. And if you don't like my questions, wait'll the cops come to call. All I can do is be rude. They can decide you're a material witness and have you locked up in a place that makes this dump feel like the Waldorf."

Fuzzy jumped out of his moldy chair and pointed his finger at me. A tiny trace of white foam actually formed at the corner of his mouth, but before he could find the right words, I asked again, "Why didn't you go to Aunt Betty's funeral? What did she ever do?"

"Nothing," he spat out. "That's what she did. Absolutely nothing." Then he sat back in his chair and crossed his arms, thoroughly hunkered down. "Get out of here," he said.

I was ready to give it another push, but when I looked over at Harry it was clear he really wanted me to back off and climb out of that creepy basement. So reluctantly, I tore myself away and let the sleazy geek get back to everything you can do with computers, no matter the death and dying going on around him.

"Sorry," I said when we were back in the car.

"Not a very pleasant fellow," said Harry.

"You tried to work around that. I probably should have let you."

I struggled to get my breathing under control. What would have helped was a cigarette or something more intoxicating, but I'd put Harry through enough for the day. So instead I sat quietly, which I was grateful he let me do for about an hour. Then he ventured a conversation.

"At least you learned something, right?"

"I learned Fuzzy was the crud I thought he was. I don't know what else."

He let that sit until we were almost back in Southampton, when he said, "So, not a little bit curious?"

"Beg pardon?"

"About the last two years of my life. That's not like you. I expected to be thoroughly grilled by now."

He was right. For some reason, I'd shied from asking. Not that I wasn't aching with curiosity, suspicion, and a few other selfish and illaudable feelings.

"I assumed you were in a coma. Though you look way too good for that," I said.

"If you don't want to know, that's okay," he said.

"You think I'm that easily manipulated? Okay, so tell me."

So on the way back to the East End he told me what he'd been doing, which was more or less the same thing he always did — move stuff around the planet. He frequently did big projects for military and government agencies, but he was just as happy moving little things as big things. Such as shipping Fabergé eggs to Mongolia or fresh internal organs for transplant in Tierra del Fuego.

He'd recruited a twenty-member family of Indonesian sailors to run a convoy of barges across the Indian Ocean to South Africa, where they were refused entry and had to continue on to the Mediterranean, where they loaded the freight on lorries in Marseilles and snuck into Rotterdam pretending to be British NGOs brought in by the Dutch government to provide cultural sensitivity training.

That's the kind of thing he does. And he told the truth when he said computers were now his business. All he needed was a laptop and a cell phone and he could run the whole show. Which meant he could live anywhere they had broadband and decent cell service. Which they have in Southampton.

"So this is where I've decided to stay," he said. "It doesn't mean I won't have to travel occasionally, but you won't find a better home base."

"I haven't looked for one," I told him, "but I believe you. I want to believe you. Because I'm here for good, for better or worse."

"So we're both here. Hm."

"Yeah, hm. Let's discuss this later on," I said, and then returned the conversation to his recent adventures, where I wanted it.

Not because I wasn't thinking what he was thinking. I just wasn't ready to think it.

I don't like the gym. I find exercise sweaty and uncomfortable. And boring. That's my biggest problem with physical fitness. I can get bored in the middle of a roller-coaster ride. After a week pedaling a bicycle that doesn't go anywhere, I find my sanity starts to erode.

The only cure is a frequent change in scenery. I've been on every machine in the gym, taken every aerobics class, invented some of my own swim strokes, and even signed up for interpretive dance after a week of yoga where all we did was stretch and clear our minds. I'm pretty limber already, and the only way to clear my mind is to do a full lobotomy.

I stuck with the dance class longer than usual. It was the interpretive part that worked for me. It was impossible for the instructor to tell anyone their interpretations stank. Plus, since I don't mind making an ass out of myself, it turned out to be the right choice.

It was close to ten o'clock when I left the gym. I was sure about that because I liked to catch the start of the ten o'clock cop shows. I've heard people say they hate seeing dramatized versions of their jobs. Too close to home. In my case, there's nothing about these shows that has anything to do with the actual thing. The shows are so much more interesting and sexy. Everybody looks great, they all live in million-dollar apartments and work out of space-age offices lit by blue fluorescents and courtrooms with carved molding and twelve-foot-high windows. What's wrong with watching that?

The gym is about fifteen minutes from my house. I usually take the back roads, even off-season, so I don't have to think about what I'm doing. The truck runs on autopilot.

My route takes me through the potato fields just north of the highway in Southampton. There's still a lot of open land up there, though it's being steadily eaten away by development, and there're no street lamps, so it's pretty dark.

My route goes due west through Bridgehampton horse country. During the day you get to look at thundering huge mansions, long lines of white fences, and well-bred jumpers trotting around looking cocky and well fed. At night it's just a long two-lane road.

Then you turn up Brick Kiln Road. My road. It takes you out of the open, rolling fields and up the hill and into the woods. You also go from this nice straight, smooth road surface to a serpentine washboard. This is where my husband found himself too drunk and driving too fast to adjust to the change in circumstances.

That night I was cold sober, and too fast was never a possibility with the old pickup. In fact, I was trying to gain a little ground speed to overcome the hill before the first curve when I saw the truck behind me. A real truck. A big truck going so fast that the headlights went from pinpricks to almost filling the mirror in the time it took me to look away and look back again.

My first thought was, Man, he's really going to have to hit the brakes. And then I realized he wasn't going to hit anything but me.

This solved the acceleration problem. I was suddenly going a lot faster, with the rear end of the Toyota now trying to pass the front end. This put the little truck in a full spin. I stood on the brakes, which might have been a bad idea, but what else was I going to do? The tires sounded like a city of the doomed on their way down to hell.

My father taught me how to cock the wheel to pull out of a spin, so miraculously, I kept control after a single three-sixty. I was so relieved by this that I almost forgot how I got there in the first place. So I didn't have the Toyota aimed where I should have when the truck hit me again.

I was able to turn to the left as I flew forward, just missing a tree. The move threw me back on the road surface. I shoved the shift knob into second and floored it.

The truck behind me recovered quickly and was bearing down on my tail before I reached the next curve. Something told me trying to race the guy was a losing strategy. So I did the opposite. I yanked the steering wheel to the right and hit the brakes.

This almost worked. He cleared my bumper, but then somehow jammed up on my side. We were now moving at about the same velocity, but he was locked on my right fender, my truck now an insignificant gnat, helpless against overwhelming horse power superiority.

So there was nothing I could do when the other truck broke free and sent me hurtling toward the big tree except to ponder, in that time-out-of-time moment before you hit something at a high speed, the lovely irony of going out just like Potato Pete. Flying free over Brick Kiln Road. Watching the gi-ant gray column come at me mighty and aloof, and thinking, All that nice work on my face, and now this.

6

People who suffer massive head injuries usually don't remember how they happened. I guess that's nature's way of shielding you from the horror, letting you heal and get on with your life without having to relive the moment over and over.

That's how it was with me after getting blown up by the car bomb. I went from being late for lunch with Sam to swimming in a gooey, hallucinogenic stupor. The shock wore off about the same time as the painkillers, which was partly by design. The doctors wanted to ask me how I felt, to get my read on the overall situation.

I said I felt about as shitty as a human being was capable of feeling, and that was before they showed me my face — what was left of it. I'm not the suicidal type, but I have to admit the question of life or death at that point was a coin toss.

If you don't smash up your head in a terrible accident, you'll probably remember everything that happened, like a movie in slow motion that lets you take in every exciting moment.

Maybe that's why I had plenty of time to jerk the steering wheel all the way to the left, which caused the top-heavy little truck to flip on its side and slide about ten feet, so instead of a head-on collision, the top of the bed hit the big tree, absorbing most of the concussion and spinning the Toyota like a top into a grove of saplings, which absorbed the rest.

That's when I learned the Toyota had an air bag, which scared me more than the impact when it blew up in my face but kept me safely pinned to my seat as the truck whirligigged through the woods.

And that's where I stayed frozen, braced for another blow from the assassin truck. When it didn't come, I discovered my arms and legs were all still working. I wormed my way around impediments, like the shift knob, until I was more or less standing on the passenger's side door. The seat belt was now half wrapped around my neck, which was better than having it squeeze the part of my chest already blossoming an angry bruise.

I unsnapped the belt, reached over my

head, and opened the door far enough to prove I couldn't open it any farther. I wedged my foot against the side of the passenger seat and pushed up, trying the door again, this time getting halfway out before it closed on top of me like the jaws of a wounded but determined shark.

I was stuck, but at least I had a view of the road, so far clear of murderous pickup trucks. Feeling vulnerable, I frantically wriggled through the door and dropped to the ground, where I looked up at the stars for a while, wondering which were the lucky ones I was supposed to thank.

A car passed. I held my breath and lay as still as a stump. As if that was enough to camouflage an overturned Toyota pickup truck. And to what end?

I stood on shaky legs and leaned back against the dirty underbody. That's when my cell phone rang, from inside the truck. I wasn't going to climb back in, stupid as it was to leave it there, so I got to listen to it trill at me for a while.

Then I reconsidered. How sensible was it to be a few humiliating and uncomfortable moments away from contact with the outside world?

After burning my hand on the muffler, I found a better handhold and a place to put my foot, and was about to hoist myself up when Danny Izard raced up with every light on his patrol car ablaze. I guess if the Town went to the trouble to put all that stuff on your car, you want to use it.

"What did I tell you about pushing turns in that toy truck?" he said, as anyone would do to comfort and reassure an accident victim. "You all right? Bleeding anywhere?" he said, sticking a thousand-watt flashlight in my face.

I reached through the light and took it out of his hand. I shut it off and told him to call an ambulance and then call Joe Sullivan. I wasn't giving my statement to Danny and then be stuck with him as the reporting officer for the life of the case. I liked him, but he was too much of a dumb kid for this one. I needed a grown-up.

He looked unsure but did as I said.

As I hoped, Joe got there before the ambulance. With one small blue light on his dashboard blinking discreetly. I hoped Izard took note.

By now I was sitting on the ground with my back against a tree. I was drinking a bottle of water Danny had given me and smoking a cigarette, which unlike my cell phone, I had the sense to stuff in my pants pocket when I got dressed at the gym.

"Good, you got a smoke," said Joe, walking up to me. "The paramedics can skip that part."

"It wasn't an accident," I said. "Some big pickup pushed me off the road."

He reached into the rear pocket of his jeans and pulled out his casebook.

"Really."

"No idea of year, make, or model, but it had four wheels and a big bumper that he used to ram me."

"Ram you? Actually physically, intentionally drove into the back of your truck?" he asked, looking skeptical.

For the first time since the crash I felt a little sick.

"We're not gonna go through that, are we? I tell you what happened and you tell me it was my imagination or lecture me on probative evidence or pat me on the head and tell me condescendingly that you'll look into it? If that's what we're going to do, get me another cop who'll stop fucking around and take this seriously."

His face fell halfway to the ground.

"Okay, Jackie, jeez. I'm not doubting you. It's just a hell of a thing to say happened."

"It's what happened. I don't know what color it was, either, but it was dark. Blue, black, gray. Maybe lighter than that, though definitely not white. Where's that ambulance? I'm think I'm going to puke."

Sullivan made me lie down on a patch of weedy grass on the side of the road and put my feet on a knapsack he dug out of his car. He took off his jacket and put it over me.

"Don't start getting chivalrous," I said through my teeth, which for no reason had started to chatter.

"If you die of shock they'll fire me. I need the job."

I didn't think the problem was physical. It was the thought of somebody going to the trouble of trying to kill me. Intentionally, with malice aforethought. Which it had to be, because random, unprovoked killings are less common than a meteor hitting you on the head. Even if I cut the guy off down on Scuttle Hole Road, and I didn't, this was an overreaction. Even for City people, and they don't drive pickups.

I hated that feeling. Nauseating fear.

I looked over at Pete's pickup, probably a total loss. So there's a silver lining, I told myself. It made me chuckle, which Sullivan probably thought was shock-induced dementia.

"So, Joe," I said. "I'm thinking the next ride's a Volvo, but I can't decide between station wagon and sedan. I'm always hauling stuff around, but does anyone date a woman who drives a station wagon?"

"Hang in there, Jackie," said Sullivan, leaning over me next to Danny Izard, concern written on their faces.

On the way to the hospital, the paramedics had a fun time listening to my heart, shooting penlights in my eyes, and squeezing body parts like my mother kneaded bread, all the while studying my face for evidence of pain, which they didn't have to do. I had no problem yelping if I needed to.

By the time we got there, they were acting as though nothing was hugely wrong, so I relaxed. Relaxed so much that I almost passed out. Which is why I didn't know Sam was there until I was rolled into an examination room, where I opened my eyes.

"Everything still working?" he asked.

"Haven't tried everything yet. Sullivan must have called."

"He told me you were okay, but I'm a bugger for confirmation."

"You're a bugger, period," I said.

"I'll check off 'Change in personality' as a 'No.'"

"This is not good."

"Markham said you were probably fine."

Markham as in Dr. Markham Fairchild,

Jamaican giant and king of Southampton Hospital's emergency and trauma unit.

"I'm talking about what happened," I said.

"Getting run off the road? Been there. No big deal as long as you survive."

I forced myself up onto my elbows so I could look him in the eye. "I need to find out who did it and have them permanently incarcerated or I won't be able to sleep, eat, or drive a car ever again in my entire life."

I like to think I'm good at reading people — interpreting their facial expressions and body language. Good luck trying that with Sam. I guess he has the same muscles in his face the rest of us have, but I'd never seen them in action. I used to play poker when my dad's friends caught me sneaking a peek at their game in the basement. That's where I learned what people meant by a poker face, and the best of them were Marcel Marceau compared to Sam Acquillo. He just sat there and stared at me. Implacable.

"What?" I said.

He stared a little more, then said, "You're not gonna let down, are you?"

"What do you mean?"

"Back off from what you're doing."

Maybe letting down is not a bad idea, I thought to myself. Better that than dead.

"Can't do that now. I have to find out," I said.

"What?"

"Why me? I must've done something to bring this on. What the hell did I do?"

He stood up from the visitor's chair and sat on the edge of my bed. He took my hand in both of his. Hands bigger than a man his size should have. Meaty, knuckly, calloused, and coarse to the touch. But careful and tender.

"Good," he said. "And don't worry. If someone kills you, I'll kill them. Simple."

I don't know why acts of kindness make me want to turn the other way and run. Maybe it's a reverence of self-sufficiency or maybe I don't work well in team environments or maybe I just can't stand the intimacy.

Sam was an exception, usually. The ledger with him still had a balance in his favor, though there were plenty of entries in both columns.

So I did the logical thing. I grabbed the poor guy's sleeve and held on until I fell asleep, a little drugged but mostly on board with his logic:

You're gonna die eventually anyway. You might as well live the life you have without worrying about who or what is going to end it.

Or how.

Later that night, after surviving some poking and prodding by Markham Fairchild, I got a pat on the head and a ride home in Sam's old Pontiac Grand Prix. The car, once a total loss after a similar run-in, was now completely restored for no good reason anyone could think of, including him. I told him Potato Pete's pickup would not enjoy the same resurrection.

Sam offered to stay with me, but I did what he really wanted and told him to get out of there and let me get some sleep. I gave what I thought was a convincing performance because he seemed to leave convinced.

It wasn't until I was alone in my house, after I'd carefully and dispassionately stripped off my clothes and taken a shower, slathered cream all over my body, and poured myself a glass of wine, that it was safe to sob a little.

I hated myself for it. Not the crying, but the cause. I hated losing control of my emotions. I couldn't afford it. Not now. Now that people were actually trying to kill me, too, it was time to get serious. I had a dead client to look after — one who might be past looking after — but that was tough.

I wouldn't have chosen the method, but I had to admit, they had my attention.

7

The next morning I couldn't move, predictably enough. Markham had given me a bottle of painkillers. The label said three a day, so I got a head start and took two. I waited another hour, then got out of bed and felt my way to the bathroom.

I pulled up my pajamas to assess the damage in the mirror. Half my left boob had turned purple, with highlights in pink and yellow. Very attractive. It actually looked worse than it felt, and it felt really bad. I checked around the rest of me and found a few more ugly red splotches, though in less intimate places.

I examined my face, calming the irrational fear that somehow the crash had dislodged all that lovely plastic surgery. It hadn't, of course, but that's why it's called an irrational fear.

When I went to get dressed, a bra was out of the question. Just looking at it made me wince. So I went for a tube top, baggy shirt, and loose jacket combo that looked so good I wondered why I hadn't thought of it before.

A little concealer from a tube — almost dried into stone for lack of use — was all I needed to dab out the welt on my forehead and be ready for public consumption.

And Harry.

"You did what?" he asked when I called him on my cell phone.

"I didn't do anything. It was done to me. I'm okay. Just a little banged around. The truck, on the other hand, is a goner."

There was a moment of silence on the line.

"I need to come over there."

"No," I said, before he barely had the words out. "You don't need to come over here."

"It's not safe."

"Yes, it is. It's safe if I keep moving," I said.

"I want to see you."

"I'm going over to the Volvo dealer to buy a car just like yours. We'll match."

He pressed me to describe the accident and my actual condition. I got him off the phone by promising to tell him everything, in person, as soon as I had the chance.

"I'll pick you up in my new car," I said.

I'm not sure where I stand on big, strong men. If you pay attention to the words, it makes some sense. Big, strong men. When you're feeling threatened, there's just nothing better. This wasn't the first time I'd attracted murderous attention, so I knew that well enough.

But if I gave in to that now, there'd be no going back. Harry couldn't follow me around all day, and Sam wouldn't. Eventually I'd start resenting the constraints on my freedom and get all twisted up in gender angst and be worse off than if the truck had done a proper job running me off the road.

So when the cab arrived, I ran the ten yards and jumped in the rear seat as if a thunderstorm was raging, but I did it on my own.

As it turned out, I picked the right mood to negotiate for a new car. Testy paranoia, seasoned with a feminist rage that would've embarrassed Bella Abzug. I got the car I wanted, at the price I wanted, and likely paved a less condescending path for the next unwed sister who wandered into the dealership.

The Internet has made it impossible to hide anymore, unless you intentionally change your identity, and that isn't easy. If you're a regular law-abiding member of society, I'll find you. The more active you are in the world, the easier it is to pin you down. I'll know when you were born and your parents' names and their parents' and your other ancestors' as far back as I have time to look. If you go to school, graduate, get married, buy a house, get a job, get a promotion, get divorced, get fired, get foreclosed on, get arrested, sued, or released on parole, I'll know about it. If you're famous, or you come from a famous family, I'll know even more and twice as fast.

Wendy Wolsonowicz would probably find that appalling, given where she'd decided to live. She was the only one of the immediate family I hadn't talked to, so I picked her as my next stop.

She'd moved to Shelter Island from Arizona about the same time as her adopted brother. Shelter Island is a big landmass wedged between the North and South Forks of the East End. You can only get there by ferry. This is one of the reasons it's escaped some of the more rapacious development out here, but there's also not a ton of land you can develop, since a huge hunk of the place is wildlife preserve. Wendy had somehow managed to buy the only piece of private property within the largest preserve, an island itself surrounded by a couple thousand acres of wilderness.

At two million dollars, a two-acre parcel boasting the ultimate in fashionable seclusion might look like a steal. Until you read the fine print, where it says she can't sell it, transfer ownership, or pass it down to her heirs. The seller was an ornery holdout from the time the Nature Conservancy was buying up contiguous tracts who negotiated a onetime private sale with the deed forfeited to the preserve upon the death of the buyer.

So this was a girl serious about her privacy.

A few minutes after turning on to County Road in my new car I was reproaching myself for holding on to the rattletrap Toyota for so long. The only similarity between the two vehicles was they had steering wheels and tires and moved over public thoroughfares. The Volvo was so quiet you couldn't hear the engine when the radio was on. In contrast to the pickup, where you couldn't hear the radio when the engine was on. I'd have to exercise more to compensate for the reduced effort needed to shift gears, steer, and brake, but on the bright side, my kidneys would probably last a few more years.

I turned up North Sea Road and headed

for the ferry to Shelter Island. The decision to go solo was looking better all the time. It was dicey enough barging uninvited into Wendy Wolsonowicz's costly isolation without bringing along a behemoth like Harry Goodlander.

Alone, I got to pay a little attention to the weather, which was exceedingly lovely and mild and sparkly, as it often gets in the fall. North Sea Road winds all the way to Noyac, where it becomes Noyac Road and goes from there up through North Haven to the South Ferry dock. Most of the trip is in the woods, except for a long, gentle curve along the southeastern shore of Noyac Bay. My heart always picks up a beat or two when I look out over the water, even after a lifetime of looking at the little lakelike bays that fill in the gaps between the forks.

Today it was fairly wavy, but no whitecaps, and bluer than usual. Probably because of the deep blue autumnal sky. This was how water at its best was supposed to look. Not British Racing Green. Not turquoise, like a '55 T-Bird. But a nice deep blue, like a shiny new Volvo station wagon.

I was halfway around the bay shore when a big pickup came up fast behind me. He flicked on his high beams and blasted his horn. I pulled onto the shoulder and he whooshed by. Then all I had to do was wait for my pulse to fall to normal range and dig my fingernails out of the steering wheel before getting back under way.

"Dickhead," I whispered into the soft silence of the station wagon.

The guys who load the ferry noticed right away that I had a new car and went out of their way to put me in a safe spot, thereby redeeming the whole class of young men with long sideburns and baseball caps, like the kid in the truck who'd almost run me down. I got out and stood at the side of the boat to look at the water and breathe in a little salt air. The channel was a lot choppier than Noyac Bay, but the stolid, flat-bottomed little ferry wasn't fazed.

When I got to the other shore I looked at the printout of the Internet map. Wendy's place was close to the ferry landing, which was at the southwest corner of the big preserve. So within a few minutes I was following a gravel road dotted with signs hysterically warning against messing with the wildlife, as if that's what people came to wildlife preserves to do.

Wendy's house was built on a rise, with a driveway that curved more than necessary up to an area in front of a separate two-story garage. The house fit on the wooded lot as if it had grown up from the soil along with the surrounding trees.

Three dogs streaked across the property the moment I pulled into the drive. A big chocolate Lab, a white shepherd, and a midsize gray-and-black mishmash of a thing. They looked more curious than aggressive, but I stayed in the car until I reached the house, where I sat and prayed none of them would jump up on the door to get a better look.

A sharp whistle pulled the dogs away from the car. They ran to the house, then came back down more docilely, followed by a tall, big-boned woman in coveralls. She was somewhere in her thirties, with dark hair afflicted by an excess of kink and wave, like yours truly. Her eyes were pale blue, her face broad and friendly, her stride strong and direct.

I got out of the car and offered my hand.

"If you can do that for me, you'll be a miracle worker," she said, pointing to my face, while reaching out the other hand to shake.

This would have been an unusual greeting for anybody, but more so for a woman who'd recently had her face rebuilt.

"I didn't think it showed," I said, unsure of what else to say.

She lingered over our handshake like my dad's awkward engineer friends would do as a lame form of flirtation.

"Are you kidding me? I love freckles."

Being the keen-witted, perceptive lawyer that I am, I spotted a miscommunication.

"I'm Jackie Swaitkowski," I said. "I'm an attorney. I was hoping to talk to you about a case I'm working on."

"You're not from the Fabulous Face?" she asked, looking bemused but no less friendly.

"Sorry, no."

She dropped my hand, looking a little disappointed.

"They're supposed to come today. I finally got up the nerve to try it out."

"Try what?"

"A full neck-up make over. They come to your house. A plus for me, because I don't have a car." She used the tips of her fingers to tap around her face. "First they give you a consult, then do things with peels and mud and face creams."

She looked around her property.

"I spend a lot of time outside," she said. "After a while I start looking like Jeremiah Johnson."

"I understand completely," I said. "For every hour in court I need at least thirty minutes in a bathtub."

The Lab had been shoving against my legs as I spoke to Wendy, and I'd been scrunching around the top of his head. The white shepherd decided to get in on the action. The other dog still held back, moving to and fro, low to the ground and looking up at Wendy with nervous eyes.

"You said something about a case," said Wendy.

"Your uncle's, Sergey Pontecello. He was a client of mine. Do you mind if we chat for a few minutes?"

She answered by walking over to a picnic table under a gnarly-looking shade tree. I followed her and we sat across from each other. I looked down at the tabletop and noticed purple and orange lumps of organic debris, obviously fallen from the tree above. Considering too late, as usual, the fate of my favorite lime green jeans.

"Because he's dead?" she said.

I couldn't tell if the question was rhetorical, so I assumed it wasn't.

"He died a few days ago."

She folded her hands and looked down at the table.

"I heard. The police told me."

"Did they come out?" I asked.

She shook her head.

"I told them everything I could think of

on the phone. They said they might call me back, but nothing about seeing me."

"Odd way to learn about a dead relative, from the police."

"I never talk to my mother. Did she send you?"

I told her no.

"You don't seem too busted up about it," I said.

She raised her shoulders, then settled them back down in a languid shrug.

"Uncle Sergey didn't mean anything to me. I didn't wish him any harm, but he was just this weird little dude who married my aunt. Who I mostly knew as a crabby old librarian who smoked like a chimney and insulted waitresses. I only saw her about once a year. What did they do, have a funeral or something?"

The gray-and-black dog had followed us, staying close to Wendy's side. I'd forgotten it was there until it startled me by jumping on the bench and sitting down next to her. She stroked the dog's back.

"Poaggie always demands a seat at the table."

"Everyone needs a protector," I said.

"Do you have one?"

I pondered that.

"If I wanted."

"We're not talking about dogs, are we?" she said.

"Not in the literal sense."

She looked at her hands again, and in the quiet of that moment, I listened to the world surrounding her reclusive corner of Shelter Island. There was a small prop-driven plane overhead and the distant burr of an outboard, the wind messing up the leafy treetops and the faint whirr of airborne pests. Not much else.

"Quiet out here," I said.

"Oh, yes. That's the point. Maybe you should tell me what *your* point is."

She looked over my shoulder, hoping the girl from the Fabulous Face would soon arrive.

"I don't know if there's a funeral planned. Nothing's been announced. It might be because Sergey's in the forensics morgue in Riverhead, which is where they put murder victims to perform criminal autopsies and sort out custody of the body."

Wendy looked only mildly interested, as if I'd told her Sergey had croaked on the golf course or died quietly in his sleep.

"Murdered? Ridiculous. Who would possibly want to murder him?" she asked.

She'd folded her arms as if to stop herself from playing with her hands.

"So you think some people are too ridiculous to kill?" I asked.

"I do. Me, for example. I live here alone and hardly ever leave. I don't even have a car. That's one of the things I miss about Aunt Betty. She used to drive me in the morning from the South Ferry to the train station in Southampton, and back again at night. I have to go into the City every August because of this dumb proviso my father put into his will. Didn't trust his little girl to look after her own money, so he forces me to prove my competence to these grubby old guys who pat me on the knee and take a fat fee out of my inheritance. Other than that, I'll go for weeks without seeing anyone but a park ranger, usually from about a hundred yards. I was scared to death the first year, but then I realized killers like more of a challenge."

I wanted to tell her killers weren't just stupid and evil, they were stupid and lazy and almost always kill people easiest to kill. A challenge was the last thing they wanted. But to what end?

"Why the isolation?" I asked. "It's pretty here, but it's got to get lonely."

"I'm not a people person," she said. "And I have Bilbo, Poaggie, and Bert. Dog people would understand."

"Not that I don't admire you," I said. "It takes a centered person to live in a place like this. In a week I'd drive myself crazy."

"Too late for me on that one," she said, smiling agreeably. "So if my mother didn't send you, who did?"

"I sent myself. Nobody else seems to care what happened to the funny old guy, except maybe the cops, and they have to. It's their job."

Wendy took a piece of half-carved wood out of her left pants pocket, and a Buck knife out of the right. It was a big knife, and she handled it like an old friend. The first pass dropped a long, curled piece of white wood on the table.

"Your brother said he doesn't talk to your mother, either. What's up with that?"

She didn't look up at me but stopped whittling for a moment, then took off another slice.

"I love the way some people talk about the traditional family as the supreme state of being, the most moral, healthy, and divine association any person could ever have. Do you believe that, Miss . . . what was your name again?"

"Swaitkowski. Call me Jackie. It's easier. And no, I don't believe that."

"Most of the world's great tragedies occur

within the family. Ever read Sophocles, Ibsen, or O'Neill? Let's take a gander at Freud to see what he thought of the family unit."

"What about Fuzzy. Do you talk to him?"

Wendy seemed to wear an impervious outer coating of amiability. It held its strength and resilience no matter where the conversation led.

"You've obviously spoken to him yourself," she said, looking at me over the razor-sharp Buck knife. "What would you think?"

"That you're not all that close?" I said brilliantly.

She smiled, taking it as a joke.

"I loved my father. He was all the family I ever cared about. When he died, that was that. So I am absolutely of no use to you whatsoever, in whatever you're doing, which I still don't quite understand."

She carved off a bigger piece of wood than she'd probably intended. It flew across the table and fell in my lap. I left it there.

Poaggie had been sitting quietly through all this, his little black eyes trained on a spot somewhere below my chin, which I assumed to be my jugular. But then he jumped up and leaped off the bench. With a look of resigned patience, Wendy told me she probably should get back to her chores.

When I didn't immediately move, some of

her patience slipped away.

"I really have to insist," she said in a way that reminded me a lot of her mother, Eunice.

I stood and brushed the colorful plant life off my pants. Wendy stood as well, and whistled. Bilbo, Poaggie, and Bert galloped up as if to herd me back to my car. I'm not good at ending things before I'm ready, but even I know diminishing returns when I see them.

The day was starting to wane, the sun closing in on the horizon. Photographers call this the magic hour because the light turns color dense enough to stick your hand into. It does great things for the complexion, and was appropriately kind to Wendy, whose slightly roughened veneer looked more radiantly and gorgeously healthy than weather-beaten.

"Don't let 'em mess with that face of yours too much," I told her. "It's pretty fabulous as it is."

She didn't believe me, of course. No woman would entirely. Unless she's one of those models who spends her young life drenched in adulation and magic-hour light.

Wendy gathered her hair at the back of her neck and pulled it to one side, giving me a look at the fullness of her face.

"That might be true if I had your freckles."

I didn't believe her, of course.

After climbing in the car, it took me a moment to find the key and the slot you stuck it in. Then a few moments more to remember I had to put my foot on the brake to make it work. There were a lot of safety features built into the Volvo that my Toyota would snicker at, if that was something old pickups could do. I found the button for the window and let it down. During all this goofing around, Wendy had been writing something on the back of a small piece of paper. She gave it to me through the window. It was her phone number and e-mail address.

"I'd really rather not have people coming to my house uninvited. It's unsettling when you're out of the way like this. You understand."

"Sure," I said. I gave her my card.

"My e-mail's on there," I said. "If you think of anything you want to tell me, feel free."

She studied the card.

"He wasn't funny," she said.

"Huh?"

"You said he was a funny little guy. He wasn't funny. He was unctuous and self-important and deluded to the point of being oblivious to everything going on around him. He was never funny."

She put the card in the top pocket of her shirt and walked back toward her house.

Bert and Bilbo went with her, but Poaggie sat at the edge of the lawn and waited for me to leave.

"Creepy little mutt," I said, loud enough for his sensitive dog ears to hear, and headed off toward the dying light of the sun, not so magical anymore.

8

After seeing Wendy Wolsonowicz, I spent the night finishing off half-smoked roaches stashed in various ashtrays around the house, brooding over dysfunctional families, including my own, and pretending not to be spooked by every random sound in the house.

The dope did a lot to take the edge off things, but I thought a little red wine in the mix would work even better. This led, as it sometimes did, to the opposite intended effect. The brooding slowly gave way to abject gloom, of the boozy free-floating variety, though it wasn't long before I passed out on the couch, too tranquilized to be afraid, too immobilized to care.

When I woke the next day, my mood matched the sky, which was on the darker side of dark gray. I felt around the side table for the telephone, in the process clearing the table of a few catalogs and grabbing a handful of ashes, but eventually found the receiver and dialed a number I hoped my memory had accurately preserved.

"Goodlander GeoTransit," said Harry as buoyantly as I'd hoped he would. "Goodlander speaking."

"Say something positive about me," I croaked, my voice clogged with the evening's excess. "What am I good at?"

"Trivial Pursuit. The only time we played you basically ran the table."

"Being good at trivia isn't what I'm looking for. Something meaningful."

"You don't give up on people, no matter how much you might want to, until it's proven beyond a reasonable doubt that they deserve being given up on. You don't give up, period. No matter how hopeless the pursuit."

A gentle warmth flowed into my chest, out to my limbs, and into my dreary, ill-tempered mind.

"Then why did I give up on you?" I said.

"We don't know for certain that you did. I'd say you were up in the air, and I left town before you could make up your mind."

I made a sound I hoped conveyed approval without commitment and slouched deeper into the overstuffed cushions. I told him he was saving my life, or at least my day.

"You can save my night tonight," I told him. "As promised."

I dragged myself out of the hole in the couch and into the shower. Soon after, reasonably restored, I made it out the door only a half hour later than the deadline I set for work days, mostly honored in the breach.

After sitting at a long traffic light, I was about to turn right onto Montauk Highway when I looked to my left at the big bank on the corner. It gave me an idea, so I turned left instead, which offended the guy behind me who'd foolishly believed my right turn signal. I rolled down my window and waved, saying sorry too quietly for him, but loud enough for my conscience.

Harbor Trust was the biggest bank on the East End. Like every bank these days, it was the product of recurring waves of consolidation, still ongoing. The names on the outside changed, and the buildings got nicer, but the people inside were all pretty much the same people who'd been there all along.

Along with agents and buyers, banks were part of the holy trinity of real-estate law. A bank was usually indispensible to the process, even though cash deals are more common in the Hamptons than elsewhere.

Consequently, I got to know a few bankers.

One of them was Elvin Graveley, who was neither elfish nor grave. He looked like he'd lost his hair in the first grade, giving him the impetus to wear thick black-framed glasses and grow a hefty paunch, completing the stereotype. He had a nice nose, however, something I rarely noticed on people, though Elvin didn't give you much else to focus on with pleasure. A nice nose and a ready smile, if you took the trouble to notice.

I found him at his station, a large mahogany desk at the back of the bank behind a privacy screen made of frosted glass.

"Hey, Elvin. How's the money game?" I asked, thrusting out my hand so abruptly, it forced him back in his chair.

"Hey, blondie, money game's good. Looking for some?"

"Sure. How 'bout a few hundred thousand I don't have to give back."

"We can do that. You book the flight to Rio while I start on the paperwork."

"Rio's no good. Can't speak a word of Portuguese."

"Then the deal's off. Embezzlers only get to fly down to Rio. Bank rules."

"Pity. Can I buy you a cup of coffee instead?"

He peered at me through his thick lenses.

"You only buy me coffee when you want something from me."

I was honestly offended.

"Not true. I buy you coffee just for the hell of it all the time. It's only later I think of something I want from you."

"I'll get my jacket."

We risked our lives running across Montauk Highway to get to one of those local places overlooked by the cars and trucks heading east in the morning — desperate to escape the traffic and get on the job — and ignored by the counterflow ten hours later, when minds were more focused on beer than caffeine.

The proprietors had worked hard to reinforce their clandestine status, refusing to post a single sign, unless you counted the local fund-raising posters yellowing in the window. Yet there were always about five or six people in the place whenever I went there with Elvin, and I don't think they were the same people every time.

They gave you a wide choice of coffees: regular and decaf, with or without cream and sugar. If you bought two cups up front, at a discounted price, it was a bottomless cup after that. Maybe this kind of merchandising wizardry solved the need for additional promotion.

The old lady with the jet-black hair who ran the floor set us up with the first of our two coffees, which I insisted she bring sequentially. I also bought a plate of eggs and bacon for Elvin and a bagel for me, which I used as a delivery system for giant wads of Philadelphia Cream Cheese.

"A full breakfast," said Elvin. "You must really want something."

"It hurts me a little that you think that," I said sincerely.

"It shouldn't. I like it when attractive women buy me off. Just don't tell my wife."

"Okay," I said, "here's what I want. The complete bank records for Elizabeth and Sergey Pontecello going back as far as you can. And the contents of their safe-deposit box."

We both enjoyed the joke.

"The dead guy? You know I can't do that, Jackie. What do you really want?"

"How close can you get?" I asked.

"Not close at all. That information is completely confidential. I can't even look at it unless I'm on official bank business. Especially when it's all tied up in probate. If I revealed anything without the administrator's permission I'd get fired. And then prosecuted. And then tarred and feathered.

Or maybe that comes first."

"The police are going to show up with a subpoena."

His curiosity ticked up a notch.

"That's different. But not for me to deal with. That's the manager's business. How do you know they're going to show up?"

"Sergey's not just a dead guy. He's a murder victim. The cops need to know his financial situation. It takes them a little while to get the paperwork together, but you can expect them at any minute."

"Like I said, the manager's business."

"But he doesn't actually pull the records and stick them in an envelope. Somebody has to physically do that. Like you."

Elvin had that look of incredulity I so often bring out in people.

"That sure as hell wouldn't be me. I write mortgages. I hardly know how to get money out of my own account."

"I don't want you to do anything even remotely improper," I said, clear enough for witnesses to hear.

"Hm."

"I just think if you happened to chat with whoever does pull the records, you might hear something interesting. Nothing improper about a little chitchat."

Elvin shook his head.

"You don't get how this works, do you? This information is going to be pulled by someone barely a notch above a regular teller. Like a supervisor, somebody who can gather it up without a lot of questions. These people stare at numbers all day long. Unless you ask them to look for something specific, those numbers mean absolutely nothing. The person will go into account files, click on little boxes, download a barrel of data to print out or put on a CD, depending on what the cops want. And that's that. Nobody looks at anything, and even if they did, it wouldn't mean anything to them without a frame of reference."

"Poo."

Elvin took a mouthful of his bacon and eggs. "Unless they had a personal banker," he said.

He could see my mood, about to slip into dejection, suddenly revive.

"I like the sound of that. Personal banker. What's that?"

"Our better customers, which means the ones with the most money, are assigned an individual who oversees all their bank business. Mostly moving money in and out, wire transfers, but sometimes managing investments, trusts, even life insurance. It's called a concierge service, which should give you the idea."

"So it includes dry cleaning and tickets to *Les Miz*."

"If there's enough money in it, probably. If the Pontecellos had a personal banker, he or she would know everything about their account. In intimate detail. And before you get too excited, personal bankers treat client confidentiality like the Air Force treats the nuclear code."

I moved off the subject so Elvin could finish his breakfast in peace, easing the possibility of severe heartburn. I worked on eating the cream cheese off the bagel with a fork.

"You could maybe find out if the Pontecellos had such a person and give me the name. That can't be so terrible," I said as I picked up the check and grandly folded it around a twenty-dollar bill.

He grinned at me, I want to think affectionately.

"I could do that under the guise of innocent curiosity. An unfireable offense, even at a bank. And the same defense will get me past Saint Peter, because in fact, I am a little curious. Though maybe not so innocent."

"You're a devil," I said, which broadened the grin enough to convince me some affection was involved.

As soon as I got back in my car I called Joe Sullivan and left a message on his voice mail. By now he'd know I was running out ahead of him on his case. He wouldn't like that. Actually, he'd hate that. He was very methodical and a little slow off the mark, but I was no more than one step ahead. The only way to stay on this was to feed him information that he might be able to use and at least give the appearance of full and free cooperation.

Anyway, as the victim of an attack myself, I had an excuse for bugging him. I knew he'd be working it as hard as he could, but it never hurts to keep top of mind.

His voice mail budgeted about two minutes a call, so it took a few installments to bring him up to where I was that morning, just leaving Harbor Bank.

"I'm guessing Sergey didn't have a pot to piss in," I said into the phone. "His sister-in-law held their house as collateral against a big loan, which might have given her standing to kick him out after all. I'm also guessing he had an account at Harbor Trust, where he might have had a personal banker. They might be broke now, but they used to have money, and that comes with a personal banker. I'm getting his or her name. I think you should maybe drag the poor dweeb into an interrogation room to scare out the nuances, so to speak. And before you start yelling at me about telling you how to do your job, these are just suggestions. Excellent suggestions, I might add. And you could repay me by letting me listen in on the interview. It might actually help, which you know is all I want to do."

That's as far as I got before the voice mail timed out again. The beep almost sounded like it was sick of hearing me talk. It was a wise machine. Another few minutes and I'd have sold past the close, as I often do.

9

My office in Water Mill was my new favorite place on earth. First off, it was a real office I have to drive to like an adult, not stagger into wearing my pajamas like I did when I worked out of my house. It has my name on a little aluminum plate screwed to the door above the name of the dour surveyors who share the second floor with me. I had the top spot, which I imagined irked the surveyors, though we never talked about it.

I'd still managed to infuse the atmosphere with a little of my domestic charm. There were lots of windows to let in fresh air and light up the overstuffed furniture, a coffee-maker, and a tiny refrigerator just big enough to hold white wine and light cream. There were also a few extra things stacked around to complete the homey feel but not enough yet to overwhelm the space completely.

Sam said it was more like a landfill than

an office, though you can't give too much credence to a guy whose house made a Shinto temple look like a cluttered heap.

I spent most of the day trying to catch up on all the client work I'd let slip while chasing down the Wolsonowicz family and being chased by killer pickups. This is where an Irish Catholic upbringing really shows its worth. There's no such thing as a casual responsibility with me. Once I tell someone I'm going to do something, it becomes an Obligation. A Sacred Trust. A Covenant Sanctioned by God. The scale of the Obligation is irrelevant. I put the same dedication into dropping your letter in the mailbox as I do into clearing the title on your new million-dollar house. Or keeping your sorry ass out of state penitentiary.

So I think it's only fair, given my commitment to managing a person's legal affairs, that I get a little wiggle room as to when that management actually takes place. Some people invest way too much importance in things like timing and schedules. Sure, you have to get to the station on time, but is that the *only* train that'll get you where you want to go?

I plowed through nearly the whole backlog before the middle of the afternoon, when I gave myself a well-earned pause for nicotine, coffee, and a good stare at the windmill across the street. I'd forwarded both my phones into voice mail, so I also checked for messages. One was from Sam.

"Call me," he said, and hung up.

So I did.

"Do you know a woman named Edna Jackery?" he said, instead of saying hello.

"Do you know who you're talking to?" I asked.

"Jackie Swaitkowski. Or somebody using her phone."

"Who's Edna Jackery?"

"The owner of the nipple. The former owner."

I'd forgotten about the nipple. Probably pushed it out of my mind. Only so many grim images you can retain at a single time.

"Wow. How'd you find that out?" I asked.

"Suffolk County forensics. They had a tissue sample on file."

"Isn't that sort of confidential?"

"The M.E. is an acquaintance of mine. He owed me a favor. It's pretty fresh information. Sullivan will get the report tomorrow."

"So I'll act surprised when he tells me."

"If he tells you," said Sam. "The cops don't usually make a habit of sharing investigative information with civilians."

"I'm not a civilian. I'm an officer of the court."

"You near your computer?" he asked.

"I'm looking right at it. I guess that's near."

"See what you can find out about Edna Jackery. The M.E. told me she was a hit-and-run. That's all I know. I'll hold."

I often thought the only reason Sam cared about me was because I looked up information for him on the Internet. He used to be a bigshot tech-head till he went off the rails and got himself fired. You'd think he'd have his own computer. Maybe he would if I didn't always do what he wanted. Jackie the Luddite enabler.

It took a few moments to log on to my favorite browser and go to a site that archived local news. Sam took it all as patiently as ever, which means not at all. I could hear him huffing into the phone.

"Just hold your horses," I said. "This doesn't happen instantaneously."

"Then what the hell good is it?"

I watched the hoped-for information fill the screen.

" 'Edna Jackery,' " I read from the news report, " 'forty-two and the single mother of a teenage son, was declared dead at Southampton Hospital, where she was taken after suffering multiple injuries after being struck by a hit-and-run vehicle on County Road Thirty-nine on Thursday night. The police are actively investigating and say there is limited information on the series of events leading to the woman's death.' "

"When was this?" Sam asked.

"About a year ago," I said, then kept reading. " 'Edna Jackery was an employee of Sydney's Snack and Scuba Shop, also located on County Road Thirty-nine, where she was a bookkeeper and occasional cashier. She reportedly worked late that night, and police speculate that she decided to walk home after failing to start her 1997 Chevrolet Malibu, which apparently had a dead battery.' There's a bunch of other stuff about the survivors, and what a good mother she was, and the memorial service, and the rest of the usual."

I looked for more recent articles, but there was only one, which said the police had yet to track down the hit-and-run driver.

"If Edna Jackery died at Southampton Hospital, Markham would've been the one to declare, am I right?" I asked Sam.

"If he was there, and when isn't he?"

"You can ask him what happened to her nipple."

"I'm not asking him," he said.

"Why not?"

"I'm on my way to the Pequot to eat fish, drink vodka, and crack a new physics text from the library. See if I can bring a little certainty to Werner Heisenberg."

"I don't know how you read stuff like that. It makes my hair hurt."

"Tell me what you find out," he said. "I'll do the same."

"Certainly."

My new car was still where I parked it. I don't know why it wouldn't be, but I was feeling overly protective.

As predicted, Markham was at the helm of the Southampton Hospital ER. The woman who sat in a little glass booth just inside the double doors, through which I'd recently been wheeled, examined me carefully when I asked to see him, looking for blood or evidence of blunt-force trauma.

"Dr. Fairchild is on the surgical floor on a consult. How important is this?" she asked.

"It's regarding a murder investigation," I said, hoping that sounded important enough.

She seemed unhappy about it, but picked up the phone and murmured into it for a few minutes. Then she looked up at me.

"What did you say your name was?"

"Jackie Swaitkowski. He knows me."

Still looking at me, she listened and nodded and pointed to the waiting room.

"Any relation to Pete Swaitkowski?" she asked.

"Widow."

"Oh. Sorry. My sister had a terrible crush on him in high school. I guess you're the one who caught the fish."

"More like a bird," I said, and went to sit down. I'd had this exchange a few hundred times since Pete and I got married. Nobody could argue with Pete's looks. Or his gentle, good-natured smile and eagerness to do whatever dopey thing anybody else thought would be fun. He'd walk in a room and all the gay men and heterosexual women would drop dead in love. I finally got used to it when I realized he was oblivious to the whole thing. Probably assumed it happened to everybody.

Half an hour later, the woman in the booth waved to me and told me to meet Markham in the canteen.

"I didn't know you were in the employ of the police," he said as I approached. He was sitting at a table with a half dozen cups of yogurt, apparently purchased from one of the vending machines.

"I'm not. The victim was one of my clients."

"And one of mine?" he asked.

"Sergey Pontecello. Found in a bloody heap in the middle of the road."

He nodded as he dug around the bottom of the yogurt container.

"I love the ones with all the little pieces of fruit," he said. "It's like finding buried treasure."

"He was declared dead at the scene, so I assume they took him straight to the forensic morgue in Riverhead."

"That's right. But I hear about it from the paramedics. They like to impress me with gruesome stuff I don't actually see, so I can't prove them big talkers."

"Not sure they could exaggerate this one. Pretty gruesome."

"I take your word for it, Counselor. How you feeling yourself? Sometimes the bad stuff take some time to show itself. That neck okay?"

Markham Fairchild was the biggest person I'd ever seen. He was almost as tall as Harry, but twice as wide everywhere else. Not fat, just enormous. I loved to watch his hands — which should have been too big to do anything other than wrench boulders out of the ground — handle delicate medical instruments or sweetly brush the hair out of a patient's face.

"I'm fine, Doc. Thanks for asking. I'm also interested in a woman named Edna Jackery. She was a hit-and-run, about a year ago. The newspaper said they brought her here."

Markham gathered three empty yogurt containers and flung them one by one with startling accuracy into a trash can easily ten feet away. He peeled back the foil on number four.

"One of the blessed, that one. Gave it up in less than an hour. Could still be on the fancy equipment in someplace to dis day, breakin' the State of New York's bank and her family's heart."

"So no hope."

Markham tapped the side of his head.

"Once the brain give up, there ain't a whole lot can happen. Modern medicine can keep the rest runnin', but that's just a technical trick."

I didn't know how to ask the next question delicately, so I just asked.

"What kind of shape was she in, otherwise? I mean, the rest of her body. Was she all ripped up?"

Markham must have found some interesting treasure, because he spent the next few moments intently digging around the bottom of the yogurt container.

"I got so much stuff to t'ink about and

paperwork to do, I never have time to t'ink about anything else, you know? But that don't mean I totally forgo my natural curiosity. So, Counselor, that curiosity is asking me, what is all dis about?"

"It's complicated."

"I once sewed a man's penis back on that was three-quarters severed by a flying saw blade. That was complicated."

"Yeah, but did it still work?"

"The saw? No. But according to my lucky carpenter, all systems are go."

"We found her nipple," I said.

"Mrs. Jackery's?"

"It was in Sergey Pontecello's pocket. So that's why I'm here."

Markham took a break from devouring the yogurt to sit back in the canteen chair, which didn't seem capable of supporting him, and give me a look both sour and perplexed.

"That lady was all head trauma. A couple small cuts and contusions from the impact, but the cause of death was a header into the pavement. I've seen dis a lot. Car hits person, person ends up on hood, driver panics and hits brakes, person, who could be fine if they only just stop the car, goes flying like a missile into the road headfirst, and the rest is up to the funeral director."

"So as far as you know, all nipples were where they should've been."

He nodded.

"For sure, presumin' they real. Got a lot of nipping and tucking coming through these days. Including nipple nipping, if you can believe it. What is it with the ladies to go messing around with their natural selves?"

"The ladies have a lot of pressure on them, I guess," I told him. "We're still figuring out how to deal with it."

He shook his head sadly.

"Dr. Fairchild," I said, "one other thing. Joe Sullivan will probably be calling you with some of the same questions. It would be oh so convenient if you didn't sort of mention that I'd gotten here first."

He went back to digging around in the yogurt container. I sat and watched in silence, suddenly feeling stupid and small, not a hard thing around the good doctor. Before I suffocated in the dead air, I thanked him, apologized, and bolted from my chair. I was almost to the door when he called out to me.

"Of course, Mrs. Jackery stop off at the same place as Mr. Pontecello."

I stopped.

"Huh?"

"All hit-and-run mandatory autopsy. Murder investigation. All done by the M.E. in Riverhead. And I thank him for it. Autopsy's not my cup of tea."

I knew that, but I thanked him anyway.

"And Counselor," he said. "Only one withholding from the police per customer. Next time, don't ask."

I thanked him again and headed out the door before I could further embarrass myself. I'd have to be more careful if I was going to approach Suffolk County Forensics, or the medial examiner, who worked in the same lab. I'd gotten to know them on some of Burton's nastier cases. They were brilliant, exacting, and as paranoid as hell, living in mortal fear of missing a crucial detail that would blow up a case. You can guess how they felt about defense attorneys, the people often decrying slipshod procedures and incompetence. I could see myself dropping in on the lab and casually asking if they'd misplaced any nipples lately.

I sensed my mood starting to teeter, which was ridiculous. One little bump in the road and it's misery. But before darkness fell I had another thought. I checked my watch, hoping it wasn't too late, and drove out to County Road, where I thought I'd find a place called Sydney's Snack and Scuba Shack.

The building sat alone in the middle of a field. It was a converted house, or more accurate, converted shack. Somebody, perhaps Sydney himself, had hand painted the sign, which was about three feet high and ran the width of the second floor. The style of lettering was late 1960s Haight-Ashbury, and the choice of colors startling in their incompatibility, which might have been Sydney's intent. A different sort of artistry expressed itself on the front door, which was covered with a three-quarter-size poster of a Dallas Cowboy cheerleader wearing scuba gear.

Inside, an avalanche of aquatic equipment cascaded down from the walls and spread out across the floor. More clung from the rafters and aggregated around freestanding displays whose original purpose was long forgotten. Flippers, goggles, tanks, regulators, weight belts, baggy trunks, snorkels, surfboards, kayaks, paddles, wet suits, underwater radios and cameras, dry bags, knives, and life preservers for small, medium, and oversize dogs. In a far corner was an island of relief, a small counter with a half dozen chrome-and-black leather stools, behind which was a single shelf with a blender, an espresso machine, and other subtle evidence of food preparation.

Zen serenity in the midst of material profusion. Couldn't be the work of the same person. I said as much to the wiry, balding, ponytailed guy in a tropical shirt unloading a box of Day-Glo buoyancy compensators. I assumed it was Sydney.

"Brandon Wayne," he said when I introduced myself.

"Oh. So who's Sydney?"

"My girlfriend. Ex. Twenty years, now."

"Sorry."

"Don't be. I booted her. Probably for no good reason. Not a bad girl. Though explaining the name of the place all the time has probably improved my memory of her."

"So which was her idea, the water gear or the snacks?"

"Neither. She wanted a hair salon, one just for men. Make 'em all look like Duran Duran. Couldn't abide that. I got into food after rehab. Don't let the empty stools fool you. Come in around December and the joint's full of Joes off the construction sites drinking joe."

He held one of the buoyancy vests up to my chest, frowning appraisingly.

"Supposed to be a safety thing. Makes you look like beach ball."

"Gee, thanks."

He caught himself.

"Not the shape. The color. I don't think divers are going to dig it. Would undermine their dignity." He dropped the vest back into the box. "So what're you looking for? Not exactly the season, unless you're heading south."

"Information," I said.

"No more training classes till the spring. I could sign you up now."

He climbed over the box and headed for the mound at the back of the room that served as a counter. I picked my way around the stuff on the floor while I tried to explain what I meant.

"Not diving information. I was wondering about Edna Jackery."

He stopped cold and turned around. "You family?"

"I'm an attorney." I handed him my card. "I was looking into another matter when something related to Edna came up. That's when I learned she'd been killed in a hit-and-run."

"Great person, lousy bookkeeper. I still don't get why you're interested."

The truth is a funny thing. It's usually the most reliable fallback, but plenty of times it can do more harm than good. Other times, it's just too damn complicated to be a serviceable strategy.

"I'm doing research on hit-and-runs. Especially those involving women, who seem to be disproportionately affected. It's too late to help Edna, but maybe my report will save someone else's life. That's enough for me," I concluded earnestly, suggesting that not helping me was tantamount to involuntary manslaughter.

He crossed his arms and nodded. "I told the cops everything I know. I liked the hell out of Edna, but she was the sloppiest person I ever knew." I forced myself to keep my eyes on his and not gaze around his shop. "A natural-born fuckup, and blissfully unconcerned about it, though like I said, a doll to be around. What can I say, I'm a sucker for the type."

"Me, too. The newspaper said she was working late and had to walk home because her car wouldn't start."

He shook his head, looking down at the floor.

"I wished she'd just called me. I'd have driven her home. She didn't want to bother her dopey kid, who was probably responsible for screwing up the car in the first place. It's dark along this part of County Road. No streetlights, and the glare from the traffic can be disorienting, even if you aren't a knucklehead like Edna. Forgive me, Lord, may she rest in peace."

"Some knucklehead ran her over and didn't bother to stop or call an ambulance."

"Yeah. Motherfucker. If I catch him before the cops . . ." He made the gesture of a quick slip of a knife across his throat. It looked fairly authentic, so I probably looked surprised.

"Naval training. SEALs," he said.

My surprise deepened.

"Where do you think I learned to dive?" he said. "Worked off a sub for four years. No big deal. Just a job like any other. What else you want to know?"

I shook off a vision of the fiftysomething Brandon Wayne climbing a cliff in a wet suit, in the dark, with a knife in his mouth, stabbing and garroting an unsuspecting sentry, packing plastic explosives under the gun emplacement . . .

"Did she know anyone named Pontecello or Wolsonowicz?" I asked.

He thought about it.

"I didn't know her well enough to know her friends. Those names are a little familiar, though. Maybe they came in the shop. Men or women?"

I ticked off the members of the happy family, throwing in the dead artist for extra measure.

He nodded.

"That's what rang a bell, probably. I knew Tony's work. I'm an artist myself," he added, pointing either toward the inspiration of heaven or his psychedelic sign.

"That's yours?" I asked, almost breathlessly. "Really something. Honestly."

"Couldn't paint like that now. Had to move on. I'm into miniatures. Like crazy miniature. Use steel microfibers and ultra-low-viscosity dyes. Kills the eyes, even with a big magnifying glass, but it's so cool."

"Did Tony ever come in here? Or any of his other family?"

He thought some more, then shook his head.

"I'd know it if he was here. Not sure about the family. I could check the archives, but knowing Edna, they'll be a mess."

I described Sergey Pontecello, but that also drew a blank. It didn't surprise me. Sergey would have been a serious fish out of water in there, if you can use that analogy in the most watery place in town.

"What do these people have to do with Edna's death?" he asked.

"I don't know. That's why I'm asking."

He studied me in a way he hadn't before.

"You know the best part about getting off

153

the junk?" he asked.

"The money savings?"

"The clarity. You realize your brain still functions almost as good as it used to, despite all the abuse. It's an amazing instrument."

"And yours is working pretty well right now. I can see that."

"It is. You know what's even more amazing? The way the junk can teach you to see things a brain that was always clean and sober would never notice."

"Like a defense attorney who's pretending to be doing a study when, in fact, she's running a murder investigation?" I said lightly.

He grinned at me.

"Yeah. Like that."

"Running an investigation is too grand a thing to say. I'm nosing into the murder of Sergey Pontecello to the annoyance of the real investigators, the police, because he was a client of mine, and I feel an overwhelming sense of responsibility for the guy even though I had absolutely nothing to do with his death. As far as I can tell. Though I'm not entirely sure."

"I sort of feel that way about Edna."

"There's a connection between her and Sergey Pontecello that's already been established, but I can't tell you what it is without compromising the official investigation and permanently alienating the cops, which would end my criminal practice, which I don't need but gives me a way to repay all the favors I owe to people like Burton Lewis and Sam Acquillo, and assuage at least some of this vague, societal guilt I inherited from my bleeding-heart mother despite all the counter-efforts of my sanctimonious, self-entitled old man."

The part of my brain responsible for putting the brakes on that other part of my brain finally woke up and pulled the lever. My mouth clamped shut, but the momentum of the unspoken thoughts caused me to lurch forward and almost lose my balance. Brandon waited for things to stabilize.

"Golly," he said.

"Sorry," I said, opening my pocketbook and rummaging around as if I were actually looking for something and not covering up my embarrassment. When I came across a stack of business cards held by a rubber band it felt like divine intervention.

"Here," I said, holding out a card. "If you come across any of the names I mentioned in connection to Edna" — I put the card down on the counter and wrote the names on the back — "please call me. That's my cell number. You should also call the police"

— I wrote down Joe Sullivan's name and number — "this guy specifically. Just do me a huge favor and don't tell him I was here. Unless he asks specifically, then tell him. Better I take the hit than you get charged with hindering an investigation."

Brandon took the card and looked at the names, then slipped it into his shirt pocket.

"Okay, Ms. Swaitkowski, whatever," he said. Though I had a feeling he'd call me if anything came up. It was that lingering sense of guilt. I could smell it on him.

I stuck out my hand and gave him the assertive, masculine shake I usually reserved for assistant district attorneys and single men I wanted to discourage. He returned the favor by nearly crushing my knuckles. Former Navy SEAL, I reminded myself.

"You never asked me about Slim," he said, still holding my hand in the vise.

I used my other hand to extract it before responding.

"Who's Slim?"

"Slim Jackery. The husband."

"Why did I think she was a single mom?" I asked.

"That's what it said in the paper. She was divorced but still lived with Slim. Edna once said something about going through with it all, then changing their minds but not wanting to confuse things even more by getting married again. Standard-issue Edna."

This was a gigantic relief for me. There's nothing you can say that's okay to a kid who's lost a mother. Not that the husband would be a walk in the park, but at least he wouldn't be wearing fresh, new skin and the unsettling ignorance of adolescence.

Brandon told me Slim had an automatic sprinkler business, but he couldn't remember the name. He'd met him only once, when Slim came in to buy foul-weather gear for his crew, hoping to exploit Edna's employee discount.

"There isn't any such thing, but I gave it to him anyway," said Brandon. "Thirty percent, so Edna'd have something to brag about around the house."

"Did she?" I asked.

"Never heard a word. That's how I normally think of my good deeds: doing the unnecessary for the ungrateful."

I took his hand back in both of mine and squeezed as hard as I could.

"It wasn't your fault," I said.

He used his free hand to rub the naked crown of his head and smooth back the long, thin remains of hair at the back.

"I told her she had to come in that night to close out the month because I only had a few hours the next day to get to the bank before taking off for the Keys. What's your excuse?"

"I thought Sergey was a silly little man. Before I had a chance to take his predicament seriously, he was dead," I said.

"So at least we understand each other," said Brandon Wayne, who should have been Sydney, but nothing's ever what it was supposed to be once you get a close-enough look.

10

I made arrangements to pick up Harry at seven. I liked the old-fashioned gender protocols about who picks up whom and who picks up the check. But not all the time. This was never a problem for Harry, another big point in his favor. And I wanted to show off my new car, which was just like his car.

The directions he gave me to his place ended with "When you see what looks like an old gas station, you're there."

"You're living in a gas station?"

"Former. More recently a vegetable stand and most recently, before me, an artist's studio. Sculptor. Liked the big doors for hauling in and out big hunks of steel."

"Big hunks in, fine art out," I said.

"We'll let history be the judge of that."

I found the place easily enough, even in the dark, which it wouldn't have been at seven, but I was running a little late. I'd made the mistake of peeking at the computer before getting into the shower. I'd typed "lawn irrigators, Southampton" in the search box.

Slim Jackery was there on the first page, three-quarters of the way down, so he wasn't the area's premier irrigator, though you wouldn't know it from the name. His phone number was there, so I called.

"Rainmakers International," said the guy who answered.

"It's good to know you can water my lawn anywhere in the world."

"Strictly Southampton at this time, ma'am, but we're always looking to expand. Where's your property?"

"Bridgehampton. Might be a good stop on the way to Marrakech."

He pressed me on the type of lawn I'd be asking him to water, but I was evasive. The type of lawn I had was a narrow strip of weeds and moss that made a border between the driveway and the woods. Pete didn't believe in lawns, and I was indifferent. Only later did I truly appreciate his vision. Not just the grounds, but the whole place was designed for low to no maintenance. It didn't look like much, but it saved a lot of time and energy I could spend on messing up the inside.

"I'd rather discuss this in person," I said. "Can we meet somewhere tomorrow?"

He gave me an address in the estate section of Southampton. He said the owners were in Europe, but he preferred I use the service entrance. On the way to Harry's I drove by, just to get my bearings. The service entrance was about a quarter mile east of the main drive. Place probably needed a lot of watering.

All this distraction meant I didn't knock on what I thought was Harry's front door until almost nine. He answered the door wearing a terry-cloth towel around his waist and another on his head, turban-style.

"Oh, is it seven already?" he asked, hand to cheek.

At moments like this, the complete character of a relationship tends to emerge, its subtleties, hazards, and enchantments exposed for all to see.

So where do I start?

My brain and Harry's are made of different component parts. Or maybe they're just assembled differently. All my life I've heard about how opposites attract — you're this, and I'm that, so here we are great together!

Not true. Opposites irritate and confuse, disorient and breed unrelenting conflict. There are times when these friction points

161

are suppressed, which is nature's way of getting us to reproduce with people who under normal circumstances we'd rather shove in front of a subway. I read once there were mathematical formulas that have tiny inconsistencies, called statistical noise, that grow every time you run the formula, until eventually they take over and blow the whole thing to smithereens. This is what happened to Harry and me. The noise of our small but essential incompatibilities grew over time until it was all I could hear.

I thought about this as I stood there on his doorstep, but not so much about what caused me to drive him away. More about what got us started in the first place. Two things, actually. His deep humanity and that gigantic slab of masculine glory now on vivid display above the towel. So while my thoughts ran amok, my breath was snatched.

"My," I said.

"That's it?"

"Okay. Amusing. And understood. I apologize. Nice towels."

"You want 'em?" he took off the turban and started to unhook the other towel from the side. I put my forearm over my eyes.

"I want you to get dressed and come out with me. Please. I'll make it up to you. As agreed, I'll drive and provide."

162

I felt him drape the towels over my shoulder and heard him walk away. I peeked just in time to catch the back half of the presentation, and it was worth the peek.

"Oh, crap," I told myself, to all of myself, top to bottom.

At Harry's request, we tossed his portable table and umbrella in the back of my Volvo, along with two folding chairs and the provisions I'd picked up along the way at the wine store and deli. I knew a spot on the beach where a tall dune had been scooped out by a storm, leaving an area protected on three sides from the prevailing breeze. It was a warm night for that time of year. The moon was out and the sky was clear, and there was no one else around.

I left my heels and reservations in the car and followed him across the sand with an armful of food and Australian shiraz. He carried everything else as easily as a normal person would carry a rolled-up newspaper.

I set the table while Harry rigged cute little battery-powered lanterns to the underside of the umbrella. Harry was completely fluent in the black arts of modern technology, without all the self-congratulation and "I can do this and you can't" attitude that guys like him usually have. Gadgets were just a natural extension of his personhood.

They were always around. And always worked, for which I was very grateful.

We spent at least a half hour exchanging ever more inflated pronouncements on how great it was to eat tasty food and drink wine at night on the beach, with the surf sounds and seagulls and fresh autumn air. And it was. So great I became almost stupefied by the sensations. That's why I nearly forgot my obsession with Sergey Pontecello and his charming family. Nearly.

"Harry," I finally said, with a change of tone signaling the shift in conversation. "You're smart. How did Sergey Pontecello get Edna Jackery's nipple in his back pocket?"

I took him through what I'd learned over the last few days, focusing on my conversation with Brandon Wayne and what he had told me about Edna's general disposition and behavior.

"I normally only know how something gets from one place to another if I move it there myself."

"This isn't normal. Think abnormal."

His face twisted a little with the effort. Then it straightened out again.

"Maybe you shouldn't think so much about the how, and think more about the why," he said.

He had a right to be proud of himself. It was a brilliant, albeit obvious, thought. Though it didn't bring me any closer to either one.

"Excellent, Harry," I said. "So, why do you think?"

"Why indeed?" he said philosophically.

I reached across the little table and plucked a pen out of his shirt pocket. I dumped the cookies out of a small white bag that I flattened so I could write on it.

"He found it," I said as I wrote. "If so, where? It was night. He was home. I assume this because I talked to him on the phone earlier on, and that's where he said he was. Phone records will confirm. Though they can't prove he was home after that."

"So he could have left the house later on and found the nipple, like, on the side of the road."

"That's where most people pick 'em up."

"In other words, highly unlikely."

I wrote down "Found it at home."

"If so, where?" asked Harry, reading the napkin upside down. "On the floor? In a punch bowl? In his sock drawer?"

"He said he was just starting to go through his wife's things. I assume that means the bedroom."

"Also the kitchen. And the living room.

Anywhere in the house. It could have been in the coffeepot, under the bed, in the medicine cabinet."

"Not likely," I said. "Eunice had locked him out of the bathroom." I told him more about Sergey's late-night call. "It was in an envelope, let's not forget."

"Then he found it in the mailbox," said Harry.

"If it was in the mailbox, it wasn't just found. It was delivered."

We left that on the table while we each took a sip of our wine. The concept took root.

"Makes a lot more sense," said Harry. "Somebody gave it to him. It was FedExed, hand delivered, tossed over the hedge, dropped off by carrier pigeon. Having the nipple in his possession can only be caused by willful action, not an accident."

I tried to remember the night Sergey called me. Was there anything at all strained in the conversation's tone or content? Given the dither he was in on being denied dental floss, it didn't seem possible that the nipple had arrived before the call.

"He got it later that night," I said. "Otherwise, I'd have known."

Harry nodded.

"Okay, how much time between his last

call to you and the call from the cops?"

I had the exact chronology written down somewhere back at my office, but I could get close.

"Between nine thirty and two in the morning. Assume the neighborhood lady found the body about a half hour before that," I said.

"There's gotta be a relationship between the nipple and his death," said Harry. "You don't have two things like that happen simultaneously without a correlation."

"Sometimes it's coincidence," I said.

"But you don't know."

"I don't know. I have too much ignorance," I said.

Harry grinned at that. "I didn't know ignorance had substance. I thought it was just the absence of knowledge. Like cold is the absence of heat."

I shook my head. I explained that, to me, ignorance was a thing that tends to produce even more ignorance as you process all the things you don't know until you generate this enormous glob of vile, worthless speculation.

"Ah," said Harry, "to put this in terms I can understand, as you bring in small parcels of knowledge, it allows you to collapse the cubic footage dedicated to ignorance storage on a geometrically declining scale. This freed-up capacity can be repurposed to accommodate the resulting growth in knowledge stock, though more frequent utilization might actually drive a net gain in total volume requirements."

"Like the man said, I store, therefore I am."

I spent the night with Harry on a mattress reinforced by a four-by-eight sheet of birch plywood suspended between two saw horses in the middle of the room the sculptor used for the final assembly of his creations. You could still smell the residue of arc welders and metal grinders and what I thought, to my pleasure, might have been marijuana. That was one of the issues on which Harry and I parted company, helping to lead to a parting of more material significance.

I smoked an occasional joint; he didn't. He not only didn't, but he also hated it, sort of the way religious people hated sin and some nonreligious people hated religion. A hate on the cellular level. Being me, of course, I had a hard time understanding this, assuming there was something bigger and nastier behind this unfettered antipathy, though every effort to ferret that out only made matters worse.

The lingering smell of dope was only one of the reasons I liked that place. The panels in the bank of garage doors were glass, so the whole wall felt like part of the outside, which the owner had generously illuminated, giving an all-night view of huge oak trees covered in ivy and blue-green azaleas and a pair of Volvo station wagons of competing vintage.

The ceilings were high to accommodate cars on lifts, which Harry said were still in the floor but long past operational. The prior resident had built all sorts of shelves and cabinets and workbenches, so the place had the feel of earnest industry, of foolishly euphoric enterprise.

There was a fair amount of euphoria of another type also expressed that night, but that's a story that'll have to stay between Harry and me.

The next morning I went directly to the address Slim Jackery had given me. He said he'd only be there till ten. I couldn't risk the trip to and from Bridgehampton, so I went in the same clothes I'd worn to go out to dinner. It was the Hamptons; nobody would notice.

The place was at the end of a street of big estates, or what looked big until you got to this place. On the western border was a grassy swatch of wetlands along a shallow bay, across which was the Shinnecock Indian Reservation.

The service entrance paralleled a privet hedge on the left, leaving the right side open to the yard. Somewhere over there, snuggled in the embrace of towering, luxuriant birch trees was the main house, a four-story brick testimony to what you can do with your money if you have way too much of it and way too little sense of its genuine worth.

I was almost halfway to where I could see a small gathering of white vans decorated with scenes of exuberant tropical growth, which I thought had to be Rainmakers International, when I spotted something more familiar.

Out in the middle of the colossal lawn was a truck with a sign on the door that said RAY ZANDER ESTATE MANAGEMENT. SINCE 1984.

So I took a hard right and drove my Volvo like a Land Rover over to say hi to Ray.

He was on his hands and knees staring down at the grass. He looked up when he heard my door slam. I walked over to him.

"Lost your contacts?" I asked.

"Found some nut grass. Don't know how the devil got in here, but sure enough there's more. The stuff is like a horror movie. You can't kill it. Spreads underground so you take out part of it, another part just pops up and thumbs its nose at you."

He stood and gazed out on the vast landscape, the implication clear.

"Maybe you can negotiate a peace accord," I suggested. "Give up a little territory in return for suspended hostilities."

"You a diplomat?"

"No, but I took arbitration in law school. Do you work a lot with Slim Jackery?"

"Who's that?"

"Rainmakers International," I said, pointing at the white vans at the end of the drive.

"Is that his name? That's a good one. No, but I don't see any of the irrigators that much. We tend to work when they're not around and vice versa. There're no sprinklers for this lawn. They'd need their own reservoir. They just do the shrubs around the house and the vegetable garden, if you can believe that. The guy probably owns a chain of grocery stores and here he's growin' his own tomatoes." Ray bent down and pulled a tuft of nut grass out of the ground. "We can do this all day and it won't make any difference. Nut grass ain't even a grass. They eat it over in Africa, use it for medicinal purposes."

"Maybe we should export it back to them," I said. "Help the balance of trade. How're things over at the Pontecellos'?"

"Strictly Wolsonowicz these days. Other'n that, 'bout the same."

"Any other ideas on what happened to Sergey?"

He shrugged and looked down at the lawn, as if trying to catch a clump of nut grass sneaking up through the lawn. "Frankly, I do have a thought, but you gotta be careful sayin' where you heard it."

"Sure."

"One of my guys told me he'd seen Sergey and Betty at the casino every time he went over there, which was a lot since the son of a bitch is always broke. They weren't slot players, neither. All table games, high stakes. Of course, you figure they could afford it, though there's no limit on what you can lose. If you're catchin' my meaning."

I was. More than he knew.

"You're wondering if Sergey got himself in trouble with gambling debts, maybe owed somebody dangerous."

"Not the casino itself. Them Indian casinos are squeaky-clean. But they can only do so much about the side betting. That's where you get them bad actors. Just a thought."

My regard for Ray Zander, which hadn't exactly started on a pinnacle, was rising rapidly.

"Which casino are we talking about?"

He told me. Of course, I'd heard of the place. There were two of them in Connecticut, an easy ferry ride from the North Fork. I'd never been to either, but most people I knew had.

I wanted to see what else Zander had growing in his fertile mind, but I was afraid of missing Slim. So I thanked him and got his cell phone number so I could chase him down for further discussion. He seemed agreeable to that.

"Jawin' is a lot more interesting than mowing lawns," he said. "Just hard to get paid for it."

I left him and drove back over the lawn and down to the end of the drive. The white vans were empty, but I could see several men waist-deep in a row of yews that bordered the west wing of the gigantic brick building. It was hard to think of it as a house, which is probably why I felt okay about invading their private property to mingle with the gardening help.

As I got closer it was easy to pick out Slim, but I called his name just to be sure. He waded out from the yews and came over to me.

Slim was as close to round as a being with arms and legs could be — maybe five foot five on the vertical and about the same on the horizontal. He had a shiny bald head like Harry's but apparently no neck. Heavy as he was, he was light on his feet, and since he looked like a balloon or a beach ball, you could almost see a stiff wind blowing him up into the sky.

"You the lady that called?" he asked.

"Yes, sir. Jackie Swaitkowski." I gave him my card. "You know, when I called you about my lawn, I realized I recognized your name. I'm terribly sorry about Edna. I knew her from the Scuba Shack."

His face showed sudden sorrow and a touch of embarrassment. I felt bad for thrusting this on him, but I was committed.

"Thanks, Ms. Swaitkowski. Still trying to make sense of it."

"I do a lot of work with the police on things like this," I said, which was a truthful statement, however misleading. "Would you mind if we talk about the accident for just a minute?"

He looked more than unsure, but eventually gave in to the full force of my sympathetic, girl-in-need, oh-please-be-kind-to-me look. As if I were the grief-stricken one.

"Sure," he said. "There's a table over on the patio. Let's go sit."

It was black, wrought-iron, with four chairs, each weighing approximately a half ton. Slim helped me get settled.

He told me he was at a meeting that night with a landscape architect working out an installation for a big new house in the Village. He said he didn't know why Edna hadn't called him or their son to come get her, except that it was like her to get a notion in her head and then act on it. In this case, the notion was they'd be mad at her about the car. As if it was her fault it wouldn't start. He said he'd gotten plenty mad at her over a lot of things but never that.

"Her mind had a funny way of working sometimes," he said. "So while it didn't make sense to me that she was walking along County Road in the dark, it didn't surprise me."

He went on to say that since she'd died he'd been thinking about how stupid he felt for all the arguments they'd had, and for all the things, formerly mentioned, that pissed him off about her. The more he talked, the more the regret grew in his voice, and the worse I felt about bothering him.

"Are the police any closer to finding out what happened?" I asked as gently as I could.

He shook his head.

"They'll never catch him now. If they don't get you within the first forty-eight hours, they probably never will," he said, which I knew to be true. "I don't care, frankly. If he's got any kind of conscience, that'll take care of the punishment. If he doesn't, we'll have to wait for God to handle things. It doesn't matter to me. Catching him won't bring her back. And it sure won't help me or Jeddy get over this. Just make it all fresh again and give me a name to hate rather than my own vision of some poor, suffering bastard I can even feel a little sorry for."

I got so wrapped up in thinking about the intricacies of mourning, forgiveness, and revenge that I almost forgot my main reason for coming to see him.

"Ever heard of a guy named Sergey Pontecello?" I asked. "Did you or Edna know him, or anybody named Wolsonowicz?"

He thought about it but shook his head.

"I don't think so. Funny names. Why do you ask?"

"Sergey was also found dead on the road,"

I said. "The cops have found a connection between him and Edna. I can't say much more without compromising their investigation."

He blanched.

"Don't say any more. I don't want to know."

No danger of that, I thought to myself. I've already dug a deep enough hole for myself.

"I'm sorry, Mr. Jackery. I really am. I'll leave you alone. I just hope you'll contact me if you come across anything that relates to these people." I took my card back from where he had it on the table and wrote down the same information I'd given Brandon Wayne.

"So what about that irrigation system for your place in Bridgehampton?" he asked.

I'd already forgotten the pretense of our meeting. I mentally scrambled, which must have showed.

"You don't really need it is what you're trying to say."

"I don't," I said. "Not right now. Maybe if I can grow a little more grass. If that happens, you'll absolutely be the one I call."

"I'll be there," he said, happy to be back in the world of positive thinking.

"By the way, where's Edna buried?" I

asked when I stood to leave. "I want to pay my respects."

Slim smiled the first real smile of the conversation.

"You like waterslides? Edna was nuts for them. She was also nuts about the Catskills, where she went as a kid. So I put one and one together and tossed her ashes down the Kaaterskill Falls. Risked my neck doing it, but I didn't care much about that."

"That's nice," I said, not knowing what else to say, though I meant it. "So you had the funeral up there?"

"No. At Winthrop's here in town. They get all the Jackerys. Had a nice service before the cremation. I guess they'll get me, too, if they're still around by then."

By the time I left Slim and his watering business, Ray Zander was gone. The sun had crept higher, which made the huge lawn look greener and as uniformly healthy as a putting green. I was sorry to know that evil lurked underneath such apparent perfection, worming its way through the dark dirt, planning the right moment to burst forth and devour everything in its path.

11

I knew it was time to go to the police. I'd already been pushing my luck way past acceptable limits. Joe Sullivan might have been overly methodical, even plodding, but he liked to be thorough and keep orderly records. Which meant he rarely missed anything and never lost a case in court over shabby procedure.

When he wasn't pissing me off, I admired him. He was a by-the-book cop in every way, as honest and dedicated to the truth as any person could be. And he never once even remotely tried to hit on me, which seemed like the favorite contact sport in the law-enforcement community. Some of those meatballs would say and do things to women that would get you sued, fined, or fired in half a second in the regular world.

I arranged to meet Joe the next morning at a diner in Hampton Bays where he liked to eat breakfast. The main attraction was an all-you-can-eat special that brought out his competitive spirit. Luckily, he was big enough that I could see him over the top of his plate, which the waitress must have brought with the help of a crane.

"The cardiology deluxe?" I asked as I sat down, waving to the waitress to bring me my usual bowl of fruit salad and yogurt, which I thought might ward off excess calories spilling over from the other side of the table.

"We gotta go through this every time?" he asked.

"Sorry. It's jealousy talking. I wish I could eat like that and not look like a hippopotamus."

He used his fork to skewer a row of home fries and a link of sausage.

"Let's get something out of the way before you say another word," he said in a dark and unfriendly voice.

I felt all the blood in my body race to my face, which was always a little pink and now likely the color of a valentine.

"What do you mean, Joe?"

"There's a state law on the books. It's called something like 'interfering with a police officer during the pursuit of his official duties' or some shit like that. But it's a real law with real penalties for people stupid enough to break it. The fines and jail time wouldn't be the most serious problem for you. It'd be the disbarment."

"If I was stupid enough to break the law," I said as calmly as I could.

"Not so much stupid as pigheaded."

"Pigheaded, sure. I can be pigheaded."

He shoveled a lumpy red-and-yellow glob into his mouth.

"Confess," he said.

"Huh?"

"Confess everything. Tell me every fucking thing you've done, everything you've said, heard, or thought as it relates to the Pontecello case and do it right now."

He dropped his fork on the table and took a sip of coffee, looking at me over the brim.

"I hear you," I said.

"I'm listening," he said.

So I told him everything I could think of, as he'd asked. Everything but how I got Edna Jackery's name, because that might expose Sam and I wasn't going to do that. That left a big hole in the story, but there was nothing I could do about that. He took out a beat-up leather-bound casebook and took some notes. His face was a blank sheet.

"That's it?" he asked when I paused for a sip of coffee.

"All I can remember right at this moment," I said. "I might've forgotten something. I can't help you holding that against me, but nobody can remember everything."

He studied his notes in the casebook, then looked up at me.

"I can't dedicate my life to any single case, no matter how much fun that would be," he said.

"Of course," I said.

"So anybody willing to put in the time can get out ahead of me."

"Sure."

"Only they don't know how easy it is to fuck up a criminal investigation. They don't know about due process or chain of evidence or the rights of the accused. And that makes them reckless and dangerous," he said.

"It really does."

"But that wouldn't describe you," he said.

I shook my head.

"Oh, no. Absolutely not. That would not describe me."

"Because you know that you have to keep the lead police investigator fully informed of everything you learn, do, or say. In real time. Or else that investigator will have your law license hanging in his family room and will make sure the only job you'll ever get again is in this place, dishing ham and eggs."

He gathered up a shovelful of said ham and eggs and shoved it into his mouth.

"I hear you," I said.

He nodded.

"This is the last time we have this conversation. I like you, Jackie, but not enough to have it again."

"I really hear you," I said. "I really do."

I'd completely lost my appetite at this point but forced myself to eat more of my yogurt anyway. I knew he was right, and I was grateful that it hadn't gotten worse, so in an odd way I was relieved. I'd dodged a bullet, though I felt the breeze as it passed by my butt.

A few minutes later, he said, "I got your message. The Pontecellos did have a personal banker. I've got the woman coming in tomorrow."

"Great. I hope you get something useful out of that."

"You can sit in."

I stared at him for a minute, thinking maybe aliens had kidnapped Joe Sullivan and replaced him with an unconvincing impersonator.

"Really?"

"You said you wanted to help. Here's your chance."

"Can I look at the file?" I asked.

"Not fucking likely."

"Okay."

"You probably know Eunice Wolsonowicz has a lien on the house. Probate'll have to work out who inherits, but the A.D.A. is telling me Eunice has a clear claim."

"Only because Sergey's dead," I said.

"All she had to do was call in the note and he'd have to turn over the keys. No reason to kill him for it," he said.

"Evictions can take a long time in New York."

"Still no reason. She could afford to wait. She can afford anything. There's no financial motive."

"Maybe he could've paid off the note," I said.

"You believe that?"

"No. I believe Eunice, who said they were broke."

"Me, too," said Sullivan.

I let him get in a few more mouthfuls before asking, "Ever wonder what happened to it?"

"To what?"

"The money."

"Yeah, I wonder. Though I bet I'm going to find out right now."

" 'Bet' is a good choice of words," I said.

"Gambling?"

"Yeah. The casino. No quicker way."

"You know this?" he asked.

"Speculation based on secondhand eye-witness testimony. But I know how to find out for sure. Or rather, how you can find out. Correlate withdrawals from the bank with their trips to Connecticut. Hotel and ferry reservations will give you that."

He nodded as he carved a crater in his mountain of eggs.

"You're thinking, Jackie."

"Like I usually don't?"

"That's something my wife would say. I don't like it any better coming from you."

I concentrated on my fruit salad and yogurt while he plowed through the rest of his meal. The place was filling up fast with tradesmen diverted from the river of traffic pouring in from the west.

"Anything else you want to tell me while you're in such a genius mood?" he asked as he used a piece of toast to complete the conquest of his breakfast.

"I appreciate getting in on the banker thing. I really do," I said. "But is there anything else I'd like to hear?"

"Probably lots of things. I've actually been investigating this case myself, you know, between rounds of golf."

"You never played golf in your life."

"I've got another reason for the Pontecellos' financial issues," he said.

He waited for me to ask.

"Okay, Joe. What other reason was there?"

"The broad was a klepto. Liked the good stuff, of course. Designer clothes, jewelry. In Southampton Village, mostly, though we got a complaint from a leather place in Bridgehampton. Cost Sergey a bundle in legal fees and court-enforced therapy to keep her out of jail."

"No shit," I said.

"No shit. The last time was about five years ago."

I'd never met the woman, but I had no trouble seeing an image of her in my mind. My Web search said she'd worked in the East Hampton library for almost twenty years. Extrapolating from Sergey's manners and her sister's pretensions, she must have had a straight posture and attitude to match. I'd known a few compulsive crooks from my Burton Lewis spillover practice. I knew it was an equal-opportunity pathology. Rich people just got in deeper than those with lesser means. The same was true of compulsive gambling. Everybody was eligible to join the club. The rich ones had farther to fall, but they could get there just as fast.

"Gee, Joe. That's excellent information. I really appreciate it."

He toasted me with a mug of coffee.

"Now you want the bad news?" he said.

"Okay," I said, back on alert.

"The trace chrome on the rear bumper of your pickup was so generic we couldn't isolate it closer than Zimbabwe, where they mine the stuff. We didn't find anything else. No tire tracks, paint, nothing that would help identify the vehicle. And no witnesses we can find. Deadest of dead ends."

That was a troubling thought but not the most troubling.

"You do believe me, don't you, Joe?" I asked slowly, looking straight into his eyes.

He looked annoyed.

"Christ, Jackie, if I didn't believe you, I'd be an asshole. You calling me an asshole?"

"I'd never call you an asshole," I lied, having on at least a few occasions used that exact word to express my feelings toward Joe Sullivan, which were admittedly somewhat complex.

"Good. So let's leave it there. I'm not giving up on finding the guy, I just want you to know we don't have much to go on."

I had another thought.

"He also caught a piece of my right rear fender."

"I know. All we got was chrome."

"But he'd have my paint, right?" I said. "And that we can match."

"To a high degree of certainty, as the A.D.A. likes us to say."

"Okay, then start examining every truck on Long Island. You got nothing else to do."

"Yes, ma'am. We'll get right on that."

Feeling stuffed by proxy, I lumbered out of the diner and joined the migration east. I didn't mind the slow pace. It gave me time to think. I was cynical enough to be unsurprised by Betty's secret perfidy. In my experience, rich people are at least as capable of criminal behavior as the next guy, maybe more so, since they have the delusion of invulnerability. But it didn't exactly fit with my sense of Sergey. This I also knew to be a delusion, that a few minutes' conversation could open a window into a person's soul.

The more I thought about it, staring at the ass end of a beat-up dump truck as we crawled through downtown Hampton Bays, a better explanation emerged.

Sergey had things to hide. As a classic old Euro fop, he was fluent in the language of discretion. It was designed to say things without saying anything, a useful skill for a man whose pretensions outstripped his means. A man who hoped to defend his position in life at all costs.

All costs. That was pretty inclusive.

I called Goodlander GeoTransit and asked for the president of the company.

"You always go right to the top?" Harry asked.

"Time is money, boss. It'll take us at least an hour to get to the ferry, and who knows how long after that to drive to the casino."

"We're going gambling?"

"Life's a gamble, Mac. You gotta go for the gusto. Get the hay in the ground while the sun's shining. Chow down on them early worms. Make dust or eat dust."

"Carpe casino?" he asked.

"You're a fast study, bub. Hope you're just as fast with a suitcase. It's a there-and-back, so pack light. Just don't forget to bring lady luck."

"So it's a threesome. I thought you'd never ask."

"In your dreams, tiger. I'm fifteen minutes away and closing fast."

The Twin Forks of the East End of Long Island are usually described as the flukes of a whale's tail, which never made any sense to me at all. Maybe if you looked at Long Island as a big fish, with La Guardia Airport as the eyeball. I always saw it as an alligator with its tail cut off, with the Twin Forks a set of jaws chomping down on a big rock.

The big rock was Shelter Island, home of Wendy Wolsonowicz and dozens of ospreys, piping plovers, and other lucky birds.

It felt good to cross over the island with Harry via the little ferries on the way to the big ferry that left from the tip of the North Fork for the shores of Connecticut.

I was glad for the company. It's one of the things I ping-pong around about. Whether to go it alone or with another human being, be it a trip to the deli or for the rest of my life. Harry told me that was my biggest problem the day before I packed his stuff and set it out on my doorstep, an event we'd thus far silently agreed wasn't worth revisiting.

The weather was in on the conspiracy, so we had lots of sunshine to warm us while we stood outside the car and soaked up the breeze. Once on the North Fork, the trip through the little New England — like towns of East Marion and Oysterponds was an unexpected delight.

The big ferry wasn't as romantic, but it was a lot bigger. And colder. I'd under-packed, though of course Harry hadn't, so I spent the trip in the luxury of an XXL sweatshirt from Penn State.

I'd never been to any kind of casino, ever. I didn't know what you did in casinos. The only mental image I could work up was from the James Bond movies, where they all wore evening gowns and tuxedos with black ties and white jackets.

This is definitely not what we found in Connecticut.

"What's the point of this again?" I asked Harry as we stood on the threshold of a huge room filled wall-to-wall with noisy, glittering machines.

"You put coins in the slots at the top and push buttons or pull levers and if you're lucky, an avalanche of coins comes out the bottom."

"How lucky do you have to be?"

"Very."

We moved on from there in search of the table games. They were harder to find than you'd think. Probably on the principle If you have to ask, you don't belong.

The room was bigger and less intimate than I'd imagined it would be. The ceiling was high and filled with shadow, and the tables were the opposite — lit like a night game at Yankee Stadium.

"Better for the security cameras," said Harry when I pointed that out.

It wasn't until I was actually standing there looking at all those beautiful, thoroughly exotic green felt tables that I appreciated how little I knew about gambling. I hadn't played a hand of cards since my dad's poker games in the basement. So what I knew was next to nothing.

Luckily, I had Harry with me.

"What do you know about card games?" I asked him.

"Absolutely nothing."

Okay, strangers in a strange land. Take that liability and turn it into an asset. Flaunt your failings.

I approached a table where a young woman in a crisp dealer's outfit stood at the ready. I asked her what exactly went on there. The first few words out of her mouth made no sense to me at all, so I stopped her and told her we'd flown in from Mars, where they hadn't evolved the art of gaming. She didn't believe me, but she tried to explain the essentials of blackjack.

I only listened with half my brain, since I knew Harry would be listening with all of his. This was much more his bailiwick — a quantitative pursuit involving statistical analysis and probability theory. Judging from a look at the other tables, it also involved cigarettes, attitude, and alcoholic beverages, activities I was far better equipped to understand.

So when we sat down at the table, Harry was briefed on the rules of the game and I ordered strawberry mojitos.

The next hour wasn't the agonizing bore I'd thought it would be. Quite the contrary. I was close to having a brain seizure from the suspense. I love it when the experience of other people's lifetimes dawns on me in less than a few minutes. Oh, of course, I said to myself. This is why gambling is so crazy exciting and seductive. With blackjack, it was partly the rhythm — the lose, lose, win, win, win, lose, win, lose, lose, lose, win. It was exhausting when it wasn't exhilarating. Harry, as cool a man as ever tapped a queen of hearts, never flinched through the whole thing, but I could see his competitive nature awakening by the cast of his shoulders and his steady, concentrated stare.

Harry had been down as far as two hundred dollars but was up about fifty when I snapped out of it and started asking about Betty and Sergey. I used the old Aunt Betty ploy, good old dead Aunt Betty. I told the dealer they'd made a lot of friends at the casino, and I wanted to spread the sad word of her demise.

"No, ma'am. I don't think they ever played at my table," she said. "But Logan Brice might've known them. He's worked table games longer than any of us."

She pointed to a slight, very dark man with a fringe of white hair and white moustache working a blackjack table across the room. He was playing with a single customer, a much younger, wider, and whiter guy wearing a T-shirt that said I'M ROOTING FOR ANY TEAM PLAYING THE NEW YORK YANKEES.

Harry took off to reconnoiter, and I headed for Logan's table.

"Mr. Brice," I said, looking at his name tag. "I'm Jackie Pontecello."

I almost stuck out my hand but realized just in time he probably didn't want to make physical contact with a customer.

"Nice to meet you, ma'am. What can I do for you?" he said without taking his eyes off the table or hesitating to deal out the guy's next card. He had very long, slender fingers and dealt the cards with the barest flick of his wrist. His features were sharply defined, with a straight nose and squared-off chin that reminded me of Sammy Davis Jr.

"Does my last name ring a bell?"

When the customer folded his hand, Mr.

Brice looked up.

"It does."

"My Uncle Sergey and Aunt Betty came here a lot to play. They both recently passed away. Before he died Uncle Sergey asked me to inform his favorite dealers. He didn't want you thinking he'd just started playing down the road. But he didn't get a chance to tell me who to tell."

"Signore Ponte Vecchio."

"Pontecello."

"I called him Signore Ponte Vecchio. A joke. He liked it, even if his wife didn't so much. You ready, sir?" he asked his customer. The guy shook his head and without saying anything or looking at us, got up and left.

"Gee, sorry," I said. "Did I do something wrong."

Mr. Brice shook his head.

"Some people are just, you know. Some people. Care to play?"

"I really don't know how," I said, sitting at the table anyway. "Can you just show me?"

He smiled.

"Didn't Melissa already do that for you?" he asked, looking pointedly over at our first stop along the way.

"You're observant."

He pointed at his right eye.

"A dealer's curse."

"So you remember what Sergey looked like. Little guy, slick dresser. Had an accent."

He smiled again and this time pointed at his sternum.

"Are you referring to me?"

"I could be, you're right. You guys related?"

"I didn't know Pontecello was Ethiopian."

"Or Brice, for that matter," I said.

"No, that's more vaudeville, as in Fanny Brice."

"Where'd Logan come from?"

"Where I first touched America. Logan Airport. In my mother's arms. It's an easier name to get by on these days than Hakim."

Of course the image he threw into my head — of a delicate, fragile child being held tightly by his terrified but hopeful mother — caused a lump to grow in my throat. I used the drink I'd just ordered, another mojito, to swallow it back down.

I told him an even more embellished story about how Sergey begged me on his deathbed to seek out all the people he'd come to know in the last years of his life and to tell them how much he appreciated their kindness and consideration. The mojitos were responsible for the story getting away from me a little bit, even though I still had a pretty clear image of the real Sergey, mangled and bloodied in the middle of the street. Between that and seeing little Hakim in swaddling clothes, I almost started to tear up.

Logan drew a handkerchief out of some invisible pocket and tossed it to me across the table.

"Clean this morning. Take it. I have plenty more."

"That is so nice of you, Mr. Brice," I said, dabbing the corners of my eyes and looking at the handkerchief for signs of dissolving mascara.

"My pleasure. To be honest, I don't know who else your aunt and uncle might have spent time with here. They usually stopped by on the way to and from the Moon Club, where the high rollers play no-limit Texas Hold 'Em."

"I guess the 'from' game was a lot less happy than the 'to.'" I made sort of a *hah* sound meant to convey the obvious in-nuendo. The bait went untouched.

"Mr. Pontecello was always a gracious and cordial man," said Logan. "To, from, and everywhere in between."

He smiled elegantly, with no sign of duplicity.

I smiled back, I hoped as convincingly.

"That's nice. He would have been pleased to hear that from you."

Harry came out of nowhere and put his arm around my shoulder. I looked up at him.

"Mr. Brice tells me Uncle Sergey made out pretty well at the poker tables," I told him.

Brice put a finger in the air.

"I said Mr. Pontecello was a gracious man. I have no knowledge of his success in the Moon Club, and here at blackjack, it's improper to comment."

I had assumed the dealers would hold their customers' success, or lack thereof, in strict confidence. I just owed it to myself to try anyway.

"What's the Moon Club?" Harry asked.

"High-stakes Texas Hold 'Em," I told him.

I drank some more of my mojito and wondered how scary it would be to play a few hands ourselves at the Moon Club. I'd promised to cover Harry's markers, assuming he'd keep things in check. That might not be possible if we stepped up to the big leagues.

Harry stood and looked at me expectantly.

"I think we're ready to move along," he said.

"We are?"

He nodded.

"Okay, sure," I said, then thanked Mr. Brice and wished him luck, which in retrospect was a dumb thing to do. The only luck he needed was the casino's statistical advantage.

"What's up?" I asked Harry as we walked through a sea of green felt.

"Gotta get some Play Money."

He wouldn't explain until we got to a large glassed-in booth in the middle of the casino floor. We were now much closer to the slot machines, whose cacophony of sirens, trills, clangs, beeps, buzzing, and bells made coherent speech almost impossible. I could see the need for the booth.

The explanation was on a freestanding sign in the middle of the booth. Play Money was a reward program where you earned points in proportion to how much you spent at the tables and slot machines. You could start off fresh with Play One, then go to Play Two, which you could join by earning more than a thousand points in a six-month period. A sleepy-looking young woman standing behind a counter told us the approximate investment needed to reach Play

Two and thus work your way up the next four levels until you reached something called Platinum Play, which she said only her manager was authorized to discuss.

In other words, if you have to ask, you can't afford it.

"When you're a member, you can check your points right over there," she said, pointing with her two-inch-long nail at a row of PC monitors. I took a closer look at the log-in screen — you just had to punch in your user name and password, which you could also do from your home computer.

"I'd love to sign you up right away," said the woman, with less enthusiasm than her words would suggest.

I went over and leaned on the counter.

"Say we got to be Play Three players. Where would we go for dinner?"

The question stymied her for a moment, but she recovered by remembering the stack of brochures in front of her. She picked up one and scanned it.

"I think you'd probably want to go to Le Canard," which she pronounced "La Conrad."

"Ducky," I said as she handed me the brochure. Inside was a description of all the stores and restaurants where we could redeem our Play Money. Without explicitly calling out which places your level qualified you to walk into, you got the implicit idea.

Eventually I realized this wasn't just a casino. It was more like a small city. A very prosperous city whose principal industry was providing a pleasant escape from reality.

And there wasn't a shred of evidence that Sergey and Betty ever shopped at, ate in, or pilfered merchandise from any of the stores or restaurants, admissible via any level of gaming success. I used real money to buy Harry and me cocktails at a place made to recall your last visit to the Amazonian rain forest and gave up the fight.

"This is stupid," I said to Harry.

"But fun," he said, ever the optimist.

"I like the cops. I respect the cops. I enjoy working with them in close harmony. I shouldn't try to be their bird dog."

"Is that what you're doing?"

"If I was an A.D.A., a half hour with a judge, followed by a phone call with my counterpart in Connecticut, and there'd be a blizzard of subpoenas falling on this place."

"Isn't that because we're blessed with sacred rights that preserve our privacy and guard against the arbitrary exercise of government authority?"

201

"That's right, Clarence Darrow, we are. Thank you for that perspective."

I kissed him on the cheek, then pulled out my cell phone.

"Hey, Joe," I said when Joe Sullivan came on the line. "I've narrowed your investigation of the Pontecellos' gambling habits."

"Isn't that swell of you?"

I told him what Logan Brice had told me, at least confirming they played the tables.

"Or, he could just ask the IRS," said Harry, speaking over the top of a brochure he'd picked up at the glass booth.

"Hold a second, Joe," I said, then looked at Harry. "The IRS?"

"Sure. If you gamble over a certain amount, the casino requires you to fill out a win/loss statement. It'll all be there."

"Why didn't you tell me about this before?"

He waved the brochure.

"Didn't know."

Sullivan also knew about win/loss statements. He told me he was requesting them from the other casino in Connecticut and the ones in Atlantic City and Upstate New York. He also told me he was bringing Autumn Antonioni, Sergey's personal banker, in for questioning at ten the next morning.

"What am I doing?" I asked Harry after hanging up with Joe Sullivan.

"Chewing the bone."

"What bone?"

"The bone Sergey Pontecello left for you, that you'll need to chew on until there's nothing left," he said.

"Interesting metaphor."

"And what am I doing?" he asked.

"I don't know. What?"

"Trying to understand you. I always knew you were a determined girl, when you're in a certain mood. You hate things getting in your way. Maybe I didn't appreciate what that really meant."

"So what does it mean?" I asked.

"That's what I'm trying to understand."

"I hate circular logic. It gets in my way."

"So where do you want to get to now?" he asked.

"Back to the real world, while we still can," I said.

"Never thought that applied to Long Island, but lead on."

On the way out we swung by Logan Brice's table so I could ask him one last question. By then there was a full table of blackjack players to whom he dealt his cards with fluid, effortless grace.

I waited for a break in the action. It came when a young woman refilled Logan's card dispenser.

"Sorry to bother you again, Mr. Brice, but I noticed you only talked about Sergey. What about his wife, my Aunt Betty?"

Logan thought about it.

"She liked to play on the way to the Moon Club, not so much afterward."

"Too tired?"

He looked at me, unsure what to say.

"Yes, she was tired. Tired enough to be a little sleepy when they came back through. But, of course, you knew your aunt. How she might be after long hours of complimentary beverages."

"Sloshed," Harry whispered in my ear.

"Ah, of course," I said to Mr. Brice, who smiled with relief when I also said, "I understand."

Before we could leave, he stopped us.

"There's just one other thing," he said. "I think I can tell you this, but please, don't attribute it to me."

"Sure. What?" I said.

"I'm ashamed to say, but I was always as glad to see Mrs. Pontecello leave as I was to see her pull up to my table."

"I know, drunks aren't a lot of fun."

"Not that. This drunk was without a

204

doubt the best blackjack player I ever dealt to. After fifteen minutes of play I could hardly beat that woman, and I have the house advantage."

He slapped the blackjack shoe and made a happy face despite himself.

12

Recent events must have conditioned me to be less vulnerable to surprise. That would explain my incredible poise when a call from Eunice Wolsonowicz woke me early the next morning.

"It's a professional matter," she told me. "You did say you represented my brother-in-law."

"I met with him, yes," I said.

"I need to discuss disposition of the remains."

"The coroner called?"

"He did. There's also the matter of his and Elizabeth's belongings. I have them packed and ready to be shipped, but to where and by whom?"

"Hm," I said professionally. "I may know of someone who could help. You're sure there are no other family members who'd be interested?"

"None I'm aware of, Miss Swaitkowski,

but perhaps that would be something you could determine."

For the first time since getting the call from Joe Sullivan that he'd found a dead guy with my card in his pocket, I felt my heart soar toward the heavens. A divine gift was about to be bestowed upon me, one I thought so unlikely I hadn't even bothered to pray for it.

"Certainly, Mrs. Wolsonowicz. I'll take care of everything. You simply need to assign me coadministrator as it relates to Sergey and Elizabeth's estate. Sandy Kalandro can handle the formalities with Surrogate's Court," I said briskly, then held my breath.

"Fine. I'll give him a call. When do you think you might begin?"

"As soon as I can see Mr. Kalandro," I said.

"Yes, yes, very well. Thank you."

Then she hung up. No good-bye, but I didn't care. I was in a near swoon over the implications. I climbed out of bed, did a dumb little dance, then called Harry.

"Goodlander GeoTransit."

"You're hired," I said.

"That was easy."

"I like your name. Sounds substantial."

"Substance is our middle name," he said.

"I'll need a substantial truck and a substantial guy to help load and unload. And a place to store it all. Big enough to spread out and go through everything."

"You're not joking."

"I never joke about shipping and handling."

I told him about the call from Eunice Wolsonowicz. I filled him in on the legal implications.

"Excellent."

"I need to sit in on Sullivan's interview with the banker lady, then get over to Atkins Connors and Kalandro. Assuming no hitches, how quick can you set me up?"

"It's already done. Call me when you're ready."

I spared him all the dumb jokes about needing hands-on customer service. It was too easy and I didn't have the time. I was already naked and ready to jump in the shower.

On the way over to police headquarters in Hampton Bays, I called Sandy Kalandro, hoping at least to have a meeting confirmed before the interview with Autumn Antonioni.

"Hello, Miss Swaitkowski. Eunice said you'd be calling," said a voice both silken

and deep. Even sonorous, and a tad reso-
nant.

"It's Ms., but you can call me Jackie," I
said, lowering my voice a notch, trying to
get on equal footing.

"I've sent a courier over to get her signature. Though I'm not sure this is the wisest
course of action."

I felt my soaring heart flutter in the wind.

"Interesting," I said. My favorite word
when talking to other lawyers.

"But Eunice feels this would be a distraction for the firm."

"I'll be sure not to let that happen," I said
sincerely.

"How long have you been working with
Sergey? I was under the impression that
Horace Golden was representing."

"Horace died a while ago," I said, and
didn't add, "which you'd know if you gave
a shit about a fellow attorney," as I wanted
to.

"Yes, of course. I think the most expedi-
tious approach here would be to do as
Eunice suggests and make you coadministrator of the Pontecello estate. This keeps it
simple."

Heart and soul both caught the updraft.

"As you wish, counselor. I want to keep it
as simple for you as possible."

"Based on what Eunice has told me, I can't attest to the estate's ability to compensate you for your efforts. But I'm sure there's enough to cover out-of-pocket."

Hah! I thought. Mystery solved. If old Sandy was on the case, Eunice would be lugging his hourly rate. Let's get the dumb girl and hook her into a contingency. Case closed, problem solved.

"Like I said, let's keep it simple," I said, and didn't say all the other things racing through my mind that on other less important occasions would be finding voice.

I wanted to get to the Southampton Police HQ early enough to avoid bumping into the personal banker from Harbor Trust. I should have thought that through better, realizing personal bankers would be cautious and deliberate people who would want to get to a strange new place well ahead of schedule. So I managed to bump into her anyway, literally, as we reached the front door at exactly the same time.

"Sorry," said a tall, big-chested woman in an aquamarine pantsuit carrying an old-fashioned Samsonite briefcase. "I wasn't paying attention."

"Me, neither. Too much on my mind."

"Me, too," she said.

I ushered her through the door, then stood back while they let her through to the back office. I decided not to tell Sullivan about the encounter. He wouldn't like me talking to his witness before he did, no matter how innocently.

Joe was just settling her down at the table when I got to the observation room behind the one-way mirror. He was explaining that he liked to record the conversation as well as take notes so he wouldn't miss anything. He said he wanted her to feel comfortable. She told him comfortable was the last thing she was feeling, but not to worry about the recording. She just hoped to get a copy.

"So I can prove to my husband this actually happened."

He told her absolutely, just had to clear it with the boss.

"All we're going to do is ask you to verify that the bank records you brought us are those we requested in the subpoena. To the best of your knowledge," said Joe. "Simple."

Autumn was doing her best to avoid looking at herself in the mirror. I'd watched plenty of interrogations where the subjects couldn't keep their eyes off themselves, the men worse than the women.

She put the old briefcase on the table and opened it. She took out several stacks of paper of different sizes and shapes, each held together with a rubber band. Each stack had a cover sheet describing the contents. Joe had her read off all the information, specifying if the reports were printed statements, correspondence, or microfilm copies of canceled checks and statements more than five years old, which was the bank's limit on holding paper. This took about fifteen minutes, and I have to say it wasn't the most exhilarating police interview I'd ever witnessed.

"These are all copies, of course," she said as they wrapped it up. "We have to hold the originals for Surrogate's Court and the probate process."

Joe nodded and said, "See, that's all I wanted to know," as he flipped through his casebook. "Simple."

Autumn looked a lot more comfortable, and stayed that way even when Joe said, still looking down at his notes, "Just a couple quick questions to establish evidentiary integrity. You're the one who put these records together on the instruction of your supervisor?"

"Yes, sir."

"We have your name already. Your supervisor's name is?"

"Meryl Johnson."

"Did anyone else assist in preparing this material?"

"No, sir. They told me I had to do it all on my own."

"Not very nice of them, was it?" he asked with an avuncular smile.

It was an odd sensation watching Joe Sullivan be kindly and reassuring.

She smiled back. "No, sir."

"So they've been in your possession at all times? No one else held or examined any of these records after they first came into your possession."

"No, sir."

"But you, of course, examined them carefully to reassure yourself that you had the right material."

"Yes, sir."

Joe looked up from his notes.

"You're a very careful lady."

"I work in a bank," she said. "We're all very careful."

"You got that right. So, what was your impression?"

"Sorry?"

"What did you think when you looked over these statements? Was it how you remembered the general flow when you were taking care of the Pontecellos?"

"I'm not sure I understand."

"I'm gonna be going through everything, of course, but it'd be helpful if you could give me the big picture," he said.

She nodded. "Oh, yes. They had an investment account when I first started at the bank. That was our Harvest Fund, document category Six B, you'll remember." She pointed partway down the stack of papers. "But last year they sold the investments and moved the funds into a cash account. This account received periodic wire transfers from their brokers in the City." She repeated the name of a well-known institution. Joe nodded.

"So, these were regular infusions."

She shook her head.

"Oh, no. Always different amounts that arrived on no particular schedule. Some quite substantial, others minor. I assumed it was just another investment account like they had at the bank. Very routine for our sort of customers."

"Okay. So what would happen to the money after it got there? Were the withdrawals on a schedule?"

She smiled a different kind of smile, more one of reminiscence.

"Mrs. Pontecello would always have us redistribute the funds a day or two after they arrived."

"You've mentioned Mrs. Pontecello. Did you also deal with her husband?"

She shook her head. "I never met him. And she never said a word about him. I wouldn't have known they were married if I hadn't seen his name on all their accounts."

Joe cocked his head and, for the first time, allowed a sidelong glance at the one-way mirror.

"Really? How 'bout that. Which document stack are those wire transfers in?" he asked.

Autumn took the top half and turned them over on the table. Then pulled off a few sheets of paper held by a paper clip.

"These are all the outbound wire transfers. Not very complicated, since they all went to the same place."

This time the stenographer and I got a full look from Joe Sullivan. It was obvious enough to cause Autumn to look over, too, then dart her eyes back to the table. Since all she'd seen was herself in the mirror I could hear her thoughts as well, which were, Oh, God, is that what I really look like? What's going on with my hair? I've got to lose some weight.

"E-Spree Traders?" asked Joe as he studied the records. He stood. "Sorry. I just remembered I had to check in with my boss," he said to her. "Just be a second."

He left Autumn to sit alone at the table. I met him out in the hall.

"Since I'm not her sort of customer, maybe you could tell me what sort of bank this is," he said, handing me the papers.

I didn't have to look. I had recognized it when he said the name.

"E-Spree is not a bank. It's an online brokerage. Everything's done on the Internet."

"I know what 'online' means."

"It's for day traders. Big and little, though all you usually hear about are the little guys after they blow through their life savings," I said as I studied the records. Autumn was right, E-Spree was the only place the money went. Lots of money. I flipped the pages to get to the bottom line: $1,286,000. Lots and lots of money.

"Those nutty Pontecellos, eh?" I said to Joe. "Loved to live on the edge."

"More like on the brink," he said, before starting back to the interrogation room. I stopped him by pinching a piece of his shirt.

"Wait a second," I said. "Is this all the stuff the Pontecellos had at the bank? Sergey said there was a safe-deposit box."

He nodded, vaguely annoyed at the complication, but he had the smile back on when he rejoined Autumn.

"I checked my records," he said. "I understand your clients also had a safe-deposit
box?"

Autumn put the tips of her fingers to her
lips.

"Oh, dear. I forgot to mention that," she
said. "Meryl asked me to tell you we can
only open it in the presence of the probate
authorities. Since no one has contacted us
yet, the box is still sealed."

Joe pretended to stretch, and as he did,
looked over at me standing behind the mirror. His face said, Okay, I asked, she answered. An answer I liked so much I barely
paid attention to his other questions, until
he got to the last one — how much did the
Pontecellos actually have left over after all
the deposits and withdrawals?

Autumn put the stacks back together,
though now at perpendicular angles so
she'd be able to get the outbound wire
transfers back into their original slot, then
pulled out the largest bound stack.

"This was their regular checking account.
If you look here, you'll see the last check,
which was for $163. Leaving a balance of
$2,618, which allows them to stay above
the minimum to receive free checking."

Not exactly broke, but close enough.

Joe put his finger on another part of the

statement.

"What's this?" he asked.

Autumn stood up from the table to get a closer look.

"Oh, that's our Special Savings. That's where Mrs. Pontecello deposited the inbound wire transfers. It's connected to their cash account, so it's easier to wire back out through a single transaction."

"Am I reading this number right?" he asked, sliding the passel of papers across the table.

"Yes, sir — $6,784,118.53."

Since there was nobody else to share this moment with, I looked at the stenographer, but she just kept typing things into her laptop.

When Joe finally joined me in the observation room, I said, "You're going to tell me what else is in there, aren't you?"

"I might."

"And what's in the safe-deposit box."

"Maybe."

"And you're going to tell me what the win/loss statements from the casino say."

"I could."

"And you're going to be as nice to me as you were to Autumn from now on, now that I know you're capable of niceness."

"Definitely not. But I will tell you if I learn anything about your accident."

"My vehicular assault," I said, pointing as if my finger were simply a prelude for something with more impact.

"That, too."

I needed to be in three places at once, which was one more than I could usually manage. I deferred the dream of diving into my computer at the office or hanging with Joe Sullivan and all those appetizing bank records and picked the place I most needed to go.

Sandy Kalandro's office was just like mine in that it was on Montauk Highway, on the second floor of a row of shops. Where it differed was in every other way possible.

The receptionist was better and more professionally dressed than I'd ever been, and things went up from there. The smell of leather and oiled furniture was almost overpowering. The cream-colored walls and ceilings were so laden with moldings and fancy trim there was almost no room for the Early American landscapes, French beach scenes, and stern portraits of men in curly white wigs. The carpet was a deep green wool, which I imagined also smelled great, but I wasn't about to drop to my hands and knees to check it out.

Though I could have since I was wearing my sturdy visit-the-cops outfit, which covered every inch of my body except for a little bit of neck and whatever part of my face managed to get through the frizzy hair. The foundation was a khaki pants suit, that I cleverly built on with a turtleneck, scarf, and penny loafers. Whether the runway model for Brooks Brothers Lady Executive Department sitting behind the walnut desk in the office foyer noticed, I'll never know because I was busy digging another business card out of the crud at the bottom of my purse. When I found it I handed it to her. She held it by the edges, looked at it through the lower half of her glasses, and nodded. She pushed a button on her phone and indicated with a quick toss of her head that I should disappear into one of the massively overstuffed club chairs in the waiting area.

We managed to get through the entire transaction without saying a word to each other, which suited us both.

Kalandro had approached so quietly over the thick pile he startled me when he said, "Of course you're Ms. Swaitkowski," as he offered to shake hands.

I jumped up and grabbed his hand.

"I am. And I bet you're Mr. Kalandro."

"I am. We have our identities straight. Follow me."

I followed him across the deep green sward into a conference room decorated in a maritime motif, complete with an actual helm from an old sailing vessel, with a gigantic oak wheel and a gleaming brass-enclosed compass.

"Oh captain, my captain," I blurted out.

"First mate, technically. Marty Atkins is our most senior partner."

"That's quite a rig. Maybe someday we can take her out for a spin around East Hampton. Check out the legal eddies and currents."

Kalandro was older than I'd thought he'd be — somewhere in his late sixties. He had a full head of unnaturally dark, wavy hair like Ronald Reagan's, and a large gut that filled out his light yellow polo shirt. His pants were some kind of light gray silk or rayon, and he wore loafers, though without a place to put a penny.

His face was well tanned from recent months on the golf course or tennis courts or sailing waters. But his skin was lumpy and dotted with dark age spots, a sign of encroaching vulnerability.

"Eunice has signed the necessary documents to confer upon you coadministrator status," he said without prelude in his basso profundo voice. I could almost feel it through the four inches of lacquer on the walnut conference table.

"I'm familiar with New York State probate," I said, not adding that my experience was purely personal and drenched in grief, and thus largely lost in the haze of painful memory. "The most important items at this stage are copies of the death certificate. I need a stack of them, since I don't know what I'll be encountering as I work through the process."

He bowed his head in gracious agreement.

"Naturally. I believe for Mrs. Wolsonowicz the important thing is to arrive at a conclusion as expeditiously as possible."

"We are in violent agreement," I said, thinking correctly that this was the sort of statement an old windbag like Kalandro would like.

"Capital," he said, upon which another well-turned-out office automaton glided in with a white legal envelope out of which she drew the necessary papers and laid them on the table. She held down the thin stack with a glossy black pen that weighed about forty pounds.

The document naming me coadministrator was short and to the point. I signed it and the photocopy first. Then I moved on to the much denser contracts that said my involvement extended exclusively to the matter of the Pontecello estate, and more to the point, stipulated that I would lay no claim to any asset, financial instrument, or property in the possession of Eunice Wolsonowicz. I crossed out "in the possession of" and wrote "belonging to," then signed that one.

"Same difference, right?" I said to Kalandro, who raised his thick eyebrows but let it stand, probably because I didn't touch the clause saying I'd be paid solely by the Pontecello estate, and should my fees exceed its liquidateable assets, then basically, tough darts.

That'd be some hefty bill, I thought, but kept it to myself as I got everything signed, back in the big white envelope, and stuffed under my arm.

Kalandro had watched me with the deliberate indifference of a man waiting for a traffic light to turn green. Now he almost came back to life, mustering the energy to hand me a separate sealed envelope on which someone had written "Will."

"Eunice asked me to secure this after her sister died. You'll note there are changes since the original was composed, so if you have questions, please don't hesitate to ask," he said as an automatic courtesy. I acted deeply grateful.

"That's very generous of you. I certainly will. Well, actually, I have a couple quick ones right now, if you have a moment."

He looked at the Big Ben on his wrist.

"A moment."

"You have looked over the nontangible assets, I presume. Bank accounts, stock portfolios, etc."

He smiled indulgently. "The police have secured that information as part of their investigation. However, Mrs. Wolsonowicz was privy to her sister's financial disposition, which was less robust than one might suspect observing her lifestyle."

"Sure. You see that out here all the time. But there's enough to pay me, of course."

The smile wavered.

"Of course."

I pretended to think about that.

"So you haven't talked to the bank yet," I said.

"They'll tell us when the accounts are released. It's the usual routine."

"But let's just say things go better than planned and there's a little bit left over. I'm assuming it reverts to Eunice as the sole surviving heir."

He shook his head.

"It's all outlined in the will. There are several charitable institutions listed, notably the East Hampton Library and the dog rescue in Water Mill. These ostensibly receive about twenty percent of the estate. The balance goes to the person specified."

"Person specified? Sergey thought it all went to charity."

"Well," said Kalandro, "perhaps a review of the document will clear up that mystery."

I could see that we were playing a little game. Let's see if the dumb girl knows how to read a simple contract, which is all a will actually is. Okay, I thought, I can take the thing out of the envelope and read the answer. My dignity will survive.

And there it was, handwritten, with Betty's signature indicating this was an alteration from the original, an answer freighted with a much bigger boatload of questions.

We hereby make, publish, and declare this to be our Last Will and Testament — *etc, etc* — after disbursement to the charitable organizations listed above, and upon completion of federal tax proceedings — *etc, etc* — we bequeath remaining assets, all stocks, bonds, cash, investments, and

like instruments, all property personal and
real, to Oscar Hamilton Wolsonowicz.

Fuzzy?

13

My father didn't go easily. He took his impending death as just another affront, perpetrated by forces indifferent to his personal dignity, not unlike his engineering clients or the clerks at the Department of Motor Vehicles.

In addition to magazine articles about women living alone, I never read inspirational tales about people who fight fatal diseases with valiant determination, turning a two-month prognosis into ten bountiful years. Probably because my father turned a ten-year prognosis, at minimum, into two miserable years of abject surrender, nicely embellished by unrelenting self-pity and complaint.

It was a display of heroic proportions, if not exactly heroic.

Given this, it was unsurprising that something like a will, the ultimate recognition of the inevitable, was the last thing he'd think about, much less compose. I should have known this was the case, but, of course, I didn't, assuming no intelligent, educated adult would be that selfish and uncaring.

I was only in my first year of law school at that point and couldn't even spell intestate, much less deal with its consequences. But I learned fast, motivated by the prospect of my mother losing thousands of dollars working through the Kafka-designed theme park called New York State probate, known quaintly around here as Surrogate's Court.

The period it took me to settle all the legal questions, negotiate the estate taxes of the state and federal governments, and lay the groundwork for the next inevitability was exactly, to the day, how long my mother lived beyond my father's death.

Having worked side by side with me throughout the process, and too exhausted to celebrate with anything more than a half bottle of week-old Cabernet swiped off the kitchen counter, she thanked me for being the best daughter I knew how to be (not exactly unqualified praise) and went off to bed to die of a massive heart attack.

Real estate was nowhere near as costly in those days as it is now, but neither was law school. So I was able to pay it all off and have a little left over to squander on the transition from frantic, grief-stricken student to frantic, dysfunctional adult. Just to spite my old man's reckless disregard.

It was that lively concoction of extreme emotion, cold-hearted reality, and sudden loss of childhood that taught me the beauty of the law. Until then, I was doing it just to prove to any doubters that I could. The only real doubter being my father, though his dying did nothing to stem my determination.

I learned it wasn't just knowing how to gin the system, how to jigger the odds. There was a solid core of brilliance in the law, embedded in thousands of years of experiences far more desperate and ennobling than my own. That everyone had at least a chance, a shot at something akin to justice and fair play. Maybe that's naïve, but you need something beyond habit to get you up in the morning. At least I do.

Thoughts like these were running wild as I walked out of Sandy Kalandro's office with my briefcase stuffed with paperwork covered in authorizing signatures. The world was now different. I had the right to play around all I wanted in Sergey and Elizabeth's most intimate affairs; I was empowered and emboldened, even employed, courtesy of Eunice's abiding belief in my client's impoverishment. Abiding and influential, since Sandy had apparently bought the same line of baloney.

As had I. In fact, that's all I'd been doing — buying everybody's bullshit. Or buying into my own assumptions. Whatever I thought I knew, I knew now that it probably wasn't true. So right when I should have felt only triumph, frustration filled my brain.

"I don't know anything," I yelled at myself after climbing into my car.

But that wasn't true, said another part of me. I knew Sergey Pontecello came to see me, then ended up dead. He was supposed to have died broke, but that wasn't true. Eunice just thought it was true. Sergey surely knew better. So then why didn't he pay off the mortgages and tell his imperious sister-in-law to go pound sand?

I couldn't ask him, I thought with a slight twist in my gut. He couldn't tell me what he knew or what he didn't know. Wendy said he was deluded and oblivious. That seemed credible. He hadn't even looked at their will when his wife died. That took some commitment to obliviousness. If he had, he would have known that Betty had gone in after the fact and earmarked the lion's share of his little European fortune for his nasty jerk of a nephew, who had nothing but disdain for his apparent benefactors.

"Okay, maybe I know some things. I just don't know what I know," I said aloud, then silently pledged to never again assume anything, never conclude anything without a freight car full of corroboration, never believe in the obvious, never fall prey to supposition. To be only what Harry had said I was:

The girl who never gave up.

The next day Harry picked me up in a big truck. Big enough to have a clattery diesel engine and a cab you had to climb up into. He looked way too happy behind the wheel. That gave me insight into his love of logistics. It wasn't just about moving stuff; it was how you moved it.

I'd called Eunice immediately after leaving Sandy Kalandro, and she was more than eager to have me retrieve Sergey and Betty's things, as if they were emitting radiation and she was in dire fear for her life. I knew the type. My opposite. People who get physically ill looking at stacks of boxes, who only see a burden where I see a playground.

Harry loved boxes but hated clutter, which I knew was one of those ugly, bubbling issues left unresolved from when I tossed him out. But now was not the time to muck around with resolutions.

Instead, I focused on one of my favorite distractions, admiring the distance between Harry's hip and knee, and subsequently from knee to ankle. Especially noticeable when he was wearing blue jeans, which he must have bought at the Gangly, Lean, and Ridiculously Tall Shop.

My blue jeans were actually green, which in the sunlight looked more sickly than I'd thought they would against the reddish flannel shirt. At least we were both dressed to schlep, which is all Eunice would care about — to completely and permanently scour Sergey's residue from her ancestral home.

In addition to the big truck, Harry brought oversize cups of coffee and gooey pastries. Harry often did things like this, pleasing me by being thoughtful and aggravating me by making me feel I wasn't.

The day was shaping up to be another bright blue East End wonder. People say the air and the sky aren't only different in this part of the world, they're also better. I haven't traveled much — almost nowhere, in fact — but I'm happy to believe them.

As we pulled into the driveway, we had to work around a pair of pickup trucks that were pulled partway onto the grass. The confident signs on the doors said it was Ray

Zander and crew. Harry drove the truck up to the front door, but before we announced ourselves, I walked across the lawn to where a third pickup, one I hadn't seen before, was backed against the base of a huge old maple tree.

When I got there I didn't see Ray, but there was a thick rope leading from a spool on the back of the pickup and into the dense foliage of the tree. I followed it with my eyes and called, "Yo, Ray. You up there?"

"Who's askin'?" he yelled back

I told him.

"You keep callin' on me my wife's gonna get suspicious."

"Not if you don't tell her."

"That'd be deceptive," he called down. "The worser evil."

I didn't ask him worser than what.

"You mind just coming down here for a sec so we can talk?"

Almost instantaneously I heard a mechanical whir and the spool on the back of the truck started to spin. Ray Zander dropped like a stone, or more evocatively, like a swashbuckler with a long branch trimmer in lieu of a sword. He was sitting on some sort of webbed seat attached to the line, and as he fell toward me, he held his legs straight out, ankles locked, with one hand on the trimmer, the other resting in his lap. I jumped out of the way. When he abruptly stopped, I saw the other hand held a small black remote.

He was grinning.

"Nifty, huh?" he said.

"Yeah. Sure," I said, noncommitally.

"Rigged it myself. Thinking of going for a patent. You're a lawyer, what do you think?"

"Not my branch of the law," I said.

"I'm lookin' for investors. You could get in on the ground floor. Mr. Pontecello took quite an interest, but his wife put the kibosh on that one. Fella was on a tight leash."

"No leash on me. I'll spread the word."

"Tell 'em it's not only convenient, it's fast," he said, and then zipped back up into the tree, disappearing into the leaves. A few seconds later, he fell back out of the sky.

"I can see that," I said.

"That's the real innovation. The power takeoff was way too slow, so I regeared the whole thing. Integrated a grappling hook, a classic boson's chair, a remote-controlled, high-torque electric motor, and bingo. Costs a fraction of a cherry picker, and I get to keep the money."

He pointed out a few more pertinent features and benefits of the system before letting me convince him to hold still for a few questions. He stayed in the boson's chair, so I climbed into the bed of the pickup to get on his eye level.

I told him I'd been out to the casino, as he suggested I should. I saw a glimmer of satisfaction in his eyes. People love it when you do what they suggest.

"I'm not asking you to reveal any confidences or denigrate the memory of Mrs. Pontecello," I said, "but did you ever notice her in a state of, ah, you know . . . inebriation?"

"Schnockered? Yeah, all the time. The more schnockered, the worse she got. Yappin' at the crew, sayin' all this nonsense with the cigarette bouncin' up and down between her lips. Kinda thing you expect to see back in Brooklyn, where I grew up, not out here. I can sure see her pissin' off the wrong people, gettin' her husband into trouble."

"Must've been tough on him," I said.

He looked into the sky, checking the weather or formulating a response. Hard to tell.

He looked back at me.

"Mr. Pontecello lived in his own little world, which suited him fine. Suited me, too. We had an understanding. I keep all this landscaping in perfect condition and he pays me. He ignores, I ignore. Square deal for everybody."

"There was that much to ignore?" I asked.

"You're serious, right?" he asked, before zipping back up into the maple canopy.

"I am," I yelled.

Getting no response, I walked back to the front door of the house, where Harry was waiting not so patiently but pretending he was. I knew the look. I became oblivious, and ignored it, à la Sergey Pontecello.

"Have you rung the doorbell?" I asked.

"Not yet."

"What are you waiting for? Come on, let's move it."

He liked that.

Eunice answered the door in a gray three-piece suit, supported by stubby sensible heels and a narrow, disapproving face.

"I can't stay to administer all this," she said. "You'll have to make do on your own."

"One of my specialties, ma'am," I said.

She looked up at Harry, vaguely disturbed by the sight of him, though not enough to keep us out of her house.

"I've separated our family things from my sister's and her husband's things. I had to make judgments as to which was which. It wasn't pleasant," she added, as if to ward off a possible challenge to her decisions. "The boxes and furniture are in the east sitting room. Do I need to sign anything?" she said. She stood several paces away with her hands clenched anxiously to her abdomen.

"You already did when you made me coadministor," I said. "I assume we'll know which things to take."

"Take everything in that room," she said, pointing down the hall. "That's why I put it there," she said testily.

I was going to ease gradually into the tough stuff, but I'd about had it with that woman. I moved in close, invading her personal space, which she seemed poised to defend.

"Mrs. Wolsonowicz, are you aware your son has been named sole heir of the Pontecello estate?"

Up close, I could see her face grappling with emotions that went far beyond impatience and irritation.

"Of course," she said.

"Shouldn't he be deciding what to do with these belongings?"

She shook her head aggressively enough to wrench her neck. "He doesn't want anything. Of that I'm certain."

I nodded and moved in a half step closer. She stepped back the same distance.

"And the financial piece, same feelings?"
She scoffed.

"The debt?" she asked. "The house settles that."

"So you haven't looked into the remaining assets."

She shook her head again, less violently.

"The bank won't release anything until authorized by the courts. Some bureaucratic nonsense."

"The murder investigation," I said flatly.

"As I said, nonsense."

She looked down at her watch, then looked at me, then looked back at her watch.

"I have an appointment," she said.

I had the bad news of the Pontecellos' unfortunate lack of insolvency on the tip of my tongue. Something more than her clipped dismissal kept it there.

"Of course," I said.

She guided us to the east sitting room, which had a wide pair of French doors that opened out on the front lawn. Harry asked if he could back up the truck to the doors, which for some reason seemed to aggravate her even more.

"I suppose," she said, turning to leave. Then she stopped, turned again, and forced herself to stand still. "Thank you for taking care of all this," she said with all the sincerity of a sixth grader reciting lines in the Christmas pageant. "I appreciate it."

Index cards with things I wanted to say started to flip in front of my mind's eye, but before I could pick out something, Harry said, "It's the least we could do. Losing a loved one is hard enough."

She softened a little at that, though not enough to improve my opinion of her. Then she spun back around and left us to administer things on our own.

The east sitting room was about twenty feet square. It was heaped almost floor to ceiling with boxes, lamps, tables and chairs, temporary clothing racks, rolled-up rugs, framed pictures, a pair of bicycles, and a lot of indescribables, such as palm fronds stuck in a gigantic blue vase and a wicker umbrella holder in the shape of an old-fashioned woman's boot.

"Stuff," he said.

"The staff of life. How do you want to tackle it?" I asked.

"We'll work that out with the crew."

"The crew?"

"You don't think *we're* moving all this crap, do you?"

About ten minutes later the crew showed up. Alejandro and Ismael. They high-fived Harry and instantly dug into the gigantic pile of personal belongings. By then Harry had backed up the truck and pulled a ramp directly into the east sitting room. Alejandro was apparently the lead guy, even though Ismael was almost twice his size.

I wasn't just going to stand there while other human beings worked, so I joined the hauling frenzy. This naturally forced Harry into the fray, so in a startlingly short period of time we emptied the place of the Ponte-cellos' belongings. I expressed my amazement to the crew.

"Ismael and myself are magicians," said Alejandro. "Make objects disappear."

"Abracadabra," said Ismael, as if they'd rehearsed the act.

With that satisfying, sweaty feeling of accomplishment, I jumped into the truck and slammed the heavy passenger door. Harry started the engine, which almost drowned out the sound of my cell phone ringing on my hip. I answered.

"I did tell you about the car," said Eunice.

"Not that I remember."

"Well, the ridiculous thing is in one of the garages. It needs to be moved."

"Ridiculous?"

"American."

Latent love of country stirred in my breast.

"Okay," I said. "We'll take care of it."

"It's a forty-year-old Chrysler, if you can imagine. Who would drive such a thing?"

"No one I know," I lied.

Harry told me he'd decided to bring everything to his rental over in Southampton, citing all the extra space, including room to set up tables and shelves to help go through the boxes. When we got there the tables and shelves — and Alejandro and Ismael — were waiting. In another wink of an eye the stuff was out of the truck and neatly arrayed in the garage bay next to where Harry had set up housekeeping. Harry paid the guys while exchanging palm slaps and mock insults in the way men seem to delight in. Then we watched them leave, Ismael taking the truck.

I washed the sweat off my face while Harry made a pot of coffee and put the Magnetic Fields on the stereo. Then we stood together at the edge of the room and took it all in.

"Let's go look at some dead people's things," I said, diving in.

The boxes weren't labeled, so Harry armed us both with Sharpies and Post-its and we set to work. He designated receiving tables and shelves by room — living room, dining room, kitchen, bedroom, bath — so as we unpacked, identified contents, and repacked, we had another layer of organization.

The living room section filled up fast. Lots of vases, ashtrays, table lamps, framed photographs, coasters, cigarette boxes, and the usual assemblage of indefinable porcelain and cast-metal tchotchkes.

The dining room saw a definite uptick in quality. The china and crystal were beautiful, ancient, and rare. And very valuable, according to what I could glean from a quick Web search. The bowls, candlestick holders, and flatware were all silver, as proven by their blackened neglect. I guessed it all came down from Professor Hamilton, which made me wonder why Eunice had let it go. Had it become contaminated by the Pontecellos' possession?

"Weird family dynamics. No explaining it," said Harry, satisfied with that.

The bathroom stuff, besides being incredibly depressing, was more notable for what was missing than what was there.

"No toothbrush," I said.

"He didn't brush his teeth?"

"No. He was holding it when he called me that night. Eunice had thrown him out of the master bathroom. He thought he was still the master and wouldn't brush his teeth anywhere else."

"So what does that mean?" Harry asked.

"I don't know. Probably still in one of the

other bathrooms."

After laying grim witness to things like denture cleaners and nail files, I needed a break before cataloging the stuff from their bedroom. We went outside and drank some more coffee. Actually, I drank coffee. Harry stood over me and massaged my shoulders.

"So what're we looking for?" he asked.

"We're not exactly looking *for*. We're looking *at*."

"And what'll looking *at* tell us?"

"I don't know. Maybe I will when we've looked at everything."

By now we'd been able to isolate all the room categories, adding two more — a library and a sewing room. The sewing equipment was from the fifties, at least, and the fabrics and thread were not much newer. So whoever sewed hadn't done it in a very long time. My guess was Mrs. Hamilton, Elizabeth and Eunice's mother, but there was nothing there to prove that.

The library was of the same vintage, and again I pegged it to the professor. Most of the books were scientific texts or books about science and medicine, and there was the occasional historical novel. Except for a stack of Pogo compilations and the complete works of James Thurber, it was a pretty starchy collection.

Why Eunice had conveyed all these things to Elizabeth was unexplained, but I didn't know if that mattered. Or if it should live under the category "weird family dynamics."

Braced and rested, we started emptying bedroom boxes.

Elizabeth, it turned out, might have gambled like the Cincinnati Kid and drunk like a sailor, but she dressed like a librarian. Not only sensible shoes, but sensible dresses, skirts, blouses, and hose. When I opened a box full of her underwear, Harry averted his gaze.

"This is where I go check my e-mail," he said.

When he left I started to lay the items one by one out on the table. It wasn't a job I was particularly keen on doing, but I'd promised myself I would go through everything. I knew that nag in my head wouldn't let me do otherwise, even if I hadn't promised.

Betty's conservative ways didn't falter at the intimate. She had all the things your grandmother wore. High waists, industrial-strength bras, slips, and even a couple of old-fashioned girdles. No secret red panties or cut-out bras, which I'd half expected to find.

I went through the first box, but in the second, the clothing only filled the top third. Below was an old mahogany box. I took it out and tried to open it. Locked. I went and got Harry at his computer.

"I have a moral and technical dilemma," I said.

"First the moral," he said, spinning around in his seat.

"A locked box."

He deliberated.

"You're the coadministrator of the estate," he said. "You have a fiduciary responsibility to determine the disposition and value of the estate's assets. That actually obligates you to open the box."

"Spoken like a lawyer."

"I've known a few."

"So bring some tools."

Harry set down a cloth tool bag on the table and picked up the box, examining the brass keyhole.

"Hm," he said after several minutes' study. "Stay put."

He disappeared for another ten minutes, then came back with a small cardboard box. He opened it so I could see what it was — a box full of old keys.

"Get out of here," I said, impressed.

"Do you know how many old desks,

clocks, filing cabinets, hope chests, gun cases, and wooden boxes a professional mover would have to open over a twenty-year period?"

"A lot?"

"I buy these at flea markets. The box owners usually like it better than a hammer and crowbar."

I tried not to crowd him while he worked through a series of keys. I liked to watch him work, deliberate but respectful. I imagined all those anxious furniture owners, like me, hovering over his patient shoulders.

Finally one took with a satisfying click. He turned around and smiled.

"Love that sound," he said.

I moved in next to him when he raised the lid. The box was apparently full, since right on top was a recent copy of *Us Weekly.*

"Now, there's a treasure worth preserving," I said.

There were two more issues, then a yellow notepad with a grocery list on the first page. I leafed through the other pages, but that was it. Next was a thin stack of tissue paper, then another curious item — a layer of wrinkled tinfoil. Under that a folded newspaper.

"If there're fish and chips under there, I'm not gonna be happy," said Harry.

I thanked him for the thought and carefully lifted a corner of the newspaper.

It took only a split second to absorb what I saw on the bottom of the box, but it took a much longer time to fully comprehend. Later on we did a thorough inventory, but in the time I had before making a run for the bathroom, I counted two fingers, a big toe, a nose, and best of all, an eyeball floating in a little Tupperware container.

14

Joe Sullivan showed up with two young women in tow, each wearing rubber gloves and carrying sleek aluminum cases. I led them to the bodily remains as I tried to answer questions about the sequence of events leading to the discovery, including what we touched and didn't touch, and in what order.

"Any prior knowledge before opening that box that you might be uncovering evidence?" Sullivan asked.

"Oh, great," I said. "Nice thought. Jesus."

"Don't start," he said.

"No," I said, "you stop. As coadministrator of the Pontecello estate, I have a legal right to examine those belongings. If that's a problem for you, take it up with Judge Simpson at Surrogate's Court. And good luck with that one."

He was distracted by sounds of subdued delight coming from the forensic women as they picked the body parts out of the wooden box with long stainless-steel tweezers. He looked back, slightly confused.

"Coadministrator? When were you going to tell me that?"

"As soon as I was done looking at this stuff," I lied, knowing I should have told him right after getting the call from Eunice and hoping to paper over that indiscretion with sheer bluster.

"Either way," he said, "I've got to ask you questions like that."

"No you don't. You have to assume I haven't fucked anything up and act like you've known me for longer than five seconds."

Then I left him and his lady ghouls and went outside to gather a little oxygen and figure out what to do next.

Forensic crime shows on TV have done a huge service to the image of medical examiners. They make the job look sexy and fun and adventurous, with cool lighting and great bone structure. The old stereotype of the weirdo M.E. who prefers the company of carved-up corpses and rarely sees the light of day has almost been forgotten.

That's why it was good to have Carlo Vendetti, the Suffolk County M.E., around to remind us of where those stereotypes came from in the first place.

It really wasn't fair to think about Carlo that way. You knew he took his responsibilities seriously and worked hard to be the very best medical examiner he could possibly be.

But, man, skeevy or what?

After Sullivan left, I called Sam, who'd had more than one encounter with Carlo — not all pleasant, but usually productive.

Sam answered the cell phone I'd given him as a desperate attempt to stop him from borrowing mine. He was just washing up after a day making wall units and lawn furniture in his shop in the basement.

"I need to go see Carlo," I said when he answered the phone.

"Vendetti?"

"Yeah," I said, and told him about our latest discovery.

"You think it's more of Edna," he said.

Something about hearing her name almost made me retch.

"I don't know," I said. "But there's a precedent. And Markham told me she was all there when she left the hospital. I gotta talk to Vendetti."

He was quiet on the line for a moment, then said, "I know where to find him. Catch him off guard. If you think you can take the surroundings."

"Dead bodies?"

"Poetry," he said.

"I'm sure there's an explanation."

"Amanda thought for some reason we needed to expand our social horizons," he said. "So she made up a list of cultural attractions. I was strongly opposed to this but had to go along, assuming if I didn't, she'd stop having sex with me."

"Finally a man who understands the lay of the land," I said.

"I slept through the plays in Sag Harbor, the folk singers in Amagansett, and almost broke my neck in Montauk trying to learn ballroom dancing, but I perked up at a poetry slam in Riverhead that featured Carlo, the Doc O'Death, Believer in the Reaper, Grand Incisionator."

"You're kidding."

"Some people play golf. He's performing tonight."

"What's the dress code?"

"Beatific."

I didn't know what that meant exactly, so I went to the default blue jeans, cowboy boots, chambray shirt, and leather jacket. I left the hair to work things out on its own, too tired and stressed by the day to do anything else.

"Where's Eddie?" I asked when I jumped into Sam's car.

"Back at the cottage, defending the shores against alien encroachment."

He'd brought a thermos of flavored coffee, two giant plastic travel mugs, and a pack of Camel filters. Sam never went anywhere unequipped.

"Expecting a long night?" I asked.

"Just enough to get us to Riverhead. After that we'll have to live off the land."

Riverhead lies at the crotch of the East End's Twin Forks. It used to be a drab little mill town; now it's the easternmost expression of Long Island's love of strip development and discount retail. But the old town itself was still there, a row of storefronts grungy enough to house Chez Slam, serving burgers, booze, espresso coffee, and lyrical improvisation.

This was not my thing. I was an English major in college mostly through default and indecision. I liked the books, but the poetry almost killed me. Some of it sounded nice when you read it aloud, but I could never understand what the hell they were talking about. If it weren't for the textbooks and lectures, where they clued you in on the secret messages, I'd have flunked out in the first semester.

On the other hand, Sam the mechanical engineer not only knew the stuff backward and forwards, he could also recite, declaim, cross-reference, and allude like Ezra Pound on amphetamines.

The woman collecting the cover charge at the door wore a pretty black pencil skirt, spiked heels, white silk blouse, and heavy black-rimmed glasses. Sam asked her if her leotards were at the cleaners, to which she simply stared, blankly bewildered. So we were off to a good start.

He managed a better rapport with the waitress. She was about his age, with disheveled gray hair, wearing a dress and apron set handed down from Betty Crocker.

"What do you have that's clear?" he asked.

"My conscience and the mortgage on this place."

"Can you put that on the rocks? No fruit?"

"What do you have against fruit?" she asked.

"All that vitamin C wrecks the mood."

"What about your girlfriend?"

"Not his girlfriend, but I'll have the same thing. Just double up on the lime," I said. "You can use his."

It was early, but the place was filling up fast. Most were young black people and young white people emulating the speech and gestures of young black people. Dotted about were older people, white, the men usually bearded and frumpy, wearing polyester shirts and sandals over socks. It was hard to tell the original purpose of the joint in the dim light, but the water rings and cigarette burns on the table testified to its longevity. So did the walls, covered in posters — some printed, others handmade — promoting singers, poets, and stand-up comedians. The faded artwork and antiquated fonts went back to a few decades before the girl in the pencil skirt had learned to use crayons.

We ordered burgers to chase down the vodka, which we finished just in time to focus on the first act, a twitchy African-American guy in a Bobby Kennedy suit and wraparound sunglasses. Every line of his bit ended in *ate,* as in stipulate, perambulate, pontificate. It was an impressive cataloging of legitimate and artificial applications of that particular suffix, but as usual, the underlying meaning was lost to me. I whispered as much to Sam.

"You gotta concentrate," he said, "and let it percolate."

The next poet, also African-American, but young, too young to be in a place serving liquor, began by sitting silently for about five minutes on a stool next to a boom box playing a rhythm track. Then he started nodding his head to the downbeat and occasionally hitting the off beat with a loud grunt. The grunts slowly picked up in frequency, to which he gradually added other mouth sounds — clicks and pops — and then strategic slaps to the knees and chest.

After about fifteen minutes of this it sounded as if there were dozens of kids up there playing as many percussion instruments. It was just great. I loved it, not just because I didn't have to speculate or evaluate.

After reaching an impossible crescendo, followed by thunderous applause, he did an encore, this time playing the William Tell overture on his cheeks. The whole thing, with perfect pacing and intonation.

During all this I'd completely forgotten why I was there, which made the shock of seeing Carlo Vendetti lope onto the small stage that much greater.

You could almost call him chinless, though not in the way some people's chins are lost somewhere between lower lip and throat. His was more of a sharp, horizontal line, like Dick Tracy's, as if he'd had part of him neatly sliced off. His eyes were covered in huge, square-framed sunglasses. His head was bald on top, but he did the tragic thing some guys do with the remains, growing it long and pasting it over his skull with what looked like Vaseline. I never realized, seeing him once or twice in baggy lab coats, how thin he was — maybe a hundred and fifty pounds. That night, wearing a black body-suit that started below his missing chin and ran all the way to his feet, it was easier to tell. And since that was all he was wearing, you could also clearly make out his mascu-line equipment, which was both appalling and impressive.

"Now I know the problem," I whispered to Sam. "Testosterone poisoning."

Like the kid before him, Carlo opened in complete silence. The audience followed his apparent wishes by settling down. When all you could hear was your own breath, he started to speak.

It's a good thing Sam has such a good memory, because I don't. So whenever I want to recall parts of Carlo's poem, I call him up. I want to remember it, because it was so beautiful and moving. He began with a low, slow cadence, but the pace of the words slowly increased, as did the pitch of his voice. It was really more of a narrative,

256

more free verse, than regular poetry. And the storyline was clear. It was about a strange childhood — I presumed Carlo's — spent on a farm on the prairie wastes of western Canada, where the only escape from the trackless monotony of wheat fields and oppressively stolid parents was a soaring imagination. An imagination rich enough in describing his world to make me want to get in the Volvo and head for Saskatchewan. And as with the kid playing his own body, I quickly forgot I was on Long Island listening to the Suffolk County medical examiner.

When his story ended, the audience was either too stunned by his performance or mindful of his opening bit to clap until he'd already left the stage.

"Now that's a medical examiner worth writing home about," said Sam.

I didn't answer him for fear he'd notice I'd almost started to choke up. Instead, I took off for the ladies' room to clean up. I was a little concerned that Carlo would sneak out before we had a chance to talk to him, but when I got back to the table he was sitting there with Sam. The sunglasses were off and his tall beer was already half consumed.

I stuck out my hand, which he took with

awkward indecision, and thanked him for his beautiful story.

"I didn't know you were such a fan of poetry," Carlo said. "I've seen you here before," he said to Sam, then looked at me as if he wished he hadn't.

"He was with Amanda Anselma, his girlfriend," I said. "Sam and I are mixed up on a project. That's actually why we're here. We'd like to ask you about something, if you don't mind a little shoptalk."

Carlo surprised me for the hundredth time that night by nodding eagerly.

"Sure. Happy to help as long as it's not an ongoing."

I started with the night Sullivan called me to identify Sergey Pontecello and how I'd found Edna Jackery's nipple in his back pocket.

"That's definitely an ongoing. I still have Mr. Pontecello in a drawer."

"Dr. Vendetti," I said.

"Carlo."

"Carlo, as much as I'd love to hear what you have to say about Sergey, I just want to know one thing. When you examined Edna Jackery, was she, you know, all there?"

This confused Carlo, of course.

"Did she have all her body parts?" I asked. "Specifically nipples, fingers, and toes?"

"And eyes and ears," said Sam.

Carlo suddenly perked up.

"We just received several samples of desiccated human tissue from Southampton. I'm running the DNA tomorrow. Is this what you're referring to?"

"We think they might belong to Edna Jackery," I said. "You've already identified a nipple as hers. It's a cold case, by the way," I quickly added.

"Not if we're checking that material now," he said.

"No chance some of her got separated in the course of the examination?" I asked. "Any reason to do that?"

He shook his head, still looking cordial and unoffended.

"What for?" he said. "I only determine COD and check for trace evidence. We like to keep all the parts connected to the bodies. Easier to ship that way," he said, enjoying his own joke.

"Of course it is, Doc," I said, suddenly struck by a ridiculously obvious thought. "I'm an idiot."

Sam looked at me, waiting for an explanation.

"I guess I am, too," he said. "Because I have no idea what she's talking about."

"They call you lots of things, Sam," said

Carlo, "but never an idiot."

"Can I buy you guys another round?" I asked.

Sam called over the waitress/owner of Chez Slam. Ordering drinks was one of Sam's greatest delights, in no way diminished by constant repetition. I waited till the whole transaction was complete before broaching the obvious.

"Okay, I'm ready," he said. "Spill it."

"What?" I said.

"What you're thinking."

"Rigor mortis."

"Huh?"

"I'm also thinking we need a way for Carlo to give his opinion of Sergey Pontecello without compromising investigatory confidentiality."

Carlo sat back in his chair and folded his arms. He looked sympathetic but unmoved.

"I wish I could help you guys, but you know how it is."

I patted his shoulder.

"Of course we do, Carlo. Anyway, I saw the body right after it happened. Somebody obviously beat him up pretty badly."

Carlo shook his head.

"Really?" I said.

Carlo nodded. Excellent, I thought. The old guessing game.

"Of course, somebody tosses you from a car, you can look pretty beaten up," I said.

That got a small tilt of the head, the equivalent of "maybe."

We ran a few more options by him, from the obvious to the absurd, yielding nothing but head shakes. Before he started getting dizzy, we let him take a break and talk for a while about sports and Suffolk County politics. Since I wasn't much interested in either, I just listened to the conversation. This probably relaxed my own inflexible brain, because that's when it popped into my head.

"Macadam. All over his face and in his hair. On his poor old Howard Hughes shirt. That's what all that grimey black stuff was. Oh my God, he was dragged."

He nodded, then looked furtively around the bar, as if his boss was within earshot. Whatever line he'd just crossed in his mind wrecked the mood, and though still friendly, he was done giving up official secrets.

Out of kindness to Carlo, Sam moved us off the subject. Which didn't stop the images of Sergey flooding my mind, of him bouncing and twisting over the gravelly road, and probably screaming for his life, while his life remained. I hoped not for too long.

261

Sam did his best at happy talk for a few more minutes, then used my pained silence as an excuse to call it a night and get us out of there.

On the way back to Bridgehampton, he said, "I know why you feel like a idiot."

"Yeah?"

"You said 'Rigor mortis.' You were thinking about corpses. The first stop is the autopsy tables. Next up, the embalmers. Edna was intact when she left Carlo's lab. What happened to her happened after that. Sometime between Riverhead and the crematorium."

He went on to almost compliment me for the way I'd handled Vendetti, but I wasn't paying much attention. It's funny how sometimes a revelation comes with the feeling that you've known the truth all along. This was one of those times. It might be just a manufactured recollection, made to make you feel less stupid for missing the obvious. Or less cowardly for shying away from what your heart already knows.

In my case, the realization came with a recrimination. Sergey might have been dragged to death, but the cause of death was me.

15

The first thing I did the next morning was get into an argument. Well, not exactly. First I had to drag my butt out of bed, shower, brush my teeth, pretend to fix my hair by patting around my head, pull on whatever clothes were within reach, and stagger out to my car.

I was on autopilot and wanted to stay there until comfortably ensconced in front of my computer in Water Mill with the largest cup of coffee the place down the road would sell me.

So I wasn't even awake enough to be grumpy. I was mostly groggy. Somnambulistic. Legally dead, by Carlo Vendetti's more liberal definition, and happy about it.

I'd almost used up the tank of gas I'd bought with the car, so the first fill-up on my own felt like a legitimate moment. The problem came when I had to open the little door covering the gas spout. The Volvo was my first experience with a modern car, and I hadn't learned all the fancy new protocols, the value of which I'd be willing to debate, but right then it was more an issue of social harmony. I'd already pulled up to the gas pump, but rather than filling my tank, I had my head stuck in the owner's manual. The guy behind me was unsympathetic.

After a few minutes he yelled, "Come on. I don't got all day," in his finest Long Island accent, the one precisely engineered to bring out the fundamental Long Island in me.

"Yo, dude," I yelled back, without looking up from the manual. "Give it a second."

A few moments passed, and I'd almost penetrated the Swedish mechanical mind when the guy behind me stood on his horn.

"Park that fucking thing," he yelled as he nudged the towering wall of pickup grill closer to the pristine butt of my pretty new car.

I got out and held up the manual.

"I'm sorry, sir, but I can't get into my fuel tank." I pointed to the bay of pumps next door, clear of traffic. "Would you mind?"

He didn't react either way, so I sat back in the car with my legs outside on the ground and my brain struggling to decipher the instructions. I had the radio on, which became an unfortunate distraction. Before I knew it my attention had slid away from "Fuel tank — access, unlock" and on to "Morning Edition." I'd also forgotten the agitated truck driver behind me. But he hadn't forgotten me.

It wasn't a big jolt, but it was big enough. My heart thrilled in my chest and I heard myself make a sound. Not a scream, more of a terrified, stifled yelp. I looked behind me and the pickup was nearly in the Volvo's cargo area. The guy had somehow thought it was a good idea to roll his truck into my rear bumper, giving it a nasty little tap.

"I told you to move that fucking thing somewheres else," he yelled out his window.

I slapped the manual shut and looked up at the heavens. The sky was blue, the air was clean, and if God was watching, so be it. I got out of my car and walked back to the truck. The imbecile behind the wheel had his baseball hat turned backward and his elbow resting out the window. I started the festivities by sticking my fingernails in his arm. He pulled it back into the cab.

"Somewheres?" I yelled. "Is that what you meant to say? You think somewhere has an s on the end of it?"

The guy was immediately conflicted. Belligerence is so much easier when you're safely strapped into two tons of motor vehicle and the person you're trying to intimidate is an abstraction. Not a genuine flesh-and-blood woman.

It wasn't just the symbolism that got to me, it was the fact of it. Another attack from the rear. And even inside a mass of mechanized metal, the guy is bigger and stronger, and thus more entitled than the woman. But maybe this time not as thoroughly and irretrievably enraged.

I grabbed the chrome handle mounted next to the door and hoisted myself up on the running board of his pickup truck.

"Do you own this gas station?" I yelled at him. "Did the pope anoint you king of all gas stations? Did the president of the United States give you special permission to be this big a fucking asshole?"

In retrospect, I might have taken things further than I would on a normal day. You run into a lot of guys like this one, young and dumb, born and bred on Long Island, or somewheres in the five boroughs, and unlike me, without the benefit of a post-graduate education to hone his social skills. It was just this particular jerk's fault for being a jerk with the wrong woman on the wrong day.

"Christ, lady, what the fuck," he said, rearing back into the cab of his truck.

" 'What the fuck' is right," I said, sticking my head halfway through his window and digging my fingernails into his arm again. "Be nicer to people. It's not that hard. And someday it might save your worthless, ugly, pinheaded life."

I yelled a few more things until I got him to say, "Okay, okay."

Then I jumped down off his running board and went back to my car. He sat there a few moments, then drove to the other bank of pumps and filled up. After that, he pulled into a parking space but stayed in the truck. I assumed to reevaluate his life's choices. Or to decide how he was going to kill me and when. Or to feel safe until the lunatic woman figured out how to put gas in her car and leave.

I know behavior like this is reckless, immature, and clearly dangerous. But I felt better for it. It wasn't the dope in the truck's fault that Sergey Pontecello had been dragged to death, or that I'd been run off the road by another pickup, but that didn't give him license to abuse me or any other woman in similar circumstances. So like the owner of Chez Slam, my conscience was clear and my debts paid in full.

With the exception of Sergey Pontecello.

■ ■ ■ ■

I was sickeningly sweet to the young man behind the counter at the coffee place, another victim of my vacillating mood, but luckily the rest of the morning I was on my computer, safely adrift in cyberspace.

Until my cell phone, vibrating in my pocket, scared the crap out of me. I thought for a second there was a giant bug in my pants. I leaped up and screamed, though not loud enough to alert the somber surveyors across the hall, something I noted for future reference.

"Yeah," I said into the vicious little thing.

"Yeah? Is that how lawyers answer their phones?" said Joe Sullivan.

"Yeah. Did you get an answer back yet from DNA?"

"Why am I talking to you again?" he asked.

"That's what Fuzzy wanted to know."

"Who's Fuzzy?"

"Oscar Wolsonowicz," I said.

"Right. The witness you tampered with."

"That conversation never came close to the definition of tampering."

He was quiet on the line. The dead air gave me time to get my mouth under control before I drove myself off a cliff.

"Sorry," I said. "You were just about to do me a favor."

"Not exactly. I got the clerk from Surrogate's Court on the other line. I need him there with me when I open the Pontecello safe-deposit box. I also need the estate administrator. That would be you."

"It would."

"You never told me how that happened," he said.

"Greed. Sometimes it's good."

"Meet me there in an hour. I'll be the one with a gun."

I hadn't dressed for an official visit to the bank but, I thought, the hell with it. Nobody would care but me, and I didn't have the emotional wherewithal to go home and search my house for a pair of panty hose that didn't have a run or a pair of decent shoes that weren't scuffed or in need of re-heeling.

So instead of going home to change, I took the time to walk across Montauk Highway to the park with the big windmill so I could lie on the grass and stare at the sky. I didn't know how to meditate or do yoga or any of those other cleansing, rejuvenating things that sound so wonderful when people who know how to do them describe the results. But I did know how to lie flat on my back and listen to the birds and passing traffic.

This worked for about five minutes. Then, being untrained in transcendental meditation, I started obsessing again over Sergey Pontecello.

I knew more about the circumstances of his life than I had before, but none of it brought me closer to understanding his miserable death.

I knew his wife, Betty, was a bit of a train wreck, but so what? Everybody's got an Aunt Agatha who worked at a job like executive secretary for some big shot in the City and who drank, smoked, cursed, and screwed her way to a ripe old age. They all had husbands or boyfriends who were less of a sport but stuck with their wild women. Sergey was her sidekick. He tried to look after her as best he could. He probably loved her. Why would anyone kill him over that?

The family itself was a dysfunctional mess, but again, so what? Whose isn't? Fuzzy was a jerk. Wendy a recluse. Eunice a bossy prig, but this was the Hamptons — we crank out so many self-appointed, überbroads like her you could probably trade them on the commodities exchange.

Then there was a little matter of the pickup assassin. What was that — a random psycho or conclusive evidence that Sergey's killer thought I knew a lot more than I did? Enough to make it worth killing me, too.

What was sorely missing was the thing my favorite judge insisted the prosecutors provide. A motive. The Big Why. There was always a reason for a murder, even if it didn't make sense to normal people or the killer himself, once he had a chance to sit down and really think about what he'd done. Usually it was more than "Seemed like a good idea at the time."

Most of the cases I handled for Burton Lewis were so open-and-shut it was embarrassing for all of us to go through the necessary formalities. Either the accused was an obviously evil or hopelessly stupid social misfit, or the cops and D.A. had been running a tissue-thin case that a third-rate pre-law college student could have blown to smithereens. There was almost never a lot of gray area in criminal justice, despite the impression given by the entertainment industry.

"I don't know enough," I said to the birds flying overhead. They didn't comment.

The clerk from the Surrogate's Court was

young enough to be my son, if I'd had a son when I was twelve years old. His chin was smudged with fine hair and his clothes were made of the wrinkle-free synthetic once favored by the immigrant engineers who worked for my father. His head was all brown curls, cut rather than combed into place. He had a tiny diamond earring in each ear and looked happy with himself, as if finding the bank on his own was an accomplishment worthy of acclaim.

Sullivan was also wrinkle-free, the result of precise and thorough ironing. You could cut your hand on the seam in his khaki pants. Ostensibly a plainclothesman, he was supposed to blend in with the general populace, which he would have done on a military base on Okinawa, but not in the Hamptons. His olive drab shirt had two pockets with flaps, one of which had a slit to let out the top of his mechanical pencil. The lenses in his sunglasses were thick and utterly black, contrasting starkly with his pale skin and platinum-blond hair, cut close to the scalp. His sport coat was a loose blue silk, selected for the way it disguised the shoulder holster and provided quick, unobstructed access to the Smith & Wesson .45. Though I had to say, it looked pretty spiffy. I told him so.

He scowled. "I'll tell the wife. Her fault."

"The wife? Does that make you the husband?"

"The spiff. Who's this?" He pointed at the clerk.

"Brad Sullivan," said the kid, sticking out his hand.

"No, it's not," said Sullivan, ignoring the hand.

"Huh?"

"Sullivan. That's my name."

"What," I said, "only one Sullivan allowed per acre? Give the guy a break. Shake his hand and let's get this thing done."

Sullivan grunted but did as I asked.

The Harbor Trust in Bridgehampton was the bank's biggest building on the East End, even though their regional headquarters was in Southampton. It was new and built with stone, marble, towering colonnades, five-foot-high crown moldings, and once-skyrocketing mortgage revenue. I'd watched them build it over two years ago, a display of extravagance that would have embarrassed the Vatican. The original headquarters was a square block of granite, solid enough for me and the rest of the bank's loyal customers, which could have saved them a lot of money if they'd bothered to ask us.

Elvin Graveley met us in the lobby.

"Elvin," I said, "how'd you draw this duty?"

"Curiosity. Autumn said she felt like she'd been renditioned to Warsaw."

I heard Sullivan let out a little puff of disdain, but he stayed quiet.

Elvin led us past a long row of tellers across from a field of elegant desks with computer screens and well-dressed people who spoke subaudible words into their phones. True to custom, the safe-deposit boxes were in the vault at the back of the bank. This was my favorite part — seeing the colossal and exquisitely beautiful round door. I don't know if I caught this from my engineer father, but I always loved the splendor of shiny machined steel. I could never be a bank robber if it meant drilling such a thing full of holes and blowing it up. I'd have to get really good at hearing the tumblers drop into place, listening with perfect concentration for the traitorous little clicks.

Elvin showed his ID to the gnarly old woman guarding the wooden gate that led into the staging area in front of the vault. Even though they'd been working together in the same office for more than twenty years, she gave it a good look, then waved to me. I gave her my license, which she looked eager to reject, running her eyes up and down my entire body.

"I had some surgery done on my face since that photo was taken," I said. "Medical, not cosmetic," I added, after seeing disapproval light up her face. I'm not sure she bought it, but I got my license back. Brad skated through, probably on the strength of his resemblance to a worthless grandson, and Joe simply stuck his detective's badge in her face. She averted her eyes and rushed him through.

While the three of us waited, Elvin secured the key to the safe-deposit box. Then we all went into the vault. Another bank employee was there with a few boxes on a table and a pad of paper on which she was taking notes.

"We'll wait until the vault is cleared," said Joe.

"That's not necessary," said Elvin, trying to be helpful.

"Yes, it is," said Joe, with that flat, dead tone cops use that usually scares the pee out of regular civilians.

"Of course," said Elvin, walking quickly over to the woman and whispering in her ear. She booked out of there with barely a sidelong glance.

Elvin gave us a strained smile and led us

to the box. He asked Brad about the protocols.

"Uh, I guess you open it and I, like, write down a list of all the stuff that's in there." He held up a clipboard to help us grasp the concept.

"You guess?" Joe said.

"I mean, yeah," said Brad. "That's how it works."

"You want to think about it some more?" asked Joe.

Brad found the courage of his convictions.

"No, sir. That is absolutely the way it works."

Sullivan nodded and reached into his pocket. He pulled out a wad of surgical gloves and handed them out.

After we were fully gloved, he nodded at Elvin, who gave him a little bow, then stuck in the key, turned it, and slid out the box. We gathered around a chest-high table and watched him open it up.

A bald, naked doll with jaundiced skin stared up at us with a crooked, maniacal leer.

"Whoa, holy crap. Fucking freak me out," said Brad.

Sullivan instantly stuck him in the chest with a stubby, rigid index finger.

"None of that stuff, hear?" he said.

Brad recovered his composure.

"Noted," he said.

"Write it down," said Sullivan.

"Yes, sir."

Elvin lifted out the doll. Under it was a bundle of yellowed newspaper clippings. While Brad made a log, I asked Sullivan if I could take a peek. He nodded. Afraid to damage the brittle scraps, I barely lifted the corners to look. From what I could tell, they were all recipes. I reported that to my colleagues.

"Write that down," said Sullivan to Brad.

Under the recipes was a box containing a gold class ring covered in Latin and a cameo, very old, picturing a stern, homely woman. Also a rhinestone necklace, the kind you could find by the bushel at any Sunday afternoon flea market.

Under that was an envelope labeled QUIT-CLAIM DEED, just as Sergey had said. After Brad logged it onto his clipboard, I asked Joe Sullivan if I could take a look. He said sure.

It was a legitimate document, with all the formal legal language, blocky typewriter type, and oversize papers. I took in the first few paragraphs and scanned to the end. It was plenty official and not overly burdened with legal jargon. In fact, it was all pretty clear.

It was written about twenty years ago and said that Eunice Hamilton Wolsonowicz had released all rights and claims to the Hamilton property in the Sagaponack section of the Town of Southampton, conveying such to Elizabeth Hamilton Pontecello.

Folded inside was another document, this one a promissory note, stating that the house and contents, the specifics to be determined, were posted as collateral against a loan to be paid as funds were requested, up to a limit of $4,685,000. It was dated a year ago.

So Betty had essentially set up her sister as a credit line with the house as collateral. I already knew where this led, but still, it was oddly depressing to see the details so irredeemably documented.

I handed both documents to Joe, who looked at them before handing them over to Brad.

"Is that it?" Joe asked.

Elvin dug around and pulled out a set of ceramic salt- and pepper shakers. The salt was in a naked breast and the pepper an erect penis. "We've seen stranger," he said, and as if to prove the point, pulled out the last item, a pint-size Ziploc bag containing a pair of severed ears.

Brad said, "Oh, Christ," then slapped his hand over his mouth.

I took the bag out of Elvin's hand and tossed it to Sullivan, who caught it in midair.

"Write it down," said Sullivan. Brad handed him the clipboard and headed for the exit. Couldn't blame him.

"Send them along to Riverhead," I said to Sullivan. "Next time, we're going for the whole head," I added, grinning at Elvin, who'd already decided the consequences of unfettered curiosity weren't all they were cracked up to be.

16

The leaden weariness brought on from the last few days pinned my limbs to the bed. I decided I needed the whole morning to gather my strength. To call up reinforcements, renew my vitality.

Or maybe just loaf around in bed playing Dead Girl. This was a game of mine growing up. On mornings when waking up all the way seemed too high a mountain to climb, I'd pretend I was dead. This was more difficult than you'd think. I had to lie there, perfectly still, holding my breath and trying to will my skin into a gray, cadaverous pallor. My mother never once fell for it, though she'd say things like, "Oh, dear. Jacqueline is dead. What a pity, such a nice little girl. Sigh. I suppose we'll just have to buy another one."

The problem with playing Dead Girl when you're my age and living alone is there's no one to fool but yourself.

After I'd tried to simulate the total lifeless-
ness of a murder victim my joints began to
rebel, making it so uncomfortable I gave up
the fight and slid off the bed onto the floor.
This position seemed more authentic, so I
lay there for a while, imagining a circle of
horrified witnesses, muttering that they'd
never seen such a beautiful dead body.

This worked for another half hour, until I
was forced to admit I was wide-awake and
bored with the idea of lying flat on my back.
Still, it was a good hour before I managed
to clean myself up and choose between the
yellow jeans and green hiking boots or dark
green jeans and white running shoes, compromising with all green from top to bottom.

I'd decided that morning to visit Winthrop's, which likely incited the performance by Dead Girl. It was a short trip to
the funeral home, one of two in town. The
other was started by a Greek guy who was
also in the pizza-shop business. Though his
name was Andre Pappanasta, he named the
place Livingston and Hawthorne, understanding that Long Islanders preferred to
think that starchy, impeccable Anglo-
Saxons, like the ones they saw on *Upstairs,
Downstairs,* would be handling their loved
ones' remains. Winthrop's was the real deal,

having been in the business forever, a selling point reinforced by the facilities themselves, housed in a lovingly restored colonial inn on Montauk Highway.

I pushed a button on a table in the lobby labeled FOR ATTENTION, which I got seconds later. He was a well-dressed man in his late forties, tall and clean-featured, with wire-frame glasses and rapidly evaporating black hair made blacker by an oily dressing pasting the defeated remains into a slick skullcap.

He stood before me with hands clasped tightly to his chest.

"Mrs. Anderson, I presume," he said.

"Sorry, no. Jackie Swaitkowski. I'm an attorney here in Southampton. I was hoping to meet with your management."

The man smiled.

"My management is my wife, so you must mean the person in charge of Winthrop's Funeral Home, which would be me."

He put out his hand. I took it, fearing something cold, limp, and creepy, but suffered hard, dry, and assertive instead.

"Alden Winthrop," he said.

"I'm looking into the death of one of my clients. I was hoping I could ask you a question or two."

He smiled another well-practiced smile.

"I'm happy to speak with you, only I can't imagine how I could help."

Winthrop still looked eager to please but now slightly uncertain.

"Can we just sit down for a second?" I said, rubbing my leg as if nursing an ancient injury. That did it.

"Oh, of course, come this way."

I felt like I was back in Sandy Kalandro's office. Winthrop's space was every bit as comfortable, though distinguished by its greater vintage, predominantly mid-eighteenth-century, with some arts and crafts mixed in. And devotedly cared for. The leather couches were a dark and supple cordovan, and the finish on the elegant veneered desk and credenza so deeply luxurious I had to sit on my hands to resist stroking the grain. On the walls were black-and-white photographs taken in the old days of Southampton Village, when the streets were mud, people dressed in black, and cattle grazed in the empty fields next to the treacherous ocean. When I was getting over my dead husband, I went to a shrink who had an office like this.

Winthrop nimbly slid around the desk and sat down. I dropped into one of the two visitor's chairs facing the desk and immediately felt the urge to talk about my

283

childhood.

"So," said Winthrop.

"Do you remember Edna Jackery?" I asked.

Winthrop furrowed his brow.

"Jackery. Familiar name."

"Your family has been burying their family for decades."

"I wouldn't have phrased it quite that way, but I understand what you're saying," he said. He leaned both elbows on the top of the desk and set his chin on top of his folded hands.

"You probably remember she was killed in a hit-and-run about a year ago," I said. "Somewhere between the medical examiner's and here some of Edna got separated from the rest of Edna. Any ideas?"

"I'm sorry. I don't understand."

"I know she left the M.E. intact and was cremated by you folks," I said. "So I'm wondering why pieces of Edna keep showing up in places where they don't belong."

"Curious."

"Does cremation happen here or off-site somewhere?" I asked.

He looked around as if the crematorium was just outside the door and down the hall.

"Did you say you were an attorney?" he asked me.

I nodded.

"Is the family aware of this situation?" he asked.

I shook my head. "No, and they won't be if I have anything to do with it. This is an entirely private inquiry," I said.

His silence seemed to say he was weighing his options. I waited him out.

"How do I say this delicately," he said.

"Not too delicately for my sake, Mr. Winthrop. I'm a lawyer. I've heard it all."

"For certain items, by-products of the embalming process, we have a small furnace at the facility. For total cremation, we have a long-term arrangement with a crematorium service," said Winthrop. "The deceased from the medical examiner usually come with the family's instructions. If Mrs. Jackery was cremated, that was her family's wish. We have no direct involvement in this beyond preparing the proper manifest, picking up the deceased, holding services, then scheduling the cremation. Frankly, this all sounds thoroughly appalling. You are sure that some of Mrs. Jackery became detached in the process?"

"According to the DNA, at least one part we're sure of," I said. "Who picked her up at the M.E. and dropped her off at the crematorium?"

"Did you say it was a year ago?" he asked.

"Yeah."

Winthrop rose slowly from his chair and went over to a tall oak filing cabinet. He flicked his fingers across the file tabs until he reached the right spot. He pulled out a file and opened it, and took a moment to read through the papers. Then he sat back in his chair and put both hands flat on the desk.

"Alden Winthrop the fourth. My son. He's just breaking into the business, learning the ropes. As I did — start at the bottom and work your way up."

"Then he's the one we need to talk to," I said.

This pained Winthrop, though it was hard to tell why. Unless it was the obvious — that here was this pushy woman, intruding on him and asking unsettling questions. In fact, he had a perfect right to tell me to take a hike. That he hadn't so far was more likely caution in the face of a threat than professional courtesy.

"I'm beginning to wonder if we should be having this conversation," said Winthrop. "I don't wish to be rude, but the irregularities are rather extreme."

It was too bad that the arms on my big leather chair were broad, solid oak, providing a hard surface for me to tap my finger-nails. I realized I was doing it when the sound drew Winthrop's attention.

"Here's the thing, Mr. Winthrop," I said, sitting back on my hands.

"You can call me Alden."

"Alden. A client of mine was killed re-cently under what the police consider suspi-cious circumstances. There's a connection between his death and Edna Jackery's remains. That's all I can tell you and I shouldn't be telling you that. You're under absolutely no obligation to talk to me about this, but I'm only a couple steps ahead of the Southampton Police, and with them it's a different story."

"In what way?"

"Let's just say, Alden, you won't find them as sensitive to your interests as I am," I said.

Color would have been draining out of his face if there had been any color there in the first place.

"Should I be reaching out to my own at-torney?" he asked.

"Not a bad idea," I said. "But should you need any help from me with the cops, you'll wait till I talk to your kid."

I said this as gently as I could, but there was no disguising the implication. After some more silent deliberation, Winthrop picked up his desk phone and dialed.

"Denny, it's your father," he said into the receiver. "Are you still in Building Two?"

He listened to the answer.

"I know you said you would be. I was merely asking. There is someone here who wants to talk to you."

Another pause.

"I'll let her explain that. She's on her way over," he said, then hung up the phone without saying good-bye, as if to thwart the next objection.

"It wouldn't be a family business if we didn't work with family, now would it?" said Winthrop, almost to himself, which probably explained something, though I wasn't sure what.

Building Two looked like a big two-story garage with a row of eight bays. There was a side door at the end of a path. I opened it without knocking. The door led into a small foyer, with another door that led into a large open area, much larger than it looked from the outside. It was brilliantly lit by banks of industrial fluorescent lighting. The floor was painted a spotless dove gray. Parked inside were a pair of hearses, a blue van, a vintage something covered in canvas, and at the far end, a Ford pickup truck, the official vehicle of Eastern Suffolk County. The vehicles that were exposed looked recently detailed, polished to a finish you could use to check your mascara.

The back wall extended well beyond the depth of the garage bays. In one corner was a virtual suite, complete with a single bed — brutally unmade — dresser, fridge, top-loading freezer, sink, and a card table with two chairs. The rest of the space was crammed with folding chairs, tents, portable pulpits, and PA systems, flower boxes on wheels, easels to hold photo collages of the departed, and other accoutrement you'd expect to be in the service of a funeral home.

Except for the half dozen surfboards, ice hockey sticks, aquarium, kayak, and diving gear.

In the middle of a small open space was a padded thing on skids being kicked and punched by a young man with a long blond ponytail and a tattoo of Groucho Marx on his muscular shoulder.

He treated me to about five minutes of vigorous pummeling of the defenseless equipment, to which he gave a bow before acknowledging me with a wide, humorless smile.

"Once I start a sequence, I have to finish. It's a discipline," he said.

He walked briskly across the canvas,

slipped through the ropes, and offered me his sweaty, taped-up hand.

"Denny Winthrop." He held eye contact and my hand longer than necessary in that reflexive way good-looking young guys always do. I knew how to hold back my gratitude.

"Jackie Swaitkowski."

I pulled back my hand until he relented and let go. He swept a towel off the floor and dabbed his face.

"What's this about?" he asked. "My old man wouldn't say."

"It's a little complicated," I said. "Can we sit down?"

"Sure, you can," said Denny, "but I have to stand. It's part of the cool-down."

He used one hand to snap open a folding chair, which he dropped down in front of me. I sat.

I gave Denny the same basic briefing I'd given his father. I watched his face as I talked but saw no change in his confident poise.

"If the old man says I shipped the stiff, I guess I did. A year ago's a long time. I don't usually get to know the cargo all that well."

His smile grew slightly, amused by his own wit.

I asked Denny to describe the body-shipping process. He said he just pulls the plain blue van up to a loading dock at the M.E.'s, exchanges paperwork with a lab grunt, and takes possession of a fully stocked body bag. After the funeral, he drives the body in a special wooden box to the crematorium in Riverhead. He said it was their job to send the ashes back by UPS.

"I never have to look at them," he said. "It's strictly pickup and drop off. Other than that, I don't do cadaver shit. I made that clear to the old man when I started working here. It totally weirds me out."

He dropped his hands to his sides and shook out his arms while doing a light aerobic dance on the tips of his toes.

"So where was the drop off?" I asked. "The crematorium?"

Denny continued to bounce around on his toes, puffing out his breath and filling the room with his dank, athletic odor.

"Why do you want to know?" he asked, putting the emphasis on "you," as if anyone else's inquiry would be more legitimate.

"You might not remember that Edna Jackery was killed in a hit-and-run. This is part of that ongoing investigation," I said.

"You're a cop? I thought you were a lawyer."

"That's right. An officer of the court."

"What the hell does that mean?" he asked.

Damn, I thought. Far brighter people had bought that line, and I'd never had to come up with a reasonable response. So I did the sensible thing and pretended I hadn't heard what he said.

"There were some irregularities connected to the disposition of Mrs. Jackery's remains," I said. "That's all I can tell you."

"Really? That's all?"

"I don't need you to tell me where the crematorium is," I said. "I can find out on my own. It would just save me a lot of time if you did."

Denny stopped hopping, apparently having achieved full cool-down.

"We use the regional place in Riverhead," he said. "Usually twenty-four-hour turnaround. Stiff arrives in the morning, a bag of dust comes out the next day. We supply the urns or gilded boxes or humidors, or whatever else the family wants. Families buy all kinds of worthless crap for dead people. Seems like a waste of money to me, but the old man says it's where all the profit is."

"So you're learning the family trade," I said.

"Fuck no. I'm working on my stash. All I need is for my deals to go the way they're supposed to go and I'm getting as far away

292

from this fucking place as humanly possible."

"I have a feeling that wouldn't please your father."

"I don't give a crap about pleasing the old man. It's not my fault he likes hanging around with corpses all day."

"Who's this old man you keep talking about?" I asked. "Are you referring to your father?"

"Who do you think I'm talking about?" he said.

"Good. Then start calling him 'Dad,' or 'my father.' "

"I'll call him what I want. What do you care?"

"I don't like the disrespect. Especially toward your father, who's only trying to keep you from turning into a worthless piece of crap yourself."

Denny's face lit up in a bright blotchy red.

"That's just rude," he said.

"You oughta know."

He stopped dancing and stood flat on his feet, executing a series of shadow punches. Then he began to advance slowly toward me until the punches began to get closer and closer to my head. Eventually, I could feel the breeze from the fists flashing by. I kept my expression in neutral, with my eyes, unimpressed, cast up to his face.

Then I stood, very slowly and carefully, trying hard not to lean outside the vertical plane defined by Denny's pumping fists. As always, my thoughts were focused on the left side of my face, the slightly numb, nicely reconstructed part. Staying in the chair probably would have kept it safer. But you can't stand your ground if you aren't standing up.

I folded my arms, partly to shrink myself down and partly to hide my shaking hands. Denny started circling me, his fists still boxing the air. I could have stayed fixed in position or turned with him. I turned so I could keep my eyes locked on his face, and so I could see the incoming blow should one eventually connect.

"Stop doing this now, and I'll pretend it didn't happen," I said.

He didn't stop. Instead, he closed his eyes and picked up the pace. My heart lit up in my chest, but I kept my concentration on the rhythm of his jabs, trying to guess the right moment to jump clear.

"If you hurt me, it'll be an assault charge. I guarantee you," I said, the timbre of my voice shakier than I wanted it to be.

He stopped abruptly, dropped his hands, opened his eyes, and grinned. Or maybe it was a leer. I was too unnerved to tell.

"Assault? I'm just practicing my patterns. You're supposed to stay still. Can I help it if you move?"

I kicked the chair I'd been sitting on out of the way. I moved into his personal space, close enough to see the pores on his nose and smell his sweat, perfumed by deodorant, or maybe aftershave.

"That sounded an awful lot like a legal argument. If you think you could sock me and escape the consequences by way of your superior command of the law, go ahead. Give me your best shot."

The leer was still there, but the confidence behind his eyes wavered just a bit.

"My best shot would put you in one of those," he said, jerking his head toward the hearse.

I just stared at him, which should have been more fun. He was one of those guys who would have been attractive if you could fit him with a different personality.

"Nothing pulls together cops and lawyers like the murder of one of their own," I said.

The tension in his frame drained off with some of his overconfidence. The leer turned into some analog of a smile.

"Nobody's murdering anybody," he said. "Just goofing around."

I backed away from him, farther away than necessary. It felt better having a little air between us, though I wasn't about to turn my back.

"Run through the pickup-and-drop-off sequence again, one more time. And fill in the names of everyone you talked to at both ends," I said, pulling a pad and pen out of my back pocket.

"You're kidding."

I clicked the retractable pen and waited. He went through the process again, this time adding a few details and some additional sarcasm. He claimed not to remember who handed off the corpse at the M.E.'s but named the people at the crematorium. He didn't add much more to what I already had, but I was more confident in the story's accuracy.

I was about to get out of there when Denny's phone rang. He picked it up off the card table and answered.

"Yeah, she's still here," he said. "Yeah, I told her what I could. No, I don't know what it's about. No idea. Yeah, sure, I'll do that. Yeah, yeah, okay," he said, then paused and looked over at me, "Dad."

I took a few steps backward, then turned and moved as briskly as dignity would allow to the door. My face was burning, and I could feel my heart lodged somewhere just south of my throat. The infuriated part of me wanted to go back into Winthrop's office and ask him, "What's up with your kid?" but the other part, the one that thought it was a much better idea to just run like hell, won that argument.

For a change.

17

I drove directly to my office. Along the way I lit a cigarette with my Volvo's virgin lighter before I could stop myself. A silly concept, I realized immediately, me trying to keep anything in my life pristinely preserved.

When I got to the office, I cleared the sofa, which had been serving as a file cabinet, and dropped down on my back. Then I worked on getting heart, lungs, and brain to slow down, in unison if possible. The cardio-vascular part went as planned. The brain, not so much.

I found myself in an argument with my-self. Actually, with my multiple selves. I'm not suggesting I've got a split personality, but sometimes I wonder how many Jackies are living inside the same body. At least one of the contenders that day was begging to me to stop what I was doing, whatever it was, and get back to honest, boring, but socially acceptable work, like taking depositions and closing on houses. To jump off the tracks before official law enforcement ran me over, which it was surely going to do.

I'd crossed the line going to see Winthrop without telling Joe Sullivan. The problem wasn't just getting in the cops' way. It was messing with potential witnesses, people whose testimony could affect the case. The element of surprise had been taken away. Both Winthrop and his meatball son were now forewarned.

This voice of admonition and common sense, however, was a lonely one. The rest of the gang wanted to jump off the sofa and go do something, anything. The more heedless, the better. Only the motivation was in contention. I was furious, that was clear. I was royally and nearly uncontrollably pissed off: at the cops for being so plodding and bureaucratic, at the Wolsonowicz family for the way they loathed Sergey — only slightly more than they loathed one another — and at myself for not understanding what it all meant.

Anger, however, can look a lot like fear. I don't like to think of myself as a fearful person. You can't be that way and live on your own in a house on three acres of woods at the end of a long driveway. Or work all by yourself when you aren't out there representing antisocial frights and grappling with judges, prosecutors, and indifferent civil servants within the New York State legal system.

But there's a limit. Getting shoved off the road was certainly bad enough. The shock and strangeness of the experience, the anonymity of the perpetrator, even the uncertainty over what had actually happened — if it was malicious intent or just some strange act of road rage I'd unwittingly provoked.

The thing with Denny Winthrop was different. This time I could see his arrogant face and hear the narcissistic banality of his words. I'd helped Burton defend people like him from charges like assault, reckless endangerment, even manslaughter. I knew how close he'd come to losing what modicum of control he had over himself and how close I'd pushed him to do just that.

This was at the crux of the internal argument. Just how much control did I have over my own actions? How close was *I* to the brink?

What I didn't do was ask myself how I'd gotten to this point in the first place. Right at that moment, I didn't know and really didn't care. There were too many other things I didn't know, and there was a computer in the room that might be able to fix that.

I got up off the couch and made a pot of coffee. Then I slipped a pre-rolled joint out of a plastic grocery bag I kept in a locked file drawer and settled down in front of the computer, the greatest friend of the compulsively curious ever invented by man.

I typed in "Oscar Wolsonowicz," and nothing came up, but there were a lot of hits on "FuzzMan." I went right to his blog. I wanted to look a little closer, now that I knew the boy was likely to inherit a bundle. When I got there, he was in his usual hateful mood. The objects of scorn were a full range of public and private figures — politicians, entertainers, neighbors, other bloggers, dental hygienists, stamp collectors, jackhammer operators, and the entire front office of the New York Mets. I looked hard to find some redeeming social commentary woven into the diatribes, but like the last time I visited, it just wasn't there. Neither was any organizing philosophy beyond the hope for the imminent demise of high-profile individuals and institutions.

I think he outdid himself with a rant against the sickening soft-heartedness of contemporary nihilists.

301

Fuzzy was also an active responder on other blogs. On one he showed up often as a guest commentator. It was called Retort and was run by another charmer named Rip. Retort was true to its name, offering a forum for any and all contrarian views, a natural attractor for Fuzzy. The commentary was chockablock with searing, scatological wrath, which might have been fun for them, but to me was a dreadful, dispiriting bore. Rip always followed Fuzzy's lead, and though neither of them was likely to be crowned the H. L. Mencken of online media, Fuzzy actually could sound reasonably intelligent despite the rancor.

I forced myself to read on and began to notice their focus was primarily financial. Both were heavily engaged in the stock market, with Fuzzy again taking the lead, offering advice and a rabid form of proselytizing on behalf of his picks. As I worked my way back through the archives on Fuzzy's blog, an even deeper read revealed that Rip had run up some serious losses. After that, Fuzzy's influence grew as Rip's self-confidence faded, and despite what sounded like the banter of equals, Fuzzy obviously ran the whole show.

This involved an emphasis on short selling, Fuzzy's favorite thing, which meant making money on a company's misfortune by betting that its stock value will fall. Short sellers were a natural and legal cog in the financial machine, but it was hard to like them any more than you like carrion birds cleaning roadkill off the highway.

I went back to Google and picked up a link to his father. The same few hundred thousand references popped up, which I started leafing through from the beginning. It wasn't until the forty-fifth page that the headline "What Makes Tony Run?" caught my eye.

It was an online magazine article examining Tony W.'s emotional and psychological motivations. It covered a lot of historical background, then drifted into his romantic habits, which started with the young initiates at his private salon in Arizona and branched out to the wives of his financial patrons and favored gallery owners. Reports of people's rampant sexual appetites are always more engaging when you don't know the players. It's an abstraction, on a par with scenes from a dirty movie or novel. A voyeuristic daydream. It's different when you've sat across the table from the guy's wife and pet his daughter's dogs. I barely got through half the article before I had to click off the page.

Before this began to depress me, I escaped into a search of Elizabeth Hamilton Pontecello. The stack of hits at the top of the list covered her death and funeral. I dug deeper and found several court documents relating to Betty's shoplifting cases and consequent adjudication. Shoplifting rarely excites prosecutorial ire, as Betty's record proved. It didn't hurt that she was a woman of a certain age, sophistication, and social acceptability. It's not fair, but these things matter in a court of law. It's a human tendency to give the benefit of the doubt to someone who looks more like your great-aunt Tilly than the hard-wired sociopath she actually is.

I spent the rest of the day searching for more on both Elizabeth and Sergey, without much result. I did learn from an article in a Manhattan society publication that Sergey was born in Portugal to a Russian mother and an Italian father, who claimed various connections to European royalty. I tried to get deeper into that, but all the relevant sites were in Italian, and all I knew was conversational French.

My eyes finally began to blur. I tore myself away from the screen and was surprised to see it was getting dark outside, lost as I'd been in the timeless wastes of cyberspace.

I went into my little restroom and splashed water on my face. I thought another joint might be the perfect way to bookend the computer time, but then I wondered if it would make me too sleepy to drive home. Before I had a chance to take up another schizoid debate, Joe Sullivan called me on my cell.

"You're done," he said.

"Hello to you, too."

"Alden Winthrop called Ross Semple, Southampton chief of police. My boss," he said. "I'm still in the process of cleaning up all the shit after it hit the fan."

"Oh."

"If you got a client you're defending for murder, you can talk to whoever you want. But not if your client's the victim. Then somebody might say you're interfering with a police investigation. Ross said exactly that, in fact."

While he was talking the question of the joint was decided. I lit it up and took a deep hit before asking, "So what did Winthrop say? Did you talk to him?"

"We're all through here, Jackie. Ross actually likes you even more than I do, but not that much. You're now officially on his shit list. Just remember you did it to yourself. I bent over backward for you, but now I'm done bending." Then he hung up.

"Asshole," I said out loud.

There was a restaurant in Southampton I'd visit with Sam when we were working our way through whatever legal mess he'd roped me into. We'd go there after a tough day to unwind and regroup over a quick drink, though for Sam there was never an occasion that didn't call for a quick drink. That day, the marijuana had fogged up my reasoning powers, but I knew I was hungry and, counter to expectations, wide-awake. So I decided a glass of wine and some bar food made the most sense right at that moment.

I almost called Harry to come join me, but then he'd want to know how I spent my day, and I'd have to lie or tell him about Denny Winthrop, and I didn't want to do either.

It was that pleasant time at the restaurant before the dinner crowd arrived when you could count on a seat at the giant U-shaped bar close to the big French doors that in warmer weather were opened on the sidewalk. While waiting for my merlot I watched the staff move around tables and spread white tablecloths, busy with the transition. The air was stirred around enjoyably by strategically placed paddle fans. There was no one else at the bar, so Geordie, the bartender, agreed to switch off the TV so I didn't have to be distracted by grown men in antiquated outfits throwing and hitting a little white ball, when they weren't standing around scratching their own balls and spitting on the ground.

I'm not a person who is easily discouraged, but the call from Sullivan, while expected, made me feel like somebody had pricked my mood with a pin and let out all the air. I'd had the feeling before, though I hated acknowledging it. I couldn't accept that a person could be racing along all flush with energy and zeal, and then one dumb stumble and they're ready to crawl off like a wounded animal, curl into a ball, and die. When I was younger, I wanted to blame these feelings on something outside myself, some other person, like my father or the sadistic prick who taught seventh-grade chemistry, but I always knew that would be a cowardly lie.

"What the hell am I doing?" I asked Geordie as he set the glass of wine in front of me.

"Drinking, which is what any sane human being ought to be doing at this hour."

Geordie wasn't his actual name; it was a

nickname relating to his English roots. He came from a place, as he told it, of limitless masculine courage and mythical consumption of warm beer.

"I'm being stupid," I said. "I need to go back to title searches and petitioning for variances and learn to be realistic about my place in the world."

Geordie considered that line of reasoning.

"I've no idea what you're talking about, love, but I'm not sure I like it."

"Which part?" I asked.

"Never been a big fan of realism. Waste of time."

"And you've never gotten yourself in something over your head?"

"Ah, that's it, then. Bit off more than you can chew?" he asked.

I nodded and took a sip of the wine, not a gulp like I wanted.

"I think I messed up on something, and I want to fix it, but the harder I try, the more messed up things seem to get. I've got a real talent for digging a hole, jumping in, and pulling all the dirt back down on top of myself."

Geordie wiped a section of the bar with a wet dishrag.

"That's your problem," he said. "You're trying too hard."

"Don't start going all Zen on me, Geordie," I said, putting my head down on my folded arms.

"I'm a barman. What do I know? Except that you can't make truth reveal itself. You have to let it come out on its own. Create the necessary environment."

"That's pretty damn philosophical. No wonder you're a barman."

"You need to stop thinking for a while," he said. "Distract yourself. Take polka lessons. Go sit on the beach. Jump in the ocean. Get in a bar fight. Just not here, if you wouldn't mind. Management frowns upon it."

"No worries," I said, my voice muffled by the soft pillow of my arms.

I spent another hour in boozy repartee with Geordie, increasingly interrupted by incoming clientele. I knew what I was doing — beating all my hopes, fears, and self-recrimination into a type of putty that I could mold to my liking before trying to get some sleep. When I thought that was achievable, I got up and left, not even saying good-bye to Geordie, who was happily engaged in further nonsense with a crowd of big tippers at the other end of the bar.

I stopped at the convenience store on Montauk Highway to buy coffee for the ride home and milk for the next day. The place had been there since I was a kid, and there was never a time when it wasn't jammed with people of every description and social standing. Which was true that night. There were four guys working the registers, and the lines led to the back, where the coolers held all the dairy products. I politely cut between two guys in muddy T-shirts buying potato chips and bent down to grab a quart. Then I heard someone call my name. When I stood I saw Ray Zander, equally muddy, standing at the end of the line.

"Whashya doin'?" he said. "Don'cha know milk'll kill ya?"

Though slightly tipsy myself, I could see right away that he was thoroughly plastered. He proved this by nearly tripping on his own feet. He grabbed on to a display to steady himself and knocked off a row of potato chip bags.

I moved closer and watched as he negotiated the difficult task of picking up the bags and returning them precariously to their rightful place. I stood about four feet away, just inside the cloud of fumes that billowed around him.

"So, Ray," I said, "been doing a little partying?"

I hadn't the right to be terribly critical,

given what I'd been up to myself, though the sight of him was disturbing. His face was a mottled purple-red. His hair, a thin collection of gray-brown curls in the best of times, was sticking out in all directions. I realized that the rest of the dirty workers were from his crew, and they weren't in much better shape.

"You're not driving, I hope," I said to Ray, and then to his boys, "You're not letting him drive, I hope."

They grinned at each other as if I'd reminded them of an old joke. Which I guess I had.

"Shit, no," said one of the them. "Not unless we're enterin' a demolition derby."

"Or goin' on a suicide mission," said another.

"Where did you go drinking looking like that?" I asked.

"You mean the cooler in the back of Ray's truck? Not that choosy far as we know."

"He got that drunk on beer?"

"Ray likes a whiskey chaser with every beer. Says it helps smooth a path."

"Fuckin' yeah," said Ray, executing another ragged stumble, which one of the crew got in front of before he completely toppled over.

I drew promises from the younger men

that they'd not only get him home but into bed, with his keys hidden in a safe place. I'd defended more than one drunken construction worker who'd tried to prove his sobriety by sneaking back out for a joyride.

I was reluctant to leave the parking lot until I saw the men lead Ray to the passenger side of his pickup. Unfortunately, he saw me, too. He broke free of the other guys' grips and staggered over to my car.

"I been meanin' to tell ya something," he said, in the sort of Long Islander's southern drawl he affected.

My curiosity, as usual, got the best of me.

"And what's that?" I asked.

"You're a mighty fine example of a woman," he said. "In the looks department. I've been thinkin' that and now feels like the right time to be sayin' it. No need to thank me."

I looked across the parking lot for a little help.

"Yo, Ray's handlers, come over here and get him," I yelled.

Something dark and alien traveled behind Zander's eyes.

"That wasn't the nicest thing I ever heard from a woman," he said, moving closer to me. "You was mine, I'd backhand you for that one."

"Stop right there, while you're almost ahead," I said as sternly as I could. Then I yelled again for the crew. A guy came over looking embarrassed and took hold of Ray's arm. "Sorry, ma'am. What'd he say? Is he getting out of line?"

I just stuck with the compliments.

"No offense," said the guy, "but when he gets like this every woman seems like a mighty fine example."

"Including his wife?" I asked.

"Probably not."

"Does he get like this a lot?"

"Like what?" asked Ray, trying to pull out of the guy's grip.

"Not really," said the guy. "Won't touch a drop for weeks at a time, but when he does, can't stop. The more he drinks, the nastier he gets. Don't worry, he won't remember anything."

"Don't worry," I said. "I will."

By the time I finally got home and into bed, I'd had fully enough of that particular day. The only good thing was a lesson in the sins of immoderation, courtesy of Geordie's merlot and Ray Zander's drunken foolhardiness, an object lesson sent to me by the agents of my fickle but resolute conscience.

Contrary to every expectation, I fell into blissful sleep, where I stayed, like a good

Dead Girl, till well into the next morning.

A gift from Joe Sullivan was waiting at my office the next day, much to my astonishment. The big envelope was leaning against the door with ANONYMOUS TIPSTER written on it.

I apologized aloud for calling Sullivan an asshole, though I didn't promise to never do it again.

Inside the envelope was a summary sheet of Betty and Sergey's financial assets, along with supporting bank statements. There was also a copy of Betty and Sergey's win/loss statement from the casino. The first sheet recorded plenty of losses, but over time, their luck reversed, and ultimately they got way ahead of the game. By about forty-five thousand dollars.

"Why?" I asked when I got Sullivan on his cell phone.

"I'm authorized to release the bank records to the estate administrators. Consider the casino info a police special of the day."

"You *are* the same cop who called me yesterday and yelled at me? I thought I was the one with the split personality."

"I'm the cop who had his boss standing next to his desk when he made that call. I meant most of it, by the way."

"So, how 'bout that win/loss statement?" I said, eager to move on to better things.

"Not what we expected. I called over to the casino. Table games supervisor told me he was glad they liked poker — wins come out of the other players' pockets, the house just gets a cut."

"Get out of here. Good old Sergey," I said.

"Wasn't Sergey. The wife was the shark. Played blackjack, but the real action was Texas Hold 'Em — girls on the floor called Betty Hamptons Holdup. Both were big on the drink tray, but Betty switched a year ago to straight tonic and lime."

I started to feel the way I used to feel at amusement parks. Only this time it wasn't the vertigo or bad food choices. It was the feeling that an important truth was there in the shadows, mocking me, lurking defiantly just out of reach.

"Any of this tell you anything?" Sullivan asked.

"What do you call an old lady who curses at the gardeners, chain-smokes, drinks like a fish — at least some of the time — has a habit of filching merchandise, and plays cards like the Cincinnati Kid?"

"A four-square crazy old bitch?"

"No," I said to him. "A librarian."

■ ■ ■ ■

I hadn't been to the East Hampton Library since leaving home to go to college. I wasn't all that crazy about the library environment. It was too quiet. People ghosting around the narrow aisles gave me the creeps, and I was afraid all the noise in my head would leak out and bother people.

I did like the books, however. If I hadn't loved to read I'm not sure I could have made it through college, much less earned a law degree. A book was the only thing I could sit still for, even a bad book. So I got to know a lot of librarians, and in my experience, they were nothing like the stereotypical pinched old matrons but rather very smart and witty if you gave them a chance to be.

As if to disprove my theory, the woman at the checkout desk told me tersely that it was against library policy to discuss employees, living or deceased. She was a pinched young woman, wearing an unmatronly top and more red lipstick than her pale complexion could withstand.

"Is that in the library employee manual? I'm an attorney. I'd like to see that passage, which I'm certain is in violation of EEO statutes," I said, and even though that didn't make any sense at all, it got me past her to the next librarian up the chain of command, who looked more the type and was as pleasant as punch.

"We don't have a library employee manual," said Head Librarian Ruth Hinsdale, looking disappointed in herself. "Should we?"

"I don't know," I said, shaking her hand. "The woman I'm here about was a volunteer. Elizabeth Pontecello. She died recently."

Ruth's disappointment turned to sorrow.

"Oh yes, she certainly did. What a pity. Would you mind if we talked in my office? We don't want to disturb our readers."

"We certainly don't," I said, and followed her through a fleet of wheeled carts stacked with books awaiting the return trip to the shelves.

We'd already run through introductions, so I dropped down in one of the visitor seats in her completely uncluttered and thoroughly comfortable office. I looked around admiringly, stifling the urge to say, "Gee, that's what horizontal surfaces look like."

"And your interest in Betty?" she asked from behind her spotless, paperless desk.

"It's more about her husband, Sergey. He

was a client of mine. He died, too, but was probably murdered."

She nodded.

"I read something in the newspaper. I'm just grateful Betty went first, if she had to go. I already miss her terribly," she said. "She was much more than a volunteer around here."

"A patron?"

"That and more. There was hardly a book in this building she couldn't find without resorting to the card drawers. She had an encyclopedic knowledge of the entire reference section, if you'll forgive the pun."

See, I said to myself, like I thought. Witty.

"I guess twenty years among the shelves will do that," I said.

Ruth's gray-brown hair, in loose beauty-shop curls, bobbed when she moved her pleasingly round face.

"I made sure all of that was in her obituary," said Ruth. "She asked me to write something a week before she died. I was a little aghast but honored that she'd think of me."

"So you knew something about her life."

"Betty was not only my colleague, my comrade in arms, but my best friend, if you want the truth of the matter."

"I do, Mrs. Hinsdale. The truth is what I

318

very much want to hear."

"Truth can be a fungible commodity," she said. "Even when it's what we're trying to express or wishing to hear."

That was when I realized Head Librarian Hinsdale was made of more complicated stuff than you'd think just looking at her plump little self. And me an enemy of stereotyping.

"So Betty looked after the reference section, helped fund the library, was a good friend and partner to you. Sounds like an amazing lady. What else did she do?"

Ruth took off her plastic-rimmed glasses and worried her temples while considering the question. It gave me a better look at her eyes, which were the palest, colorless gray.

"Do you know what they mean when they say a person has a photographic memory?" she asked.

I told her I did — the extraordinary ability some people have to remember things they see in near-perfect detail for long periods of time. Where the rest of us have to rebuild the memory from associations and with elaborate mnemonic triangulation, these people literally saw a photographic image.

"Betty not only cataloged and shelved about a million books, she read almost the same number and remembered everything. And I mean everything. It took me years to fully appreciate this about her. Testing her — subtly, mind you. She never missed a trick."

"That would come in handy around here," I said.

"Naturally, though my point is she was an uncommonly knowledgeable person. It seemed there was little she didn't know, or when she didn't, where to find the answer."

That's how I regarded the World Wide Web. I expressed as much to Ruth. She liked that.

"I hadn't thought of that, but you're right. Oh dear, now every time I Google something I'll think of Betty."

"Not so bad. I wouldn't mind being remembered like that."

She smiled with more warmth than our time together deserved. I smiled back as warmly as I knew how. And then to build on the good feelings, I asked her about Betty's drinking problem.

Ruth was undeterred.

"People like Betty do everything more intensely than the rest of us. I suppose that includes personal excess. I do know she'd made great progress combating her addiction. She was blessedly sober in the final year of her life."

"She was?"

Ruth looked slightly annoyed for the first time.

"Friends know a lot, but not everything," she said. "All I know for certain is she looked better and seemed livelier on Mondays than she had in years. She told me herself she'd been less afflicted, and I believed her. There was no reason why I shouldn't."

This made me feel lousy, of course.

"I'm sorry. I didn't mean to imply anything. I've heard different opinions on that score. I'm sure you're in the best position to know the truth."

Her face relaxed, her restored beneficence matching the shot of bright sunlight that came in over her shoulder through the tall colonial window.

"That's right. The fleeting, ephemeral truth."

18

On the way back from East Hampton I managed to call Harry before he had a chance to call me. I wanted to prove to him that he didn't have to do all the work when he was in a relationship with me, even though we weren't really in a relationship at this point. But maybe in the beginning stages of a renewed relationship, even though we'd never talked about that as a possibility, which I knew he wanted, even though there were plenty of times I wondered what he wanted, exactly.

And people wonder why romantic engagements are so complicated.

"If you found any more body parts, I don't want to hear about it," I said when he picked up the phone.

"No, but I found their tax records. Apparently Betty did the returns herself. Nice handwriting."

"Really. Are they handy?"

I had him read me the critical figures from the last three years.

"For destitute people, they're pretty rich," I said when he was done.

"They had a lot of nice stuff, I can tell you that. In fine detail."

He then went through a complete inventory of the Pontecellos' belongings, read from a manifest he'd prepared using a program normally used to track freighters filled with tons of materiel.

"You didn't have to do all that, Harry. It's wonderful, but I didn't mean to impose."

"I might be an idiot, but I liked doing it," he said. "It's what I do. I can't help myself."

Now I felt like an idiot.

"I don't deserve a friend as thoughtful and kind, and considerate, talented, engaging, handsome, and —" I paused.

"And?"

"Tall as you."

"Hah. The truth revealed. Size matters."

"The truth matters, big boy, even if it's fleeting and ephemeral. Size is worthless if there's nothing to back it up."

"So when are you coming over for a demonstration of my materiel-handling expertise?"

"Tonight. Promise. Don't expect the dazzling Jackie. I'm deep in stress mode over this whole thing. You'll have to be patient and understanding and indulgent with me."

"Aren't I always?" he asked, which I had to admit he always was, no matter how loony I got, never considering that he might have his own worries or anxieties or existential fears to deal with, since I never tried to find that out.

The fact was, I'd kept the relationship with Harry brutally unbalanced in my favor, without even knowing, or caring, since we'd met. Yet there he was, ready to give it another go.

I stopped at the office to make copies of the documents Sullivan had given me and to write up a cover sheet that summarized the information. I put it all in a manila envelope, then drove over to see if I could catch Eunice Wolsonowicz at home.

The day had started out cloudless and bright, but now a gloomy gray was forming over the ocean and heading our way. Perversely, my mood was moving in the other direction.

As usual, I hadn't called ahead, so I was glad to see Eunice was there when she opened the door, though the feeling was hardly mutual.

"I'm sorry," she said. "Did we have an appointment?"

"I was just in the neighborhood. I have some things to drop off for you." I held up the envelope. "And was hoping I could ask a single question."

"I'm really very busy."

"I think you'll want to see what's in here."

I wiggled the envelope in front of her face, then stuffed it under my arm, implying that I came with the contents.

She let the door open the rest of the way and walked back into the house. I followed her to a small sitting room and took a seat, forcing her to do the same. She perched at the edge of the cushion, suggesting there was no need to get comfortable for such a short conversation.

"Before we go over this, can I ask you again about your sister's financial situation? I understand from Sandy Kalandro that things were somewhat dire. And I can surmise from the lien on this house that you stepped in to help."

"Must we go into this?" she asked.

"As the coadministrator of Betty's estate, I think I need to know certain basic information."

Her sigh came from somewhere deep in her chest.

"Elizabeth called me about a year ago, extremely upset. She said Sergey had made some unfortunate investments, causing them to essentially lose their entire life savings. I don't know which was worse for her — the loss of the money or having to call me for help. And before you ask, no, we were not close. Never were, even as children, and if we hadn't had occasional family business to deal with, we never would have spoken to each other. Nothing overtly rancorous, we were simply different people."

"So in exchange for a lien on this house, you gave her a credit line up to the limit of the lien."

"That's correct. Frankly, I was grateful she came to me rather than borrow that money from some other source. One of my deepest regrets was giving up this house. I let my husband, and Elizabeth, convince me we'd never be back East again. Oscar and Wendy surely proved that wrong. More the reason to preserve this house for *my* family. Not some foreign interloper. And thankfully, that is exactly what happened."

"Sort of," I said.

She leaned even farther out of her chair.

"I beg your pardon."

"It stays in the family because Fuzzy inherits it."

She smiled an indulgent smile.

"My son is in no position to cover a loan

of that size. He'll gladly share ownership with his sister and myself."

I took the cover sheet out of the envelope and handed it to her. To make it easy, I'd highlighted the pertinent figure at the bottom of the page.

She looked at it, then looked at me, then looked at it again. Some people express shock by turning all red. Others, like Eunice, go white.

"This is some sort of ridiculous joke," she said.

That's right, I thought. A joke on you, honey.

"Predictions of the Pontecellos' financial demise were grossly exaggerated," I said. "They were actually in great shape. As a result, so is Fuzzy, who's the only one in the will. Which begs the question I came here to ask: How come?"

Eunice literally leaped to her feet, the cover sheet crumpled in her hand.

"This is outrageous. It's absurd. Impossible."

She stalked over to a window, then stalked back. It looked like she was going to throw the wad of paper at me but thought better of it and sat down instead.

"I will not accept this," she said in a cold, hard, quiet voice.

"I think you'll have to. I'm not a big authority on Surrogate's Court, but there's nothing ambiguous about the legal issues. The will is clear and unqualified, the bank documents legitimate. You can probably claim whatever funds you advanced to her, but there'll be enough left over to cover any debt on the house. How're you getting along with Fuzzy these days?"

"His name is Oscar," she said through clenched teeth.

"Sorry. Oscar," I said, but she was already on her way out of the room. I followed her to the kitchen, where she was already talking on the phone to Sandy Kalandro. She looked at me and put her hand over the receiver.

"He wants to review those documents immediately," she said.

I dropped the envelope on the kitchen table.

"Sure. These are your copies. The key account information is in there. The bank has all the backup if he wants to go that deep. I also have their tax returns supported by a casino win/loss statement that's pretty interesting. I haven't reviewed the details, but apparently they support the other information. I'll have copies of those sent over tomorrow."

Eunice was distracted by something Sandy must have been saying to her. She took her hand off the receiver and said to him, "See that you do," and slammed the phone back on the hook.

She stood as still as a statue, with her fists clenched, staring at me. It was slightly scary.

"And to think what I did for that woman."

"You didn't know," I said. "Helping her out was a good deed. Like I said, you'll get that money back."

"I'm not talking about the money. Damn her."

She picked a Wedgwood serving bowl off the counter and threw it against the wall. It exploded into a thousand pieces, some of which ricocheted back and hit my cheek. I put my hand up to my face and she immediately apologized.

"I'm sorry," she said, though not entirely like she meant it. "I'm just very upset. I need to ask you to leave. You've accomplished your mission."

"I didn't come here to upset you. I have a fiduciary responsibility, which, by the way, you gave to me."

She shook her head and dropped her shoulders, probably in time to avoid bursting a blood vessel. "Of course. I know. I didn't mean to imply — This is all just such a shock. Please."

I didn't know what else to do but leave as she wanted. So I did, but not without asking my question one more time as she held the front door open for me.

"Why did Sergey and Elizabeth leave everything to Oscar?"

She shook her head.

"I'm certainly not going to discuss that. It's a question for Oscar and Oscar alone."

She was about to close the door, so I put my hand on the jamb. Flying chinaware aside, I didn't think she'd close the door on my hand.

"Just one more thing," I said. "Sergey's car. Where is it? It's part of their estate. I need to take possession."

She was annoyed by my persistence, but the prospect of getting rid of the car might have been the one bright spot of her day.

"It's in the garage behind the house. Feel free to remove it as quickly as you are able."

I moved my hand out of the way and she closed the door. I walked around the house and across the backyard to the freestanding garage, surrounded like the house itself with beautiful, luxurious foliage. It was built in the same shingle style, with two bays and an apartment above. I picked the left bay and pulled up the door.

It was empty. So was the right bay. I searched the inside of the garage with my eyes as if the ten-ton relic might have slipped into one of the dark corners.

I decided not to bother Eunice again. I'd freaked her out enough for one day, and I couldn't afford to completely alienate her. I also needed to clear my head, and that meant getting away from that house.

I needed a theory. Some people insist any problem can be solved if you have an operating theory. A set of assumptions that, if proven, lead inexorably to a solution. It's the scientist's approach to things. I envied their orderly, calculating minds. Mine was the other type, but sometimes I liked to pretend it wasn't.

I drove back to Bridgehampton, passing by Brick Kiln Road, my street, and down Scuttle Hole Road another few miles to stop and look at the horses grazing in the middle of a hundred-acre horse farm. The gray sky overhead had cleared again, and the sun was getting close to the horizon, making the grass look greener and the horses more elegant.

I concentrated on one really big brown boy who caught my eye when he broke into a trot. He rocked his head from side to side as he ran, came to a near stop, then took off

again. Sheer joie de vivre was how I interpreted it, since there were no equine experts
to ask. It was a rare and beautiful thing to
see, and a genuine gift to behold. As I stood
there transfixed, a revelation burst into my
mind.

Stupid, stupid, stupid, I said to myself as I
ran to the car and went directly to my
house. I kicked off my shoes, stripped down
to the buff, wrapped an ancient kimono
around me, and poured a glass of wine. I'd
burned through all my cigarettes but found
a few half-smoked in the ashtray.

I climbed over a pile of boxes that somehow had grown in the middle of the hall
leading to the rear porch, where I had my
old home office. This was not the ideal
environment for unfettering one's con-
sciousness, but it was mine, it was private,
and it had the old reliable HP.

I took a swig of the wine, lit a stubby
cigarette, and booted up.

The investigative software I launched
wasn't as top secret as the programmers'
hype wanted you to think, but it was pretty
dicey. Legal search engines had become so
powerful, I'd almost forgotten I had it,
stored in a folder marked RECIPE FOR
SWEDISH MEATBALLS. I got it from a professional geek named Randall Dodge, who'd

spent a few years in air force cybersecurity. He gave me the application after I helped him out of a drug rap he'd only gotten into to save his little brother, who had half Randall's brains and one-quarter of his character. Randall lived on the Shinnecock Reservation and ran his own specialty computer hardware/software shop in Southampton called Good to the Last Byte, with the proud slogan, "If it's got a screen and a keyboard I can fix it. Maybe."

The software allowed you to skip over the usual entry points and slip directly into lots of useful databases without the inconvenience of user names and passwords. Randall was up front about the questionable legality when he offered it to me. I accepted it with outward reluctance and inward glee.

As soon as the little window said I was up and running, I was on the hunt.

What you want when chasing people down is a complicated name. The best defense against invasion of privacy is to be John Smith or Mary Jones. For my purposes, it was better to be Oscar Wolsonowicz.

It also helps to be hunting someone young enough to have had his vital statistics loaded into a database. A remarkable amount of legacy information has been scanned in and rendered searchable, but it's not as reliable.

Oscar was the right age and right where he was supposed to be.

I'd been so focused on the adult Fuzzy, on what a standard Web search had to say about him, I'd neglected the basics. The vital statistics, such as: born New York City, New York; educated at the Spenser Academy, a boarding school in Massachusetts, and the University of Arizona, B.S. in business administration. All of this I could get anywhere. What I wanted then I could only get from confidential hospital records. Again, not a big challenge with a name like Wolsonowicz.

All it took was a few keystrokes to get to the link and the following information from New York — Presbyterian Hospital obstetrics unit: Oscar Wolsonowicz. Male. Blood type O+. Seven lbs., three ozs. M. Elizabeth Hamilton. F. Antonin Wolsonowicz.

That Betty. Full of surprises.

19

You can't go wrong with basic black and a string of pearls. This is the priceless wisdom passed down from my namesake, Jacqueline Kennedy, to the undeserving couture-challenged in need of something fast and foolproof.

The earrings turned out to be a time-consuming component, but I didn't let that keep me from showing up at Harry's at exactly the moment I said I would.

When he opened the door he looked at his watch and scowled.

"Who are you and what have you done with Jackie Swaitkowski?"

"I've been on time before."

"Don't try to fool me. I know you're an imposter. Though frankly, a very nice-looking one."

"So invite me in, because this is the only Jackie you're getting tonight."

He was still making up a tray of hors

d'oeuvres, but the wine was chilled and ready. As he poured I said he had to hear about recent events, in painstaking detail.

"I need to talk this through," I said. "I hope that's okay."

"Only if I can tell you about shipping yellowfin tuna from Pacific Costa Rica to Kyoto."

"I'd love that," I said, settling back in my chair with a handful of crackers and Brie. "You go first."

"I was kidding."

"I know. But I'm interested. Really."

Caught off guard, it took a moment for him to ramp up the story. The saga was actually incredibly involving, which was always true. I loved both the particulars and the way he told a tale. I was ashamed that I'd rarely asked him about his work, but when he launched into one of his stories, before I knew it I was swept away.

Best yet, once he was finished, my story was utterly clear for takeoff, conscience-wise. But just to be sure, I let the small talk fill the transition.

"So out with it," he said. "What've you been up to?"

"Oh, me?" I said, and then dove in with both feet.

This took us through a full tray of goodies

and most of the white wine. Along the way we studied the Pontecellos' tax returns, which Harry gladly volunteered to copy and send overnight to Eunice and Sandy Kalandro, browsed through the materials manifest, and generally had a swell time, leading to an uncontrollable affection for my host starting in my heart and heading south.

As a result dinner was postponed for a few hours, though not all appetites are indulged in the same way.

"I'm glad I came back," said Harry when he finally had a chance to say anything.

"I am, too."

"You are?"

"Yes. Let's leave it at that for now, okay?" I said.

"Absolutely. A great baseline."

"What does that mean?"

"A starting point. A foundation upon which to build."

"Okay. The first part of the building needs to be steak, asparagus, and salad, if my memory of your refrigerator is what I think it is."

After dinner I went through the manifest more carefully, checking it against the actual belongings. I was half braced the whole time for what I might find, but for better or worse, it was just stuff — the accumulated detritus of long and decidedly idiosyncratic lives.

It eventually got to that awkward time of the evening where a person has to decide to stay or go. These are not minor decisions for those of us in complicated, unresolved situations. I opted to stay, with a proviso.

"I'd like you to come with me tomorrow to see Fuzzy again. Now that you've been introduced and formed a bond."

"You're afraid of him," he said.

"If I wanted a thug I'd ask Sam. I need a tagalong I want to spend the day with, who also showed remarkable diplomatic skills the last time. You can entertain me in the car with tales of logistical derring-do."

As I faded off to sleep that night, I almost got into another debate with myself over whether I was using Harry, taking advantage of his tireless good nature, or if I thought I needed to create artificial conflicts to distract me from confronting the real possibility that I felt something for the towering mensch.

I'm sure this sort of thing causes 90 percent of the insomnia suffered by women between the ages of eleven and eighty-five. I decided to put a stop to it right there and willed myself into a troubled sleep filled with anxious dreams and unresolved quandaries.

It was a repeat of the last time. Harry drove his Volvo, and I did my best to provide coffee service and onboard entertainment. I was glad to be going against the crush of traffic coming in every weekday morning from less expensive habitats to the west, tradesmen and service people heading for jobs in the Hamptons. While not a development alarmist like other natives, it did make me wonder where it was all going to end. Maybe when the cliff dwellers of Manhattan realized they weren't coming out to the country anymore, with small towns and unpretentious, happy people like Potato Pete, but rather to a gilded suburb, where everyone had signed on to the fantasy that their expectations and anxieties could be left back in the City.

The transition to the Up Island sprawl had blurred in recent years. But in my child's mind, I could still tell when I entered that other world, the Western territories, entangled with stop-and-go highways, shopping malls, and hysterical neon enticements. That trackless terrain of frenetic enterprise and vast, anonymous neighborhoods, like Fuzzy's.

As a general strategy, arriving unannounced at people's homes had the advantage of surprise, but was worthless if the subject wasn't there in the first place. So the hour-long trip from Southampton could have been for naught. And it almost was.

Just as we were heading down the street to Fuzzy's subterranean abode, we saw him pull away in his old Datsun. Following was not that big a challenge. All we had to do was keep track of the billows coming out of the tailpipe. "Follow that smog," I said to Harry.

We wound our way through the mazelike housing development and out to the strip. Traffic was heavy, which made following Fuzzy even easier. He made two or three turns, then pulled into the parking lot of a shabby row of storefronts with a liquor store, a Laundromat, and a pizza parlor.

When Fuzzy went inside, Harry asked me what the plan was.

"I don't have one."

"Okay. What if you did?" he asked.

"Is that one of those Zen logic puzzles?"

"Sometimes it's good to know what you're going to do a few seconds before you actually do it."

"Sure, if you want to spoil the spontaneity," I said, jumping out of the car.

We found Fuzzy in a remote corner of the restaurant with his face in a BlackBerry, punching at the tiny keys as if he were trying to stick a hole in the device.

We waited for a break in the action, but when it didn't come, Harry reached out a long arm and tapped Fuzzy on the shoulder, making him jump like somebody'd stuck a firecracker down his pants.

"Holy crap, freak me out."

"Sorry," said Harry.

A crowd was forming around the counter where you ordered your pizza. Waitresses were milling around, dropping off people's meals and filling trays with dirty dishes. Teenagers were playing video games and trying to attract one another's attention in the bad-mannered way teenagers like to do. It wasn't the environment I'd have chosen to discuss the sensitive things I was about to discuss. On the other hand, Fuzzy looked perfectly at home. In his natural habitat.

"What was your name again?" he asked when we sat down.

I reintroduced myself and Harry.

"Oh, yeah. Uncle Sergey's lawyer. I didn't know you could work this hard for dead people."

"You can for their estate," I said. "That's why I'm here."

Fuzzy smirked at the thought, something I'd gotten used to. " 'Estate' is a big word for a lot of nothing," he said.

"You should know I've been appointed a coadministrator of that estate. Your mother and myself. How're you getting along with her these days?" I asked straight-out, not knowing how else to ask.

"I told you. I don't talk to her. But before you start jumping all over me, she's not my real mother. I'm adopted, something she never tires of reminding me."

Right at that moment, for no apparent reason, he sneezed, with a violent shake of his head. He wiped his nose with the sleeve of his shirt.

"Fucking allergies," he said.

"I know these are personal questions," I said, "but they're germane to me being here."

"I thought germane was some feminazi chick."

"You're thinking of Germaine Greer," said Harry. " 'Feminazi' would be an unfair characterization. Germane means pertinent. Relevant."

"Okay, so what?"

"You're the sole heir to your aunt and uncle's estate," I said. "After donations, taxes, and legal fees — meaning me — you get all the rest. House, investments, personal effects. And a 1967 Chrysler 300, if I can find out where it is."

For the first time Fuzzy looked less than completely dismissive. Not exactly impressed but curious.

"No shit. How about that."

"Your mother was named as the original administrator, but now that we share that role things could get sticky. However, my legal duty is clear. I have a fiduciary responsibility both to Betty and Sergey and to you, as the estate's beneficiary. In other words, Fuzzy, I'm technically working for you."

"No shit."

"And in that capacity, my first bit of advice is to use a handkerchief when you sneeze. Surrogate's Court likes a certain decorum on the heir's part. I also need to know why there's a conflict between you and your mother. That could have an impact on probating this thing, even without the complication of Sergey's murder."

I could see Fuzzy's bitterness etched directly into the contours of his face. As he sat there at the sticky Formica table — insolent, disheveled, and poorly bathed — I saw in his intelligent blue eyes a fury so boundless and primal it made me sit back in my seat and send thanks to whatever impulse had caused me to invite Harry along, exploitation be damned.

"I don't have anything to say to Eunice," Fuzzy said, his voice flat and hollow. "She should be happy that's as far as it goes."

Harry had been holding back from the conversation until then, but he started catching the vibe and pulled his chair closer to Fuzzy and me. I put my elbows on the table and leaned forward.

"Fuzzy, do you know why Betty and Sergey made you their sole heir?"

Fuzzy's eyes narrowed.

"Do you cross-examine witnesses in court, you know, like they do on *Law and Order*? Jack McCoy circling like a shark, setting up the poor schmuck, then pouncing on him, making him confess everything, like a complete fucking idiot, when all he had to do was sit there and take the Fifth or lie like a bastard and nothing would've happened? That's why I hate those shows."

"That's why I love those shows," I said. "But I'm not trying to trap you in anything. I'm trying to help you."

"Then quit asking questions you already know the answers to. I don't think you're stupid; don't treat me like I am."

I sat back again.

"Okay. But it would be better if you just

said it, because I can't," I said, thinking of how I'd explain accessing confidential hospital records. "Just remember, I've got your financial future in my hands. If you're going to get into a fight with Eunice Wolsonowicz, you might weigh the value of having her coadministrator, a lawyer by the way, on your side."

I gave him a look that said, "Your move, buster."

He looked over at Harry.

"You know, she doesn't need to always bring you along," he said. "Just because I disgust women doesn't mean I'm dangerous."

I didn't dignify his comment with a response. I let the silence — what there was of it in the din of the restaurant — build between us.

"Since you obviously already know," Fuzzy said, in a singsong voice more defensive than defiant, "my father fucked his wife's sister. I'm the result. Whoopsy doodles. Trouble is, no way is Betty going to raise a kid. She's a single girl running around Europe, fucking barons and dipshits like Sergey. So she says to Eunice, Here's the deal. I tell the world Tony is the cockswinging son of a bitch you know he is, or you can take this kid and raise him.

Wouldn't you like to be a fly on the wall during *that* conversation? Anyway, everybody bought into the deal. Only problem is, nobody bothered to tell me."

He shouted the last sentence, half raised out of his seat.

"But they did eventually," I said as quietly as I could.

He sat back in his chair and into his slouching, disdainful indifference. He shook his head.

"Betty told me. But only when she was forced into it," he said. "So what's this got to do with the estate shit? What's the germane part?"

"Eunice was pretty upset when she found out what her sister's estate is actually worth," I said. "She might decide to contest the will. I have to decide what my part in this is going to be, and that depends on knowing the facts. Right now, I can tell you honestly, I don't want much to do with any of you people. All I want to know is who killed Sergey Pontecello, who might have been a dipshit, but who wanted to be my client and I let him down."

Obviously, Fuzzy heard only the first part of that speech.

"What do you mean, what the estate was really worth?"

"You're rich, pal," said Harry. "Get used to it. Your mother might've ditched you, but give her credit for trying to make good on it in the only way she could."

"Yeah, yeah," said Fuzzy. "How rich?"

So I told him. After all, he was my client, sort of.

"Millions. More than one, less than ten. Somewhere in the middle."

Fuzzy burst out laughing, on cue, like a stand-up comic or a trained actor.

"Ah, that's so great," he said. "That fucking brilliant, conniving, selfish bitch, it's no wonder she was my mother."

And then he kept laughing until it was clear he really meant it, as if the act of laughter was so alien to him he didn't quite know what to do with it.

And, God preserve me, it became so infectious Harry started to smile, and before I knew it, both of us were laughing, too. Right there amidst the lunatic clamor and chaos of the pizza parlor, only one of us knowing what was so funny, but all of us enjoying the moment on its own terms, just for the hell of it.

When sobriety returned, I told Fuzzy what he needed to do in the lead up to entering Surrogate's Court, including getting a copy of his birth certificate. I also told him that if

Eunice got aggressive he'd have to find his own lawyer. A good laugh aside, I wasn't about to spend the next few years with Fuzzy litigating a complex legal issue I had next to no experience litigating.

That done, I was ready to get out of that irritating place and head back to Harry's converted gas station in Southampton. As we got up to go, Fuzzy had a request of his own.

"Hey, uh, you could do me a favor on the whole mother thing," he said. "Eunice doesn't like to talk about it. Neither does Wendy. I don't care that much about Eunice, but with Wendy, it's like, you know, really bad."

I reassured him.

"I'm a lawyer, Fuzzy. I don't share a client's information with myself without prior authorization," I said, and even though that really wasn't true, I liked the way it came out.

20

I slept in my own bed that night. For some of the night. Then I pretended to sleep for the rest, until the first pale signs of daylight woke up the birds, which made lying there seem that much more futile.

After showering and getting dressed, I killed time until seven-thirty, then drove over to the estate section in Southampton where I thought Sam might be working. I'd noticed trucks belonging to Frank Enwhistle, one of Sam's favorite contractors, lining the street. I called it right. Parked with the trucks was a late 1960s Grand Prix, another popular construction vehicle.

It was a cool, hazy morning, but Sam wore only a white T-shirt, warmed as he was from wrestling with a big triangular hunk of fancy molding above the front door.

"It's a pediment. We have the ancient Greeks to blame," he said through gritted teeth as he tried to keep a level steady with one hand and tap a slender finish nail with the other.

"I thought it was postmodern architects."

"For them we've reserved a new circle of hell."

He twisted around on the stepladder and pointed to the ground.

"Could you hand me that hydraulic nailer?" he asked.

"What's a hydraulic nailer?"

"The thing with the hose attached. Look lively, Swaitkowski. Can't hold this position forever."

"Good thing I came along."

"You're decent help," he said when I handed him the nailer. "I can get you steady work." He popped a dozen nails into the inside curve of the molding. "You could specialize in setting pediments."

"Easier than setting precedents."

"That's right, I forgot. You're a lawyer."

He climbed down the ladder.

"How's the case?" he asked.

"That's why I'm here. I know more and understand less. I'm in need of clarity."

"I'm in need of caffeine. Let's combine the two."

I drove him to a coffee place nearby. We took coffee and croissants out to a park bench in front of the shop. I briefed him on my time at the library with Ruth Hinsdale, the friendly chat with Eunice, and what I'd learned about Fuzzy, including the conversation at the pizza parlor.

I told him what I thought was clear. That Elizabeth Pontecello was a very intelligent woman living in the company of an army of demons, though she definitely manned the helm at the Pontecellos'. That her personal banker at Harbor Trust had never dealt with Sergey. That all the bank records and legal documents, the will, the tax returns, every scrap of paper we'd come across, was in Betty's name and handwriting. "And how do you jibe chain-smoking ace poker player with little old lady librarian?" I concluded.

"Birds gotta fly, fish gotta swim, eidetics gotta memorize," he said.

"Okay. That clears up everything."

"That's the technical description of people with photographic memories. Eidetic," said Sam. "It means just what you'd think it means. Their brains store and process information as images. A lot of people can do this, but with some, like Betty, they remember damn near everything, in perfect detail. It might sound like an affliction, but for people like Betty, it's a compulsion. The more stuff to memorize, the better. I had one of these guys working for me as a chemical engineer, a Pakistani trained in Edinburgh. He didn't have a lot of imagination, but he could build a polymer plant out of his head. I never saw him without a bag full of technical papers."

"So what better place to spend your days than a reference library."

"And your nights at the blackjack table," he said.

"Counting cards. But they mostly played poker. Texas Hold 'Em. Card counting doesn't work."

"It works with blackjack until you're caught. Which will happen eventually. Then you're out of the casino forever. Every casino. Her memory still gave her some advantage over the other poker players, but she had another dodge going on there, the oldest one in the book."

I hated it when Sam made me guess the thing he'd already figured out.

"Goddamn it. Do we have to do this now?"

"Come on, Jackie. Tonic and lime. Looks like a gin and tonic. Establish yourself as a drunk, then stop drinking. The other players don't take you seriously, don't hide the tells, the facial expressions and body language that a good player can read like the Sunday paper."

352

Betty didn't just run with the demons, I thought, she was one of them. I remembered the look on Fuzzy's face when I broke the news of his inheritance. Clearly enough to make me start laughing all over again. I finally got the joke.

I smacked Sam on the arm.

"Betty was a con," I said.

That's what she really liked to do, play tricks on the world and everybody in it. I can see her as a little girl, realizing she could do things the other little girls couldn't imagine doing. But she kept it to herself. It was her secret weapon. She had a lifetime of deception. She could be all these different things because none of them was really Betty. It must have been particularly satisfying to play one last trick on her overbearing, self-righteous older sister, taking her money when she didn't even need it.

I dropped Sam off at his job and drove a block to the corner of South Main Street and Gin Lane. If you're going to find yourself at a crossroads, you might as well do it in style. I pulled the car under the shade of a huge birch tree and started chanting, "Eeny, meeny, miney, mo," under my breath. When I landed on a choice I didn't like, I took the other one, and turned up Main Street and headed toward Riverhead and the regional crematorium at Great Lawns Cemetery.

Since I was already in such a great mood, why not spend the rest of the day with the dead?

Though Riverhead isn't the most beautiful place on the East End, it is the source of fond childhood memories. Back then, you could save a fortune on groceries and regular household products at the Riverhead shopping centers at the edges of town. It was as if they'd created a little outpost of American suburbia within easy driving distance of the Hamptons, just to give us an idea of what the rest of the country had turned into. My mother liked having company, so she always made routine shopping expeditions to Riverhead feel like a special treat.

With that memory along for the ride, I half enjoyed the drive to Great Lawn Cemetery, which was just that: a great big lawn with big old trees and paved walkways and curving roadways and plaques on the ground instead of headstones. I liked the concept, which is why both my parents were there. I hadn't been back to visit since I'd buried my mother. They were on eternal time, so I thought I could wait a few more years to muster the courage.

The building with the crematorium was at the other end of the grounds. It was another stately colonial building, the architectural standard of the mortuary industry. The front door was unlocked, which I took as an invitation. Inside was a foyer lined with closed doors and filled with colonial furniture, mostly uncomfortable-looking wooden chairs, and a small pine desk. I buzzed the buzzer on the desk.

Minutes later a young woman emerged from one of the doors. She was slight and pretty, even with a pair of thick glasses and short brown hair cut to accentuate the conservative. She wore a light blue shirt and khaki slacks, not unlike what I was wearing, which we both noticed immediately.

"Well, at least I got the dress code right," I said, sticking out my hand. "I'm Jackie Swaitkowski, an attorney from Southampton."

For better or worse, it was always helpful to get the lawyer part out early. Most people find it hard to blow you off without at least finding out what sort of trouble they might be in.

"I'm Sarah Simms, cemetery director. What can I do for you?"

I told her as much of the Edna Jackery

story as I could without implicating anyone or implying that I was about to implicate her. This wasn't easy, but I'd told the story so many different ways by then, it was getting easier.

"So, if I understand," she said, "pieces of Mrs. Jackery were removed from the body prior to cremation?"

"That's the long and short of it. I know it was a while ago, but I was wondering if you remember anything about her."

She was too polite to say something like "Surely you jest," but the result was the same.

"You must keep records," I said. "Do you examine the body before it's cremated?"

"We require it. We run the person through a metal detector and do a hands-on examination. There's often jewelry that's been overlooked at the funeral home, and we can't allow things like pacemakers into the retort. They can actually explode."

"Into the what?"

"The retort. The cremator furnace. Who did you say you were representing?" she asked.

"The estate," I said, not specifying which estate. "So this hands-on examination, who does that exactly?"

She smiled at me.

"I do. My family's in the funeral business. I grew up helping my father with the embalming."

There's a bonding experience, I thought.

"But you don't keep records?"

"I didn't say that. I just wouldn't remember any specific person. We serve hundreds a year."

"But you could look it up?" I asked.

"I could. But I would need the family's written permission. That is confidential information. Even in death, people have the right to privacy."

I folded my arms and studied Sarah Simms like Betty Pontecello would, trying to read the tell.

"Would it be more or less pleasant for you if I arranged to have a police detective arrive here before the end of the day with a subpoena?"

"I wouldn't find that pleasant at all."

"Me, neither. I'd much rather wait here while you go check your records. Just give me the gist. I don't have to look at anything."

"Then I'm sure that'll be fine," said Sarah, relieved to have a compromise.

She turned and left the foyer by a different door from the one she used to enter. I sat and waited, my stomach turning into a lead ball as I imagined her looking up Slim Jackery's phone number and giving him a call. Slim or Alden Winthrop, or Ross Semple.

She came back after only a few minutes.

"Mrs. Jackery had been in a terrible car crash," she said. "She was disfigured nearly beyond recognition. There were no personal effects or medical devices. This is what the computer said; I frankly don't remember the individual. If you have specific questions, you're likely to learn more by speaking to the Winthrop people again."

"That's a splendid idea, Ms. Simms. I think I'll do exactly that."

"Mrs. Simms," she said demurely. "I'm old-fashioned that way."

On the way back down to Southampton my cell phone rang. It was Harry.

"Where we going today?" he asked.

"You're a little late for that. It's already afternoon."

"I've been catching up on paperwork. You?"

"I've been chasing dead bodies." I told him about my trip to the regional crematorium and my conversation with Sarah Simms. He drew the same conclusion I did.

"You have to go to the funeral home

again. Not you, exactly. You need to call the police and they need to go to the funeral home."

There it was again, that little twitch in the pit of my stomach, the one I started to feel two years ago that eventually grew into a giant ball of distress. I didn't know what it was then, and I still didn't know, exactly, but at least now I had a theory.

For all his wonderful thoughtfulness, his easygoing, jovial nature, his apparent tolerance of my manifold inadequacies, Harry liked to drive the car. Though hardly a control freak, it was in his nature to control. How else could he move massive quantities of complicated stuff all over the globe, orchestrating it all from a computer in a converted garage?

I'd kept his protective nature at bay after the run-in with the pickup, just barely. It's not that I didn't like it. More that I might like it too much, that old fear of losing my sense of self if I got too close to Harry's gravitational pull. That sense of self might be scattered all over the universe, but at least it belonged to me. All of it. I once gave up pieces of me to the son of a potato farmer and only through tragic intervention got them all back. I couldn't lose them again.

"You're right. Sullivan is mad enough at me already. I'll see if I can track him down," I said, though I had no intention of doing so.

"Then you can come see me," he said. "I'll make it worth your while."

"You always do, Harry. That's one of the things I love about you."

"Watch it, Jackie. You almost said you love me."

As usual, right at the moment I felt most like running away from him, I felt a wave of warmth and affection flow over me.

"I do. I love your Harryness."

"Okay, I'll take that."

"But I'm not sure about tonight. Let me call you later."

"Okay, I'll take that, too. I'll be waiting. You know me."

"I do," I said to myself after getting off the phone.

I was going to head directly to Alden Winthrop's office in the main house, but since I was closer to Building Two, with its long lineup of garage bays, I decided to stop there first. I knocked on the side door and waited. Nothing happened, so I let myself in and knocked on the next door. Nothing happened again, so I let myself into the main area.

All the vehicles were there except the pickup. I called Denny's name a few times without a response. I walked into the corner where he'd set up his living space. It was less of a mess than the last time I was there. The table had been partially wiped clean, and the sheets were pulled up into a loose approximation of a made bed. From closer in, I could see a cubicle created by three movable panels borrowed from the portable ceremony supplies. The panels were covered in posters of a Japanese kickboxer inscrutably named Don Wilson.

Inside the space was a table with a computer. The computer screen was off, but a green light shone on the CPU under the table. I went over and tapped the space bar, and the screen lit up. A dialog box popped up in the middle, requesting a user name and password. I looked around the garage, holding my breath and listening for sounds of Denny. Hearing nothing, I sat down and stared helplessly at the dialog box. Knowing the statistical odds of the right guess were far greater than the number of tries before the computer's security system locked it up, I didn't even try.

I walked down the row of cars to where the one with the canvas cover was parked. I had to untie a drawstring that tucked the cover under the left rear bumper, which took some effort. The string had been knotted into a hard ball, and I had to kneel on the floor to get both hands engaged in untying it. Two busted nails later, I got it loose.

I stood up and pulled the cover over the bumper. The license plate had been removed, making the wide slab of chrome look even wider. I walked around to the front of the car and pulled up the cover. The front fenders were also shaped into big slabs, with right angles top and bottom protruding beyond the grill, in which four round headlights were embedded. I didn't see anything identifying the model until I flipped the cover up over the hood ornament.

It was a little round piece of chrome, inside of which was the number 300.

The hand that grabbed a wad of my hair at the back of my head came out of nowhere. In the instant it secured its grip and shoved my head onto the car, I was able to literally turn the other cheek, so the right side of my face smashed down onto the hood, not the left side with all the lovely handiwork by the nice plastic surgeons.

Still, it hurt like hell. I felt my limbs go weak and start to crumple. Then the hand in my hair yanked me away from the car and I saw Denny Winthrop, his face a mask set in a mindless rage. He shoved me toward the back of the garage, dropped into a boxer's stance, and looked me over as if he were picking out the perfect spot. I screamed, put my hands up to protect my head, and ran for the side door at the end of the building.

I almost made it. The door was partway open into the foyer, and I only had a few feet to go when he came out of nowhere again and grabbed another handful of hair.

I have a lot of hair to grab, which Denny yanked hard enough to pull me right off my feet and back into the garage. I hit the floor shoulders first, then my head whiplashed smack onto the concrete with a sound I heard inside and out.

I closed my eyes and became Dead Girl, one of my easiest performances. I felt dead, or near it. I watched a swirling kaleidoscope on the backs of my eyelids and scolded myself yet again for my stupid, reckless curiosity. I could hear Denny breathing as he moved in front of the door and stood over me, deciding what to do next.

"Fucking lawyers," he said, almost too quietly for me to hear, especially through the *thump thump* inside my skull. "Scum-

363

sucking, bottom-feeding, elitist pigs."

That last bit sounded closer. I felt the edge of his shoe brush against the outside of my calf. I opened my eyes and got a fix on where he was standing. I wasn't looking at his face, so I don't know what he thought was happening, but his reaction time wasn't up to professional kickboxing standards.

Mine was. Straight up into his balls.

As he went down, clutching at his groin, I stumbled to my feet. It took my head a few seconds to catch up with the rest of me, but I kept my balance. Denny was pulling himself off the floor, breathing hard. There was no room to get around him and through the side door, so I turned to make a run for one of the bays, but he dove after me and caught my ankle, and with the help of my forward momentum, caused me to sprawl across the floor. I landed boobs first, which knocked the wind out of me. I gasped for breath as I rolled over onto my back, hoping to get my feet back into the action.

Denny stood up. He said some other nasty thing, which I couldn't quite make out, then loped forward, swinging his right leg to get maximum momentum behind the impending kick.

Then he abruptly stopped and flew backward, his arms and legs thrashing wildly.

"Excuse me," said Harry, holding him by the back of the neck. "What do you think *you're* doing?"

Denny twisted in Harry's grip, swinging wildly with his fists. Harry tried to bob his head out of the way, telling Denny to knock it off, but when one of the punches grazed his cheek, Harry pulled back his own basketball-size fist and drove it straight into Denny's face.

Harry held Denny's limp body for a moment, shook him as a terrier would shake a dead rat, then dropped him to the floor. He walked over and knelt next to me.

"You okay?" he asked. "What happened to your face?"

I grabbed him by the shirtfront and made him get close enough for me to plant a kiss on his cheek, then used the purchase on his shirt to drag myself to my feet.

I walked over to Denny and checked to see if he was still breathing, relieved to see him pop open his eyes. I squatted down and grabbed a handful of his own hair. I used it to smack his head on the floor.

"User name and password," I yelled at him.

He looked at me, then over my shoulder at Harry, glowering down from a hundred feet up.

"Tell me now or you're all his," I said.

"User name RipMan," he said. "Password dragon. Like Don 'The Dragon' Wilson."

I looked over at the kickboxer posters and thought, Of course.

I stood up again, a little unsteadily, and told Denny to stay put.

"Shouldn't we be calling the police?" Harry asked.

"Just give me five minutes. If Denny makes a sound, step on his head."

I went over to the computer in the make-shift cubicle and logged on. The desktop had a blurry image of Denny surfing down the side of a wave. I searched out the browser icon, clicked on it, then waited an agonizing few seconds for the home page to come up. It was a site that aggregated blogs. I clicked on "My Favorites." Fuzzy was right at the top.

I clicked on the link and Fuzzy's blog jumped onto the screen. I clicked on "Discussion," and there he was, ranting away as usual.

I tapped in, "Hey, FuzzMan, it's Rip. Code red, dude. Make contact like now."

"Fuck," Fuzzy wrote. I waited as long as I could stand it for him to send more, then cleared away all the open pages, revealing the desktop photo with RipMan ripping a wave.

I found a mailbox icon and clicked on it. I gripped the terminal with both hands, willing the e-mail to show itself. Another dialog box popped up. I prayed Denny was too enamored with his noms de plume to use a different user name and password.

"We really should call the police," said Harry.

I leaned back in the chair and shouted, "Two minutes."

Before I could touch the keys again, an instant message box popped into the upper left corner of the screen.

"What the fuck?" said the message from FuzzMan, the screen name in blue letters.

"Hot times at the homestead," I wrote. The IM filled in "RipMan," in red.

"Explain."

"Two pigs from Shampt were just here talking to the old man," I wrote.

The response took about twenty seconds. I couldn't know if Fuzzy was hesitating or the IM was just finding its way around the world and back to Long Island.

"Did you lose the clunker?" he finally wrote back.

"No worries," I wrote back.

Fuzzy came back much quicker this time.

"Lose the fucking clunker."

"FuzzMan, Big C's a righteous ride. She's spick-and-span."

Fuzzy came right back.

"You don't watch fucking CSI? You can't clean up enough. It's humanly impossible. Lose the fucking car or Rip's account is gonna seriously shit the bed."

I waited a minute, then wrote back.

"Chill, brother. Consider it done."

I thought that might end the exchange, but he came back one more time.

"And hands off the lawyer bitch," Fuzzy wrote. "At least until she delivers the bucks. More to fund the RipMan's fuckups. Can't whack the hand that feeds you."

It took a moment for that to sink in.

"Oh, Christ," I said, before typing in "10-4," and snapping open my cell phone.

21

Danny Izard was the first on the scene, followed immediately by Alden Winthrop. Denny was awake again but lying still, breathing shallow breaths and looking disoriented. Alden tried to run to his son, but Danny stopped him.

"Wait for the paramedics, sir. They know what to do."

"What on earth happened?" he asked.

"The kid fell and hit his head," I said, cleaving to a shortened version of the available facts.

Harry was leaning over Denny's freezer, putting ice cubes in a plastic bag, which he wrapped in a dishtowel. After I had it pressed to my cheek, I said more gently than the words would suggest, "What the hell are you doing here?"

"Being a butt-insky," he said.

"You're not butting in when you're saving my life."

"I knew you'd come here on your own. I tried to pretend it didn't worry me, but I couldn't concentrate on my work. Sorry."

Two more cops showed up, then the paramedics, whom the cops let in through one of the bay doors. They pulled in a gurney loaded down with equipment and started working on Denny. Izard walked over to us after the other cops took Winthrop off his hands.

"I bet you'll be explaining this," he said to me.

"Absolutely," I said. "As soon as Joe Sullivan gets here. While we're waiting, let's take a walk."

I had Danny and Harry follow me down the row of cars to the Chrysler 300.

"How many of these do you think there are in the Hamptons?" I asked.

"Man, it's ugly," said Harry.

"But well-maintained and sparkling clean."

"Whose is it?" asked Danny.

"The late Pontecellos'. It's supposed to be in their garage."

"Any idea how it got here?"

"No, but I have a theory," I said, shifting the ice bag on my cheek. "Wow, that hurts."

"We should take you to the hospital," said Harry.

"If I turn white and pass out, do that, will you? In the meantime, I've got to talk to Joe Sullivan."

Who showed up a few moments later. He strode into the room with his hand resting on the butt of his service revolver, as if expecting to interrupt a full-out firefight. He saw us standing next to the Chrysler.

"What do we got here?" he asked Danny Izard, who looked over at me. Sullivan frowned and redirected the question.

"So, Jackie, what do we got here?"

I pointed at Denny Winthrop, whom the paramedics were locking into a neck brace.

"You can start with assault with intent to kill. I'm the intended." I jerked my thumb at Harry. "He's the witness."

"Which one of you subdued the assailant?" he asked, looking up at Harry.

"We both did," I said. "While exercising remarkable restraint."

"Save it for the civil case, Counselor. What else we got?"

I pointed at the Chrysler.

"You can add grand theft auto. This vehicle belonged to Sergey and Elizabeth Pontecello. As coadministrator of their estate, I'm prepared to assert that it was removed unlawfully from their garage, an assertion supported by the fact that young

371

Mr. Winthrop, the person lying on the floor over there, attacked me when I discovered it."

Joe pulled out his casebook and started to write things down.

"Okay, give me a second to record that, then you can make your closing arguments."

"The son of a bitch tried to kill me, Joe. And he's got a pickup, I'm guessing outside somewhere."

He looked over his shoulder, trying to divine the truck's exact location.

"I'd have forensics go over the pickup and this Chrysler with a fine-tooth comb," I said. "If they don't find anything, tell them they suck at forensics and to go back and look again."

"They'll love that."

"Remind them me and Carlo Vendetti are like this," I said, crossing my fingers.

"I wouldn't be too eager to advertise that one," he said.

Remarkably, another thought found its way into my battered brain. I asked to talk to Sullivan for a second in private.

"Say, Joe," I said. "Can you keep Denny off the grid for a little while?"

We both watched as the paramedics wheeled out the gurney.

He frowned. "He gets a phone call. The

lawyer call."

I told him who I didn't want Denny to contact. Sullivan shrugged. "Like I said, he only gets one call and that's to his lawyer. Anyway, it'll take Dr. Fairchild a while to determine if the human colossus over there did any permanent damage."

"Be nice to Harry, Joe. He rescued me. More important, I'm dating him."

He snorted and walked me back to where we'd left Harry and Danny Izard.

"Take her to the hospital," he said to Harry. "Then both of you get to the HQ as soon as possible so we can take your statements."

On my way out an ashen-looking Alden Winthrop tried to engage me in conversation, but I cut him off more curtly than I wanted to. It might have been my eagerness to flee the scene, or maybe I was afraid I'd tell him what I thought of his child-rearing skills. I've never had to rear a child, so that was probably unfair, but he wasn't the one holding an ice bag to his face.

Markham was tied up with Denny Winthrop, so one of the other trauma docs looked me over. She was a tight little woman with short hair and a clipped, professional manner. She did a thorough job, I'm sure, but I wasn't used to being examined at Southampton Hospital by anyone so small.

Neither of us thought any good would come from making me stay the night, so she wrote out a prescription for painkillers and shooed me out of there. Harry followed me to my house. He wanted to, and I didn't think it right to discourage him after what had happened. Further soul-searching over the loss of personal identity would have to wait another day.

"I know you have things to do," he said. "Just get me a beer and I'll stand at the ready. Or maybe sit."

I got beer for both of us, and after stripping down and pulling on my kimono, dragged him out to the porch. He stood patiently while I shoveled out a space for the two of us to sit at the HP.

A few minutes later I used Denny's user name and password to log in to his e-mail provider. I found the instant message icon, clicked open the box, and wrote to Fuzzy:

"Got a plan for the Big C."

Fuzzy came right back.

"I told you to get it the fuck out of there."

"Chill. I moved it to another shed. Can't complete the plan till it's dark out."

"They have another shed?" asked Harry.

"They do now," I said.

"What plan?" Fuzzy wrote.

"Journey to the bottom of fucking Wood Pond," I wrote.

Fuzzy didn't write back right away. I felt my heart clench in my chest. I'd read a lamentable amount of their correspondence on the blog sites and thought I knew their style of discourse. But IM was different. They could use a whole different approach when it was just the two of them. A shorthand I wouldn't know. The longer this went, the more likely Fuzzy would smell a rat.

I held my breath.

"Don't get wet," he finally wrote back.

I started breathing again and wrote, "I could use a ride. Long walk back from North Sea."

"Not in the contract, RipMan. FuzzMan never strays far from the crib."

"No honor among jerks," said Harry.

"10-4," I wrote.

I knew I should log off while I was ahead, but I hadn't learned anything new. As I wondered how I was going to keep up the RipMan act and simultaneously tease out information, Fuzzy wrote, "What about the perdues?"

Oh, hell, I thought. Just what I feared. A question I couldn't answer.

"What about 'em?" I wrote imaginatively.

"The frozen cutlets. Secure?"

"Is Denny supposed to buy him dinner?" Harry asked.

"Secure, per contract," I wrote, not knowing what else to do.

I had another nervous wait.

"Seek out and destroy. Too much heat."

This time Fuzzy had to wait because I didn't know what to write back. I looked at Harry for inspiration. He shook his head.

"Acknowledge," Fuzzy wrote. I imagined him yelling the word at the computer.

"Acknowledged," I sent back as quickly as I could.

"Don't need anymore. Chuck the whole batch in the fryolator."

"I'm starting to get hungry," said Harry, and that's when it hit me.

"I've got a cure for that," I said as I typed in "On the case, post-haste."

Then I clicked out of the box and called Sullivan on my cell phone, which I'd slipped into the pocket of the kimono.

A second later, he came on the line.

"I'm at the hospital with the punk perp," he said. "Cell phone's not allowed. I'll have to call you back."

"Who's at the scene?" I asked.

"What do you mean?"

"Who's at the funeral home?"

376

"Danny's waiting for flatbeds to haul the vehicles up to Riverhead. I got to call you back. The nurses are looking very unhappy."

"Call him right now and tell him to bring along Denny's freezer," I said, the words tumbling out.

"Sure, boss. Now remind me how you like your coffee. I'll bring some right over."

I groaned loud enough for him to hear.

"Joe, listen. You are the best cop on the East End. I respect you. I admire you. I will gladly grovel even more later on, but please, could you just call Danny, then call me right back?" I said, then hit the end call button.

Harry looked puzzled.

"Sullivan's going to call me back in about one minute," I said. "I can explain after that. I think."

"I was just in that freezer," he said. "Nothing there but a bunch of Tupperware and frozen burger patties."

"I'm glad you didn't use them as ice packs," I said.

The phone rang.

"Mission accomplished," said Sullivan when I answered the phone. "Awaiting further orders."

"Are you somewhere you can talk on the cell?" I asked.

"I'm outside with a crowd of health professionals. I'm the only one not smoking a cigarette."

"Do you have your casebook?" I asked, though I knew he did. He probably took it with him into the shower.

"I do."

"Good. Here's what I think," I said. "Oscar Wolsonowicz, a.k.a. Fuzzy or Fuzz-Man, has some sort of financial hold over Alden Winthrop the fourth, a.k.a. Denny, a.k.a. RipMan. I'm guessing it's related to day trading, which is what Fuzzy does when he's not polluting the Internet with his vile opinions."

"That's the price we pay for freedom of speech," said Sullivan.

"Denny was the one who rammed me on Brick Kiln Road. With his Ford pickup. I'm sure the front end's been done over pretty thoroughly, if the condition of the other vehicle is any indication. I think Fuzzy ordered him to make the hit after Harry and I paid Fuzzy a visit. I must have thoroughly spooked him. Why, you might ask."

"Yeah. Why?"

"That relates to the contents of Denny's freezer. And the old Chrysler 300. I could tell you my theory, or we could let forensics do their thing and take it from there. If I'm wrong, I haven't wasted your time."

I'd saved the instant message exchanges between the FuzzMan and myself as Denny Winthrop. I copied the file and sent it to Joe's e-mail address.

"Look for me next time you're on your computer," I said to Sullivan. "If I'm right about the Chrysler and what's in the freezer, it'll make sense. If I'm wrong, you can mock me and never trust another thing I say for the rest of our natural lives."

"I might do that anyway. By the way, the kid's checking out fine, maybe a minor concussion and a broken nose. He's screaming lawsuit."

"Happy to litigate that one. My suggestion, and it's only a suggestion, is to hold him until Riverhead can thoroughly check out the goods. I'm phoning in a favor with Vendetti to speed the process."

"What does he owe you for?"

"Listening to his poetry."

Sullivan called back a few minutes later and confirmed what I'd thought about the contents of the freezer. He passed along Danny Izard's personal thanks for almost making him lose his lunch.

He also told me we could wait a day to give our statements, since forensics would be busy nailing various things down. So I took a shower. It was only late afternoon, but I needed something to wake me up and calm me down at the same time. And a place to think without distractions beyond noticing even more grout had worked out from between the tiles and that sections of the shower wall were bulging in unpromising ways. Pete had built the bathroom himself, all the carpentry and tiling, on his first try. Doing your own construction was expected of the men in his family. It didn't matter how much money there was from selling the potato farm, you didn't pay people to do things God gave you two hands to do yourself. That was where the concept broke down for Pete. The only thing he was worse at than skilled craftsmanship was skilled reasoning. Though he did tell a good joke and was never mean to children or pets.

I eventually decided what I wanted to do next but didn't think I was up to the technical challenge. I needed to call on Randall Dodge. I dialed the number and was unsurprised to hear he was on the job, getting ready for a long night's work. Harry looked like he'd much rather stay put, whip up dinner, and recuperate from the wild day. I had to break it to him that the wild day was still in progress, and we had to go.

In addition to being an interesting racial

mix, with brown skin, green eyes, and high cheekbones, Randall was also sort of tall, though when I saw him standing next to Harry, he'd shrunk a lot. I made them both sit down so I could have a conversation without wrenching my neck.

"So, Randall, how hard is it to hack into E-Spree and download all the historical information from a specific individual's account?"

"Impossible," he said in his silky, softly modulated voice.

"Come on, how long would it take you?"

"Forever."

"You're disappointing me."

"All the big online services have state-of-the-art security encryptions," he said. "Especially a brokerage operation like E-Spree. They mess up on that stuff, the liability exposure would sink the ship."

"Okay, but what if you wanted to break into an account, what would you do?"

"Guess," he said.

"Guess?"

"Go to the log-on page and try to guess the user name and password," he said.

"That sounds impossible."

"It is, but you asked me what I would do."

"Okay, let's try it."

It took only a few seconds to find the

log-on page on the E-Spree Web site. Randall looked up at me.

"You could have up to five chances, but maybe only three," he said. "Do not try to force it. Free our mind."

"Yes, master. User name is cap F-u-z-z, no space, cap M-a-n."

He typed it in.

"We won't know if that's right till we put in a password."

"Denny thought he was the Dragon like his kickboxer hero. Fuzzy must be the Grand Warlord," I said.

"Too many letters. We need between six and ten."

"Then plain warlord."

He tried it, and the password came up invalid, but not the user name.

"Gwarlord," said Harry, spelling it out.

No-go, but the log-in box was still giving us a chance. "Could be only one try left," said Randall. "My humble suggestion is you abandon the warlord theme."

"That should have been it," said Harry. "If he's not the Grand Warlord, what is he?"

"He shorts stocks," I said. "He missed Betty's funeral because he was afraid one of his plays was going to shoot up, catching him in a short squeeze." Then I nearly shouted, "Shirt seller. Why the hell did I

382

read that into his license plate? It's Short seller. S-H-R-T-S-L-R. Write it in," I said to Randall.

The screen went to gray-white. I waited for alarms to go off, sirens coming down the street, the door to Randall's shop busted in. Cops in flack jackets yelling "Freeze!"

"Welcome, Oscar Wolsonowicz," it said at the top of the screen.

Everyone whooped at the same time.

"Shirt seller, for Pete's sake," I said.

It took a lot longer to figure out how to navigate the account. It was what Randall called "application rich." I called it confusing.

I deferred to Harry at this point, as he was the only one in the room who'd actually done any day trading. I stared at the screen while he toured Fuzzy's account history. Randall watched, mesmerized. I fidgeted.

"What if Fuzzy decides to log in?" I asked.

"I don't know," said Randall. "The account might allow multiple visitors, or it might say he's already logged in and shut him out," said Randall.

"Hear that, Harry? Keep 'er movin'."

"How do I print?" he asked Randall.

Randall reached across the keyboard and a second later a bank of printers was buzzing and clicking and paper covered in data was squirting into paper trays.

"We'll have to live with monthly reports for now," said Harry. "The backup would be printing forever. I'm also copying the stuff we print to a separate folder that we can save electronically."

My heart sank when I saw the printouts. They were crammed with numbers and stock codes and long, ragged columns and all that other junk I've spent a lifetime trying not to know anything about.

"Do you know what any of this shit means?" I asked Harry.

"Sort of."

With Randall's help, he kept every printer in the shop busy for about twenty minutes. I stacked and collated.

"I think that's all that's practical," Harry said eventually. "If I go to another level of detail, you'll need a truck full of office paper."

"Kill it," I said. "I can't take this anymore."

Before Harry quit the site he copied all the reports to an external hard drive. Then the three of us organized and bundled up the printed records. It took another two hours, but it was fun working between the Twin Towers of Southampton Geekdom.

Randall pulled out several banker's boxes, which we filled nearly to capacity. I was seriously daunted.

"A two months' analysis is not what I want," I said.

"We don't need two months. Give me two hours in my office" — Harry looked at me — "alone, and undistracted."

"When have I ever been a distraction?" I asked.

22

The next day I convinced myself of two things. One, I no longer had to fear being killed because Denny Winthrop was the sole threat, and he was in jail. Two, I'd been pushing myself mercilessly for days and if I didn't take a break, I'd die of a seizure or something.

Now my only job was staying out of Harry's way, so I took Geordie the bartender's advice and went to sit on the beach. On the way I bought a bathing suit, beach towel, and sunscreen, all on postseason sale, commencing the process of mind-clearing therapy. I also bought a bottle of white wine with two glasses in a gift pack, a pack of cigarettes, a small bottle of mouthwash, a tub of fruit salad, and a book of quotes by Saint Teresa of Avila. And a sweat suit, in case it was too cold to sit on the beach.

Buoyed by anticipation, I felt relaxed all the way to the beach and through the first glass of wine. Then I started to feel edgy and restless, my mind running in circles. A law professor once said that in the absence of evidence, all you can do is process your ignorance. So don't waste mental energy drawing conclusions when a simple fact could render moot not just the answer but the question itself.

I looked at Teresa's book and saw she had some interesting things to say on a variety of subjects, though not enough to keep my brain from wandering around the life and death of Sergey Pontecello. Increasingly, it looked like the life part existed entirely in the shadow of his wife. It was her family's house; she handled all the family's finances and kept herself busy as a librarian, as well as managing various intrigues and chicaneries. Sergey looked more and more like a cipher, not just ineffectual but, as Wendy said, oblivious. His independent wealth supported the marriage. It was relatively humble as fortunes go, but adequate, allowing them to assume at least some of the requisite trappings. Like a 1967 Chrysler 300.

Contrary to Betty's smoke screen, a chunk of that wealth had survived. Their original investments had been sold and the money transferred into a cash account, which still amounted to a few million.

At the same time, a new revenue flow developed from two sources — a fifty-thousand-dollar home-equity line, and the credit line from Eunice. Some of this money was dispersed. Nearly all those dispersals went to their E-Spree account.

No. They went to *an* account. We didn't know whose.

I jumped off the blanket as if I'd been bitten by a green fly. My cell phone was in the car, and I was about to run for it when, strangely, better judgment took hold. Bugging Harry with this now would only slow him down. Waiting another hour and a half wouldn't change the answer to my question. It would be there when I got back.

I just had to relax and casually kill the time. Easy.

Instead of running to the car, I ran into the ocean, another one of Geordie's prescriptions, if I remembered it right. It was a little late in the year to be doing this, though the water was much warmer at the end of September than at the end of May, and I'd been swimming in cold water since I was five years old.

I wasn't the only one with the idea. Two little kids were sloshing around in the surf while a Spanish nanny in a white uniform watched from ankle depth. She occasionally tossed out instructions in Spanish, which the Anglo-looking kids seemed to readily understand. Probably part of their preparatory training, strategically calibrated to the times.

I dolphined through the waves and swam out to flatter water beyond the break. I looked back at the nearly empty beach and the grassy dunes, behind which gigantic houses in a variety of architectural motifs — from plain gray boxes to gable-laden, postmodern shingled mansions — stood in arrogant defiance of undefeatable nature.

I'm not only a great swimmer, I float like a cork. Maybe that's why I'm a great swimmer. If I keep my head back as far as I can without getting water in my nose and stay fully relaxed and control my breathing, my whole body will bob on the surface like it was made out of Styrofoam. This was a good project to work on that afternoon, encouraging a Zenlike absence of striving, since the key to successful floating was letting go of one's natural desire to kick one's feet or flutter one's hands.

I was so comfortable in flotation mode, my eyes closed and brain blissfully unfettered from the recent frenzy and free to roam, I almost fell asleep. Which must have been how it was able to roam into a new line of conjecture.

There was something about the recent financial maneuvering that seemed inconsistent with Betty's style. It was too big and busy and reckless. I figured she liked to keep her head down, moving quietly and subtly, favoring the long term over the quick hit. The call for help to Eunice had the stink of desperation, not conspiracy.

She knew Eunice wouldn't cough up that much money without a lien on the house. So she really needed the money. That was a clear-enough assumption to build on, I thought, because it begged an important question.

Why?

That the answer might already be back at Harry's gas station apartment caused an unfortunate lapse in my state of repose, and I immediately began to sink.

I let my feet drop and looked around, seeing with some alarm that I'd floated a fair distance from the beach. I could barely see the backs of the breakers as they spent their energy in a final gasp of spray and foam. I put my face in the water and started to swim to shore, using an old, reliable ocean crawl that involved a look toward land every three or four breaths. With any greater interval, you could be forty degrees off course before you knew it, and too much looking could wear you out.

I still didn't panic after noticing I'd made little progress in ten minutes of swimming. I just put my head down and stretched the periodic look-see to six strokes, betting on a gift for single-minded persistence to keep me on course.

And it did. I could feel the rise and fall of the swells increase in depth and frequency, and hear the rumble of the surf through the churning of my swim stroke. I poked my head up in time to see a spray of water off the top of a breaker about fifty yards away. I put my head back down and began to sprint. Minutes later, I felt the surge of the water as a wave caught me and shoved me up and over, and then down the face of the curling break. I swung both arms in front of me and rode the violent turbulence most of the way to shore.

I stopped at the towel just long enough to gather up all my stuff and went back to the car, drying off as I walked and swishing around a mouthful of mouthwash so I wouldn't offend Harry with cigarette breath. Along the way, I somehow managed to pour and down another glass of wine. Ah, Scope with a chaser of Chardonnay.

As planned, I went directly to Harry's place. He didn't answer when I knocked, so I just let myself in. I went to where he worked on his computer, but he wasn't there. I called his name and he called back from an area of the garage designated as the living room. He was sitting on the couch. His own bottle of wine was on the coffee table. He had his feet up and was sipping comfortably.

"You're actually here when you said you'd be here," he said.

"Why aren't you still deep in analysis?"

"I ought to be in analysis, dating you. Just kidding."

"Did you compare the account numbers?" I said.

He nodded. "One number. Fuzzy and Betty had the same account. She started feeding in funds a year ago. Fuzzy still has some skin in the game, but most of what's there came from Betty."

"So how is he doing?" I asked.

"No danger of Fuzzy becoming a Grand Warlord of E-Spree Traders. I know he's in love with short selling, but the results hardly justify the devotion."

"Really." I sat down next to him.

"Before Betty joined in, he was a two-bit dabbler, honing his money-squandering skills. The problem with Fuzzy, like most day traders, is he trades too much. It doesn't matter if you're betting on upswings or down, all that frenzied in and out almost never goes well."

I put my hand on his knee and looked him in the eye.

"Can you see our Betty staking an endless, reckless losing streak?" I asked.

He shook his head.

"No. I can't. Not at this rate."

"At the same time she's dumping money into Fuzzy's day trading, she goes crying to Eunice. Secures the credit line. Turns their investment funds into cash. And if you believe Ruth Hinsdale, her homey at the library, goes sober. After which followed a lucrative run at the poker tables," I said.

I crawled up on top of him, straddling his midriff with my knees. I gripped his six-foot-wide shoulders and tried to shake him, impressing myself that I did, just a little.

"I think I know what happened," I told him.

"Really."

"I don't know if I can prove it. The law requires more than wild speculation. I know this because I'm a defense lawyer and I've been well advised by the imperious, self-loving blowhards who make up the criminal judiciary."

"So what are you going to do?" he asked.

"Take a shower, wash off the salt, and have a little more wine."

"Okay. And then you're going to tell me what happened?"

I actually didn't want to. I didn't know if what I thought was real or an arrogant delusion, that I'd only succumbed to my own clever speculation. And there was a bit of superstition mixed in — that if I gave voice to my thoughts, some malevolent force would change reality and take it all away from me.

"I will. When I know for sure," I said.

I brooded my way through the shower and all the after-shower rituals with stuff I'd brought along for the purpose — drying off with oversize fluffy towels, fine-tuning toenails, slathering on skin cream, putting concealer on the welt on my formerly good cheek, checking for things in my teeth, averting my eyes from the mirror.

When I was done, I called Joe Sullivan. He was back at Southampton Police Headquarters with Denny Winthrop, preparing for the interrogation.

"How would Ross feel about me sitting in?" I asked.

"You know how he'd feel."

"You can change his mind. Convince him I need to be there," I said.

"He's not in the mood for convincing."

"You can do it."

"Give me an hour."

When we got to the HQ, Sullivan brought me to a little attorney-client room off the reception area, leaving Harry in the civilian lounge with an anxious Alden Winthrop. I briefed Sullivan on what I was thinking. He briefed me on how he'd persuaded Ross Semple to let me in on the interrogation, which boiled down to waiting until he knew Ross would be out of the office and taking his chances.

"That's a big chance. I'm grateful," I said, "though I don't entirely get it."

"I knew when I saw you looking at that dead guy in the middle of the road I wouldn't be able to keep you out of this thing. I know what you're like when you got a bug up your ass. The only question's been how I keep that ass out of worse trouble than it deserves."

"Joe Sullivan, you actually care about me."

"Don't flatter yourself. We all do things for our own reasons. Now shut up and listen."

He briefed me on what he'd learned so

far from forensics on the Chrysler and the contents of Denny's Tupperware. Based on this, we quickly worked out a game plan.

"You're my fairy godfather," I whispered as we walked to the interrogation room. "I knew it."

"If this costs me my job, you can go to my house and explain it to my wife. Come armed."

Denny was already there with his lawyer, a regular competitor of mine from East Hampton named Isaac Fine.

"Izzy, waz up?" I asked, setting my briefcase down on the table.

Fine looked at Sullivan, concern on his face.

"I'm sorry, I don't understand why Miss Swaitkowski, the alleged victim, would be part of these proceedings," he said.

"Ms. Swaitkowski," I said.

"Because I want her here," said Sullivan. "You want a legal justification, we can work that out" — he checked his watch — "maybe two days from now. Meanwhile, based on your request for a delay, we'll bring Denny to the maximum holding pen in East Meadow. They love that fresh, young blood."

Izzy surrendered with a weary nod. He took out a yellow pad and a Montblanc pen. He always looked so at home with luxury accessories and wildly expensive clothes, as if toting around four thousand dollars on your back was the most natural thing in the world. Maybe because he was such a good-looking guy, if you like perfect grooming and meticulousness bordering on prissy.

I pulled out a pad of my own and fumbled around in my purse for a two-dollar Bic with the end half chewed off.

I was glad to have Izzy there. It allowed me to ignore Denny, though I was pleased to see an ugly sewn-up cut on his upper lip. It went nicely with the bruise on his cheek, unlike mine, visible to the world. Missing was the air of imperious entitlement — with any luck, never to return.

"We have preliminary information from the forensics lab in Riverhead," said Sullivan to kick things off.

"Would it pertain to the freezer?" I asked.

"It would," he said, looking at Denny.

Izzy threw up his hands.

"Whoa, hold the phone. I need to get up to speed here," he said.

"That's what I'm doing," said Sullivan. "Riverhead has discovered a collection of severed body parts in a freezer removed from your client's place of residence."

"Can I say something?" I asked Sullivan. He nodded.

"I believe that forensics will prove the body parts belong to a woman named Edna Jackery," I said, "who was the victim of a hit-and-run, vehicular homicide, August a year ago in Southampton. The driver of the vehicle has never been apprehended. Forensics will also determine that the vehicle itself was found at your client's residence."

Izzy held up his hand again so he could finish writing something on his legal pad.

"Sounds like pure speculation. What vehicle are we talking about?" he asked.

"An old Chrysler," said Sullivan. "We're also checking your client's pickup for evidence of an attempted vehicular homicide perpetrated upon Ms. Swaitkowski."

"Since when?" Denny blurted out. "What are they talking about?"

Izzy told him, gently but firmly, to shut up and just listen.

"At this point, Izzy," I said, "I'm definitely speculating. I don't know what this could mean for your client. But you might be interested in hearing anyway, because I'm going to pass it along to the D.A. With Joe's permission, of course," I added, getting Joe's subtle nod.

"Just remember," said Izzy, looking at Denny, "we're only listening, not commenting. Silence does not suggest consent in any way."

Denny sat back and crossed his arms, probably happy to keep his sore mouth shut.

"So," said Joe.

"So," I said, looking down at my pad, "that old car is a 1967 Chrysler 300. The late Sergey and Elizabeth Pontecello owned a 1967 Chrysler 300. I know this because I am the coadministrator of their estate. When inventorying their personal effects, I discovered the Chrysler was missing. And now it turns up in Mr. Winthrop's garage. I was in the process of making that discovery when Denny jumped me and tried to smash my head into the hood of the car. Actually, he succeeded in smashing my head into the car, but fortunately that's as far as it went."

Izzy said that wasn't only speculative, it was prejudicial.

"Relax," I said. "We're not in court. I'm just talking here."

He sat back in his chair, still wary, but attentive.

"Your client might think his maintenance and repair skills would obliterate the evidence. But you know as well as I that if there's a single twisted DNA strand on that car, those people in Riverhead will find it and identify where it came from."

"They already found trace," said Joe. "Blood inside the arm that holds the windshield wiper. Replacing the blades wasn't enough. Spatter just gets everywhere. They're running the DNA now. They might've already sent the ID to my computer."

I couldn't help looking at Denny, whose eyes widened just enough to tell the tale.

"You could save Officer Sullivan the trouble of walking back to his desk and tell us right now," I said to him.

Izzy put his hand on Denny's forearm and said, "Hey, that's not the deal."

I shrugged. "Fair enough. He's not talking, just listening. So I'll do it for him. You remember Edna Jackery?" I asked Denny. "You were in her store plenty of times, buying wax for your surfboard and kayak paddles. Did you know she had a son not much younger than you, and a husband who risked his life to dump her ashes off Kaaterskill Falls? Ashes from that part of her you hadn't snipped off and stuck in your freezer."

"Hey," said Izzy again.

"It came to me talking to Sarah Simms at Great Lawn Cemetery," I said to Denny. "Her family was in the funeral business, too. That's how a lot of people get into it. They

400

grow up around it, like you. Hanging around dead bodies, even helping out Daddy in the embalming room. Maybe you don't have the stomach for it anymore, but you're way ahead of the rest of us when it comes to dismembering cadavers. The really sick part is carving up a woman whose death you're responsible for."

Denny unfolded his arms and leaped to his feet. "Whoa, what're you talking about? I didn't kill her."

Izzy grabbed Denny by the shoulders and shoved him back into his seat.

"What did I tell you?" he said, barely raising his voice.

"The car was in your garage," said Joe. "The body parts in your freezer. You attacked Ms. Swaitkowski to prevent her from disclosing these facts. How much more do you think we need?"

"Man," said Denny, looking pleadingly at Izzy. "That's just wrong. I've only had that car a few days."

Izzy looked on the verge of despair.

"I think we need to end this," he said to Joe.

Sullivan had been balancing his bulk on the back legs of his chair. He dropped back to all four.

"Here's the thing, Izzy. We don't really

think Junior Kung Fu here ran over Mrs. Jackery. But we do think he knows who did. You're a pretty good defense lawyer, you might convince him to cooperate with us on that. Which could put me in a lenient mood. Though make it fast. I'm known for sudden mood swings."

"Damn fucking right I'm cooperating," said Denny.

Izzy did everything but slap his hand over Denny's mouth.

"I understand what's going on here," Izzy said to Joe. "Can I just have a minute with my client, and could you turn off the mikes? So we don't have to go to another room?"

"Sure," said Joe, escorting me out of the room. "I'll signal when they're off."

When we got to the observation room, he flicked off the mikes and knocked on the one-way mirror. Then he sat down to watch.

"Didn't say anything about observing," he said to me.

"Riverhead really got that DNA back in a hurry," I said.

"It would've been a hurry if it was true."

"You lied."

He turned around and looked at me.

"I'm allowed to lie in the course of an interrogation. I'm just not allowed to strike the subject or his lawyer, or speak disrespectfully about the bastard's race, creed, or favorite color."

Watching the two of them told us everything we needed to know. Izzy was grilling him and Denny was dumping out all the information he could think of. After a while, Izzy did all the talking and Denny just nodded. Then Izzy looked up at the glass and waved to us to come back.

"Knew we were watching," said Joe. "Crafty son of a bitch."

We went into the interrogation room and assumed our same seats. Joe leaned back again in his chair.

"I assume you honored our confidentiality," said Izzy.

"Hey, that offends," said Joe.

"My apologies," he said. "My client would like to share some information that may assist the police in their investigation. We simply hope that in doing so, his own situation will be taken into account."

"No assurances," said Joe. "Tell us what you got and we'll think about it."

This set off alarms in Denny, which Izzy calmed with a pat on the forearm and a wise nod. I'd used the same approach myself, more than once. It was meant to say cooperating was good for you, even though that wasn't always the case.

"Denny?" said Izzy.

"About trying to run over Ms. Swait-kowski — I don't know anything about that. I never saw her till she barged in on me at Building Two."

"We don't care about that now," I said. Sullivan looked over at me, more surprised than annoyed. "We want to know about you and Fuzzy. All of it."

"We went to boarding school together," said Denny. "He was a lot older than me and kind of a dweeb, but more interesting than the jocks I hung with. So we stayed in touch off and on and started e-mailing each other a few years ago. I haven't actually seen the guy in the flesh since school. But that's what the Internet is for. We both started blogs, kept e-mailing, the usual shit."

"No profanity," said Joe. "That also offends."

"Okay, sorry. Anyway, Fuzzy had been into day trading for a long time, and he liked to rant about it, but it wasn't exactly my thing. Then like a dope, I let him get me interested, and he starts feeding me tips, and I get into it pretty heavy. I don't know why they don't call it straight-out gambling, because your chances are about the same going to the casino. But guys like Fuzzy think they're smart enough to beat the odds, and that's why they keep losing."

"You both lost money," I said.

"Oh, yeah. Trouble is, he had a lot more of it to lose. I got caught in this margin call that basically screwed the pooch, but Fuzzy stepped in and covered the loss. I let this happen a few more times, and before I knew it, I was into him for a healthy chunk of change."

"Then a year ago August the bill came due," I said.

He looked down at the table.

"Dead bodies are dead bodies," he said. "It wasn't that big a deal to me. I'm just not that into the work. It's boring and messy. And all the fluids stink. But Fuzzy had this thing he wanted me to do, and I said, sure, if he could draw down the tab a little."

"He told you to carve parts off Edna Jackery before you took her to the crematorium. Then freeze them and wait for further instructions," I said. "Soon after, he asked you to start sending the parts, one at a time, to a particular person. No letter, no explanation, just the part. He'd take care of the rest."

Denny looked up at me.

"If he's already told you that, then you know all I know. He didn't tell me why I

405

was supposed to do this, and I didn't ask. It was freaky fun and it saved me a boatload of money, so that was fine with me."

"Fun?" said Sullivan.

Denny almost looked apologetic.

"I know it looks sick, but Fuzzy's an extreme dude. It didn't feel like he was just blackmailing me into doing what he wanted."

"He made it seem like a goof on the power elite," I said, interrupting him. "The lazy rich, the exploiters of the truly righteous. The hopelessly craven upper-class snobs whose greed was destroying the world. Who all deserved to burn in hell anyway. Isn't that what the FuzzMan said?"

He looked back down at the table again.

"Yeah, something like that."

"So who'd you send the parts to?" asked Sullivan.

Denny looked at Izzy, who nodded.

"His own fucking aunt, excuse the French. Betty Pontecello. The one who got all drunked up and took out the snorkel shop lady with her old Chrysler 300."

His own fucking mother, I thought to my-self.

Joe Sullivan got out of his chair and left the room. In a few minutes a call would be put through to his counterparts at Ata-pougue Police Headquarters, and a pair of patrol cars would be dispatched to pick up Oscar Wolsonowicz, a.k.a. FuzzMan.

I was left alone with Izzy Fine and Denny Winthrop.

"How's Janette?" I asked Izzy.

"Quite well, thank you," he said. "She's been busy with the Field School fund-raiser. I assume you've bought your tickets."

"Wouldn't miss it. Who's the entertain-ment this year? Hard to beat Jimmy Buf-fett."

Denny listened to this incredulously, then rolled his eyes — another suspicion con-firmed. The power elite were all in this together; the righteous didn't stand a chance.

Sullivan came back in the room.

"We can get this bird back in his cage," he said to me. "Unless there's something else you want from him."

"One thing," I said.

"Have at it."

"Was Sergey in the car with Betty when she hit Edna Jackery?" I asked Denny.

He looked at Izzy and Sullivan, then back at me.

"Who's Sergey?"

"Betty's husband."

He shook his head.

"Fuzzy never said anything about any Sergey. He just told me to get the car out of their garage in Sagaponack. Said it was hot and needed to go bye-bye. I just couldn't bring myself to trash the old bomber. Got a four-forty with a giant quad under the hood. The torque'll tear your head off. Obviously a stupid move on my part."

"Son, you've invented more stupid moves than most stupid dopes pull off in a lifetime," said Sullivan, standing up and dragging Denny by the collar to his feet. "Let's go find a comfortable place for you to write it all down. Maybe you can publish it in *True Stupid Crime Stories*."

I exchanged a few more pleasantries with Izzy, then went back to the visitors' lounge to rescue Harry, who was busy using his oversize thumbs to write messages on his PDA.

I was thankful that Alden Winthrop had already left to meet with Izzy and his son. I didn't know what I could say to him that he'd want to hear.

I waited until we were in Harry's car to tell him what had transpired in the interrogation room. Since a lot of it was new information for him, I had to go back a few steps to fill in the whole picture.

"Okay," he said, turning the ignition, "where we going now?"

I looked at my watch. Still plenty of time to get to Shelter Island and back while it was still light, I thought.

"Home for you," I said. "I got an errand to run."

He nodded.

"Okay," he said. "I understand."

"Understand what?"

"You need to do things on your own."

"I do. Is that bad?" I asked.

"I don't know. Doesn't always work out that great for you."

"No. It doesn't."

"Okay. I'll just go home and worry," he said.

"No, you won't. You'll just go home. Keep your cell phone on and a light in the window."

"Ten-four."

Harry dropped me off at my car and I drove up North Sea Road to the ferry to Shelter Island. I rode across the channel on the South Ferry, standing outside the car to catch the salty breeze and watch the sea birds dive-bomb for fish. Once I reached the other side, I made the trip to Wendy's in about ten minutes.

I thought about Bilbo, Poaggie, and Bert. Poaggie was the smallest dog, yet the biggest threat, based entirely on the weirdness factor. Though, for all I knew, Bert and Bilbo were actually trained killers disguised as goofy fur balls.

I'd promised Wendy that I'd call her if I wanted to see her again, but I'd been through a lot lately and couldn't muster the necessary remorse over violating the pledge.

Wendy was in the front yard, digging around one of her flower beds. Her face showed alarm over the approaching car, but it was too late to do anything about that.

Bilbo, Poaggie, and Bert charged the Volvo en masse.

"Nice doggies," I said after rolling down the window. Dogs are impressed by size, I told myself. Try to make yourself look bigger.

I got out of the car and waded through the barking, sniffing canines, following the path to where Wendy was tending her flower garden. I dropped to my knees to get on her exasperated level.

"I thought you understood you aren't supposed to come here without my permission," she said.

"I understood. I chose to ignore it. That's a public street. I'm a free agent. I'm here to talk. You can try calling the cops, but like I'm always telling your family, the cops are friends of mine. They're going to look closer at you than me."

She was wearing a blue work shirt, jeans, and a flowered bandanna. She used the back of her forearm to wipe the sweat and streaks of mud off her brow. In the same hand she held a small garden trowel. I felt like I was in a scene from *The Good Earth.*

She looked grim but rose to her feet and led me to the same picnic table we'd sat at the last time.

"So I suppose the police haven't decided what happened to Uncle Sergey," she said.

"No. But some other interesting tidbits

have surfaced along the way. Mostly about your family."

She smirked. "Can't imagine what would be interesting about that."

"You told me last time I was here that the family unit was the root of all pathology."

"I was just making conversation," she said, looking back at where she'd just been messing with her flower garden, as if wishing she were still there.

"You also said Sergey was oblivious. Oblivious to what?"

She studied me with her brilliant eyes, as clear and hard as blue diamonds.

"Maybe you already know something," she said, more inquisitive than defiant.

"Why did you tell him?" I asked.

"Who?"

"Fuzzy."

"Tell him what?" she asked, her face blank except for her eyes, which had widened just a little.

I'd smuggled in a pack of cigarettes in the front pocket of my pants, a loose-fitting pair of pleated slacks that were just right for the purpose. I pulled them out and lit one up, just to be sure Wendy understood that she and I were as different from each other as two people could be. She'd charmed me once before; it wasn't going to happen again.

"About the accident. About your Aunt Betty hitting that woman on County Road Thirty-nine. You had to know he'd do something ugly with the information."

She sat at the table in silence, looking at me, deliberating.

"I still don't know what you're talking about," she said finally.

"Yes, you do. You were in the car a year ago when Betty hit Edna Jackery, the lovable knucklehead who was walking along the road in the dark, and Betty, half bombed as usual, didn't see her. She was picking you up at the train station, like she did every August. You promised her you'd never tell a soul, yet you told Fuzzy, the one person on earth who would use it as a weapon against her. His own mother. What the hell were you thinking?"

Bilbo decided that was a good time to come up to me and shove his meaty shoulder into my leg. I reached down to stroke his back and scratch under his ears.

Wendy took on the mantle of her mother, Eunice, Antonin's genetic influence disappearing behind a cloud of haughty self-importance.

"They lied to us, all of them. We always knew Fuzzy was adopted. They just didn't bother to tell us his parents were Betty and

Tony, my aunt and my father. Which means we're half siblings, but we didn't know that. Not until Betty caught us one summer at the house in the Hamptons. In bed. Not sleeping, which I hope you're proud of yourself for making me say."

I was hardly proud of myself. I hadn't expected that at all. It might have been there, hiding out with all the other family secrets, but I hadn't seen it or ever thought it was a remote possibility.

"I don't talk to Fuzzy very often," she said, folding back into herself. "But I don't have anyone else in the family to talk to. It was such a shock when Betty hit that woman. She barely understood what had happened. I asked his advice, and he said to just stay quiet about it. That sending Betty to jail wouldn't bring the woman back. I was a little surprised by that. Fuzzy hated Betty for what she did to him. To us. Made him so crazy with anger he was never the same again. He was such a beautiful boy growing up, so sweet. I know it's hard to imagine now, but you didn't know him then."

She tried to stifle the tears, but they came anyway, silently rolling down her cheeks. She held her head up, and the set of her mouth showed her determination not to allow any further emotion to follow those traitorous tears.

With my own emotional state teetering between triumph and shame, I left her where she sat, surrounded by her dogs, otherwise alone in her island exile.

Someone had to tell Eunice what was going on. I wanted it to be someone other than me, but after leaving Wendy's, I found myself heading for Sagaponack to get it over with.

I had a pretty sticky moral dilemma on my hands. Wendy telling Fuzzy about the accident was a triggering event, but she had nothing to do with the extortion that had followed. She didn't kill poor Edna.

Then I thought about it from Slim's point of view. That for him, the driver of the car suffered enough just knowing what they'd done. He was right about that. It knocked Betty sober. That and the threat of ruin at the hands of her sadistic bastard child.

Though even in that situation, I could see Betty coming out on top. She was feeding Fuzzy a lot of money, but nothing like she could have, given the loans from her sister and the bank, plus her existing funds, now converted into handy liquidity. On top of that, she'd been on a tear at the casino, pumping even more into the kitty.

If I'd been a gambling woman like Betty, I might have bet she was up to something. One final caper.

When I got to the house, Ray Zander's truck was parked on the front lawn. The line for the hoisting device that fed from the spool on the back of his truck ran up the front of the house and disappeared over the roof.

I walked around to the back of the house and found Ray dangling in front of a window on the second floor, applying a tan compound dug out of a small pail to a section of the window trim.

"Hey, Ray," I called. "What're you doing up there?"

He looked down.

"Just filling in some cleaned-out rot with this epoxy. Been workin' on these windows all summer. Whenever I get the chance."

"Is Eunice home?" I asked.

"Think she is."

I was disappointed by the answer. So much so that I almost walked back to the Volvo and drove away, so little did I look forward to the impending conversation.

As I thanked Ray and turned to walk back to the front door, I looked down. There was a toothbrush on the ground between a pair of low-cut yews, half buried in mulch. I squatted down and picked it up.

I looked at it for a moment, then looked up at the side of the house.

"Hey, Ray, you ever been inside?"

He looked back down.

"Sure. Lots of times."

"What's behind those windows?"

He used a foot to push himself away from the house and looked from side to side.

"Well, there's a bedroom here, here, and here. And in the middle — this window here, actually — is the big bathroom."

To emphasize the point, he slapped another wad of epoxy into a hole.

I looked down at the toothbrush, then back up at the window and said, "No," too softly, I thought, for him to hear.

"Yeah, it is. The main bathroom for the floor. There're some sinks and johns off the bedrooms, but if you want a shower, you walk down the hall."

I thanked him and went back to the front of the house and rang the doorbell. A year later, Eunice answered the door.

"Don't you ever call ahead?"

"No, ma'am."

"Well, I'm sorry, but I'm busy."

I hoped my body language showed my

concern for her demanding schedule. "Of course. I just thought, as a courtesy to you, you'd want to know that your son Oscar's been arrested on a host of charges, including extortion and conspiracy to commit murder. To murder me, actually, which is a little creepy, though nothing you have to worry about. Well, okay. See you."

I turned and headed back to the Volvo.

"Miss Swaitkowski," she said, as if burdened by world-weariness. "Please come back."

I turned again, but kept walking backward.

"You got things to do," I said. "Not a problem. We'll catch up some other time. Oh, and he was blackmailing your sister, who killed somebody in a hit-and-run."

"Miss Swaitkowski," she nearly yelled as I headed briskly toward the car. "Please come back."

I stopped and turned.

"Ms. Ms. Swaitkowski."

"Please."

I shrugged and did as she asked. She let me into the little sitting room we'd used earlier, the receiving area for irritating intruders bearing bad news. I sat down earlier, she had a chance to offer me a seat. She listened attentively while I ran through the story as coherently as I could. It was the first time I'd had to lay out the whole deal, so the narrative was a little choppy, but the key facts were intact.

I finished by telling her I was sure Betty was planning her escape from the devil's dilemma — having to choose between a vehicular manslaughter charge and Fuzzy's extortion. Sacrifice the house but take most of the value out of her sister's hide, add to the other cash, and reformulate their lives somewhere else, somewhere outside Fuzzy's clutches and the long arm of the law.

Eunice took the news better than I thought she might. The absence of throwable objects might have helped. She was either toughening up or slipping into a state of resignation. Either way, she was at least a little nicer.

"Ms. Swaitkowski, do you honestly believe Elizabeth would be that wicked?"

" 'Guess' is a better word. She might've been working in that direction, but we'll probably never know. I haven't come across plane tickets or rental agreements with Argentine haciendas. It just explains the other facts and fits with Betty's style."

"Betty's style?" she said. "What style would that be? You have no idea what it was like growing up with her. She was not only more clever, she was prettier and much more fun to be around. My role was the good girl. The serious girl who studied hard and acted like a grown-up. My parents depended on it."

"Raising the child she conceived with your husband was a remarkable act of generosity," I said.

The expression on her face continued to sag.

"Antonin made it clear from the beginning that fidelity would never be a feature of our marriage. I was willing to accept that, though I couldn't have imagined one of his lovers would be my own sister." She looked at me, hoping maybe for some kind of sympathy, which I didn't know right then how to deliver. "Oscar might have turned out differently if someone else had taken him, someone outside the family. I'll never know."

It wasn't for me to comment on that, so I didn't. There was something I was much more interested in discussing, now that I had her in a weakened state.

"Mrs. Wolsonowicz, the night Sergey was killed, he called me complaining that you'd locked him out of the bathroom. Do you remember?"

She looked like she didn't at first, then nodded her head.

"Yes, that's right. He had a perfectly good bathroom of his own. I had the smaller bedroom and consequently felt entitled to the better bath. All I did was lock the door and put the old key on my dresser. He thought I was actually in the bathroom, and was creating a ridiculous scene. I didn't want to dignify his behavior with a response, so I merely sat in my room and waited for him to withdraw, which he did."

"And that was it?"

"No, actually an hour later he became positively enraged over something. He pounded on the bathroom door again, and then on my bedroom door. I never thought of Sergey as much of a man, but I admit I was becoming concerned. He sounded like a maniac."

"Do you remember anything he said? Even if it didn't make sense."

"Not specifically. The gist was I wasn't going to force him out of his house no matter how much I tried to" — she searched the air for the recollection of his words — "frighten him, disgust him, intimidate him. I do remember wondering what he could have meant by those things. I was never anything but civil to Sergey, despite his own fulminations. I certainly hadn't tried to frighten the poor man away. Though I suppose that might have been easily done."

I stood up and walked a few paces around the room, unable to control the sudden gush of energy flooding my nerves.

"After he stopped pounding on the doors, Mrs. Wolsonowicz, what happened?"

She struggled to recall an evening she likely preferred to forget.

"This is going to sound strange, but I actually thought I heard him bellowing at me from outside my window. I know that's impossible, but that's what I thought at the time. There were a few other sounds, and I was about to go look, but when they stopped, I went back to my book."

Since I was already on my feet, I kept walking — out of the room, through the front door, and around to the back of the house. Ray was still up there, scraping and filling in holes. A section of roof shingle, where the rope connected to the boson's chair passed over the ridge of the house, was torn away. I walked back to the other side and got a better look at the yew directly behind the truck. A large piece of the bush was turning brown. I picked up the top branches and saw where many of the lower branches were split and broken away. Some had been tied up in an attempt to keep some shape to the bush.

I went around to the front of the truck and saw for the first time that he'd installed two slabs of heavy timber in place of the bumper. It was freshly sanded and varnished.

I went back to Zander and called up to him.

"Come on down, Ray. We need to talk."

"I can hear you okay."

"Come on down."

He put the handle of the putty knife in his pocket and dug the remote control out of his pocket. He kept his eyes toward the ground as he made his descent. I stepped back to give him plenty of room.

"Do me a favor and get out of that thing for a second, would you?" I asked him.

It made him unhappy, but he did as I asked.

I examined the boson's chair, which was actually a webbing made from extremely heavy canvas to which equally heavy nylon lines were attached. Originally off-white, it was now a soiled beige with various stains and scars. A large section, comprising most of the lower strap that gripped the operator's butt, had been patched with new-looking material.

I dropped it to the ground and walked over to Zander and shoved him in the chest with both hands, with as much force as my increasingly hysterical nervous system would allow. It knocked him back a few steps, but he stayed on his feet.

"Hey, lady. What the Christ?" he said.

"What did you do, Ray?" I yelled at him. "Did you go on a bender that night, what, in the woods over there, or in one of the outbuildings? Alone, huh? So none of your boys could take away your keys?"

"I don't know what the hell you're talking about."

I took my phone out of my pocket and hit one of the speed dials. Zander watched, heated and confused.

"Joe," I said when he answered. "I'm talking to Ray Zander at the Wolsonowicz place. Send somebody quick. If anything happens to me, it's him." Then I flipped the phone shut.

"When did you realize you hadn't reeled in the hoist?" I asked. "The next morning? Or along the way?"

He took a step toward me. I stepped back.

"I want to think you blacked out like usual," I said, "so you didn't remember stopping the truck when you noticed it was handling funny. Getting out and seeing the line, following it back in the dark to where Sergey was lying in the road torn to shreds.

I want to think he was dead by then and that you didn't steal his last chance at survival."

He looked like a man trying to make a quick decision, weighing the options. He wasn't tall, but his arms were ropy and his hands coarse and gnarled from years of hard, dirty work. I wouldn't be much of a challenge, and this time there were no handy giants waiting in the wings. He took a step toward me.

"Hurting me isn't going to change anything," I said. "Just make it worse for you. What'll help is telling me what happened." I checked my watch. "You got maybe five minutes, tops, before the patrol car gets here. Onetime offer."

"You gonna defend me?"

"Hell no."

"Then I got nothing to lose," he said, moving a little closer, his face a blank wall.

I scolded myself again for improperly managing timing and conditions when confronting desperate drunks and criminals.

"Use your head, Ray. You heard me call the cops."

What I wanted to say is, if you lay a hand on me, my friends will run you down like a dog, and if you aren't dead when they're done with you, you'll wish you were.

"Okay," I said, instead. "I'll defend you."

He stopped his advance.

"You mean it?"

I nodded enthusiastically. "What you heard me just say is legally binding. It's canonized in English Common Law. If I violate it, it'd be like violating the Universal Code of Legal Ethics. I'd be instantly disbarred."

He liked the sound of that.

"That's like it should be," he said.

"So now you can tell me in complete confidence what happened. Tell me everything."

Remorse crept back into his expression.

"I don't know, exactly. Like you said, I didn't see anything until the next day, with the chair all torn up and bloody at the end of the line. Wasn't till the news of Mr. Pontecello got out that it crossed my mind. But nobody said anything, so I figured lay low and it'll blow over. Then you show up over here asking all kinds of crap. Later on, when I seen your Toyota go by, I thought I'd just follow you for a while, but then something took over me. I been drinkin' a little, of course. Wouldn't've hit you otherwise, I swear. I'm not like that."

"What are you like, Ray? Do you even know yourself?"

He looked over my shoulder, suddenly even more crestfallen. A Southampton Town Police patrol car, lights flashing, streaked across the lawn. Ray watched with wide eyes, as if expecting to be run over where he stood. The car stopped instead and Danny Izard jumped out, his right hand snapping open the safety strap on his holster. I told him I was okay but to keep an eye on Zander until Joe Sullivan arrived. I told him he'd just confessed to killing Sergey Pontecello and trying to kill me, which wasn't technically what he'd done, but there wasn't time for a nuanced explanation.

Not that I had much to worry about. As soon as he was approached, Zander stood with his hands out in front of him, waiting to be cuffed.

After Danny Izard ran through Miranda, I said, "All that stuff about the Universal Code of Ethics? Pure bullshit. Get your own goddamn lawyer."

Sullivan flew in a few minutes after that. I ran through the chain of events as I saw them. I gave him the toothbrush and showed him where I thought Riverhead would find the physical evidence to support the case. Partway through the process, Eunice appeared, standing at a distance, her arms wrapped in a knit shawl against the cooling breeze, watching intently. After I was done with Sullivan, I could have filled her in, but I didn't feel like it.

"All the guy wanted to do was brush his teeth in his own bathroom," I said to her, but she was too far away to hear.

24

I'm not sure why I wanted to do this, but there I was, floating in the Little Peconic Bay with Harry and Sam. Perhaps because I was the only one in the group who could actually float on her own. They weren't only lousy swimmers; life jackets were all that kept them from sinking like lead statues.

Thus I had a physical advantage for the first time, a certain leveling of the playing field, psychologically at least.

Sam's girlfriend, Amanda, had opted to stay ashore with Eddie and take advantage of the last warm day of the year to preserve her tan, a glorious deep reddish bronze, offset perfectly by a scant white bikini, all of which Harry claimed not to have noticed.

Sam had let me unfold the story of Sergey Pontecello's final hours in my own way, in fragments, slipped into the general conversation. But out there in the bay, bobbing on the little bay waves, he asked a direct question.

"How much did Sergey know about the blackmail?"

"Nothing," I said. "Betty kept him encased in a bubble. You want to think she was protecting him, but it was probably just the way she was. By all accounts, they got along fine, but Betty ran everything and kept all her secrets to herself."

"Like Edna Jackery's occasional visits, one piece at a time."

"Finding that nipple pushed Sergey over the edge," I said. "So to speak."

"Where did he find it?" Harry asked.

"When I saw him earlier that day, he told me he'd been going through Betty's unopened mail. It must have been in there with the electric bill and come-ons from credit card companies. The conflict with Eunice was terrible, but the nipple in the envelope was enough to drive him crazy, literally," I said. "He thought it was her doing. Like I said, crazy."

"Though sane enough to operate Zander's invention," said Sam.

"Ray was wooing him as an investor and had shown him how to use it. Sergey was desperate to confront Eunice, so he rode it to the second floor. What he thought when

Zander took off with the thing still hooked to the truck, I can't imagine."

"Finally took a little initiative and look where it got him," said Harry.

I held my breath and sank all the way into the water, committing myself to an hour or two of wet hair. But it was worth it to feel the salubrious properties of the salty bay.

When I surfaced, I sought a cleansing of another kind.

"After Sergey found the nipple in the envelope, he called me," I told them, "but he couldn't get through because I turned off the cell phone. If I hadn't done that, he'd probably still be alive. For some reason, I've known this from the beginning — that I was somehow culpable, an accessory to the crime. And it turns out I was right."

Neither one of them was particularly happy with me for sharing this insight. Harry looked at a loss for words. Sam came to his rescue.

"Crap, Jackie," he said. "Ray Zander killed Sergey when he decided to kill a bottle of booze. Fuzzy killed him by terrorizing Betty. Eunice helped torment him to death, in a way even colder and more calculating than Fuzzy. And Betty killed him when she killed Edna, kicking off the whole thing. They all made decisions, and took actions, with malice aforethought or callous disregard — something you couldn't have done because you didn't know anything. If you're that desperate to feel guilty, save it for when you actually do something you deserve to feel guilty about. You'll get the full effect. Trust me on that one."

With that he started to thrash his way back to shore. Harry cocked his head in that direction, and I nodded. He kissed me, a glancing peck made so by his encumbering life jacket, then followed Sam. I let them get a decent head start, then happily swam after them, not exactly absolved, but close enough.

3L 11/10
HS
Brad 2/11
Kap 3/11
MT 5/11
Crof 6/11
CC 2/11
GCC 3/12
SO 11/12
AHR
OK 2/13
3L 6/13
Blen 8/13
FAIR 9/13
TAP 10/13
CG 2/14
WR 6/14
KOP 7/14
SGR 12/14
BRAD 4/15
TER 5/15
COOP 7/15
SO 5/14
ST 6/16
HAR 10/16
MT 2/17
BLEN 7/17
GGR 12/17
RAC 3/19